THE MONTANA MARSHALLS

KNOX

BOOK ONE

SUSAN MAY WARREN

D1287811

SDG PUBLISHING
A division of Susan May Warren Fiction
Minneapolis, MN

Knox
Montana Marshalls series
ISBN-13: 978-1943935260
Published by SDG Publishing
15100 Mckenzie Blvd. Minnetonka, MN 55345
Copyright © 2019 by Susan May Warren

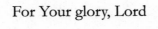
For Your glory, Lord

1

Oh goody, now Knox got to watch his troublemaking little brother break his ornery neck.

"Tate, this is a bad idea." Knox said it in his big-brother voice, but Tate hadn't a hope of hearing him over the cheers as he walked into the straw-padded arena under the hanging lights of the beer tent toward the mechanical bull.

His renegade brother nailed the rough-edged charm of a cowboy, complete with his faded jeans, a black Stetson over his dark brown hair, a scrape of off-duty dark whiskers, dusty boots, and a swagger that suggested he'd been born on a bull.

Tate always did know how to put on the game to charm the ladies.

The organizers of the after-hours entertainment of NBR-X, the professional bull-riding tour, knew their crowd—beer-gesturing, cowboy-hatted rowdies who spent the evening watching young men pit their lives against angry, thousand-pound animals hoping to crush their rider into the dirt or against the rodeo boards.

The scent of blood spilled today turned wannabe cowboys into daredevils.

The crowd knotted around the circle, shouting smack

and laying bets for or against Tate's success. The ruddy rodeo aroma—horsehide, dust, hay, and plenty of craft beer—only added to the trouble brewing in Knox's gut.

Probably Tate would survive. Knox had seen Tate ride—had taught him how to stay on the back of a real bull, and frankly, a smart man would ante up a Ben Franklin to the bookmaker collecting cash in an oversized boot.

But Knox worked too hard for his cash, and to his knowledge, Tate hadn't been on a bull in years.

"C'mon, Tate, let's go," Knox said, a last-ditch effort to put a halt to the crazy. But when Tate got something in his head, he practically turned into one of those bulls in the nearby barn. Red-eyed, focused, and lethal.

The crowd exploded with fervor when Tate handed his red Solo cup to a blonde wearing a hot-pink Bull Riders Know How to Hang On T-shirt. When she grabbed a fistful of his shirt and pulled him to herself for a quick good luck kiss, Knox just wanted to shake his head.

He should probably hightail it out of the Tent-o'-Trouble and back to his room at the Hyatt where he could take a shower and whisk off the grime that seemed to hover in the air.

Not that Knox didn't savor a good rodeo, with bareback riding, bulldogging, tie-down roping, barrel racing, and maybe even good old-fashioned mutton bustin'. But NBR-X had taken the glitz of the sport and turned it into a rock show. National Bull Riding eXtreme, a traveling, rowdy weekend event that included a thrill-ride carnival, a craft beer tent, and a high-decibel concert to cap off every night.

And this was their yearly kickoff event. They were bringing their A game to the early March springtime weather in south Texas.

If it weren't for Tate, Knox would have left right after

Hot Pete's performance, headed back to his hotel, and looked over the contract, ready for tomorrow's negotiation.

The way Hot Pete bucked tonight, Knox might be able to raise the lease price with the contractor. And line up futures for the other four prime two-year-olds back in the barn in Montana at the Marshall Triple M.

Hot Pete, his prize bucking bull, was in rare form this year—poised to net even more than the $350K in prize money that he'd earned last year. The best bull to come out of Gordo the Bonebreaker's line since Knox had pastured the champion. Gordo had his own pedigree from years in the ring, and his straws went for $1,000 a pop. Hot Pete's stats boded well for the future of the Marshall Triple M.

Not that any of Knox's siblings seemed to care. In the last three years since his oldest brother, Reuben, had come back home, made peace with the family, and decided to give Knox his blessing, the rest of the family—his other three brothers and two sisters—had drifted away. Honestly, Coco wasn't a birth sister, but she felt like one, the way she'd merged into their family after her mother's death, so she also counted. But she'd drifted, just like the rest of them.

Knox was losing them to places and futures unknown, and he hadn't a clue how to knit them back together. Hold on to the legacy his father had mantled upon him.

Family first. Family strong.

So, of course, when he'd pulled into San Antonio, he'd texted his brother. Yes, Tate was still working security. Yes, he'd meet him after hours for a beer to catch up.

And yes, his next-youngest brother hadn't changed a bit—trouble coursed through his veins and pulled everyone in his vortex with him.

Knox stepped up to the circle. The organizers of the crazy bull riding gimmick had added real longhorns, with blunted ends, and the hairy red hide of a Braford bull, hopefully engineered, although Knox doubted it. It looked dangerous enough, if Tate were to fly over the horns, get hooked.

The guy could just as easily dislocate his shoulder not to mention land on his head and get a concussion. Or even worse—break his neck.

For all the malarkey…

Tate slid onto the bull's back, one hand gripped into the leather strap. If he'd been straddling a real bull, he'd wrap the bull rope around the chest and over the shoulders of the bull, slip his hand under the rope, and wrap the loose end of the rope once around his hand. Knox saw his own actions in his mind, breathing instructions to Tate.

Scooch your body up, until your hand is between your upper thighs. Position your feet forward, above the rope, and grip the bull's body with your spurs. Except, Tate wore no spurs, and the body had no give. No breathing from the animal, no snorting, no shaking of his angry head.

Tate lifted his hand and stuck his chest out. Nodded.

The bull began to shift.

From here, it was all instinct. Feeling the animal, getting over its front end when he reared. Keeping your backside down when he kicked up his hind legs. Using your spurs to hold on.

Tate gripped the machine with his boots, his body rocking forward, back, twisting as the bull spun. In one quick second the machine went from a rocking twist to a full-out thrashing, jerking Tate hard, forward, back, simulating a spin, then another rear—

Tate flew over the horns.

He landed with a breath-clearing whump into the straw, lying dazed for a moment before he scrambled to his feet.

Knox hadn't realized he'd been holding his breath, white-gripping the railing until Tate raised his hat above his head, waving to the crowd.

Six point four seconds. Not terrible, but he wouldn't win any awards. Tate's gaze landed on Knox and he grinned, as if he'd ridden Gordo into a championship spot at the NBR-X finals. And the blonde in the ring only added to the fuss. She grabbed Tate's shirt and gave him another full-on mouth kiss.

Disgusting.

Tate wrapped his arms around her and dipped her.

Knox was out of here. His crazy brother hadn't changed a bit since he'd left home on his Kawasaki and not looked back.

Maybe Knox hadn't a prayer of figuring out how to bring the family back together again. They were happily living their own lives.

Leaving Knox to carry on a legacy he didn't want.

He was pushing his way through the crowd when a hand caught him on the arm. He turned.

"Where'ya going?" Tate bore a smudge on his chin from his close encounter with the earth. "Your turn to ride. You know you want to. And the pot's up over 1G!"

Tate must've stuffed a C-note into the collective pot to ride—winner of the eight seconds takes all.

"I don't think so," Knox said, watching a skinny kid barely over twenty-one climb onto the back of the machine.

Tate slapped a hand on his shoulder. "If anyone can stay on that toy, it's you, Knox. None of these other yahoos won the national junior bull riding championship."

"That was a long time ago," Knox said, glancing at the kid in the ring, now spinning off the machine. Two whopping seconds. He earned a few boos. "Besides, I have work to do."

"You're always working—loosen up, bro. Live a little."

He considered Tate. The man had inherited their mother's blue eyes and her easy smile, but the renegade attitude was all Marshall genes. It seemed everyone but Knox had answered the call of the wild—big brother Reuben into smokejumping, Tate into personal security, Wyatt, the hockey star, Ford into the Navy, and Ruby Jane turning travel agent and seeing the world. Even Coco—or rather, Katya—had returned to her father's country, Russia, to work as a diplomatic aid.

And it wasn't that Knox didn't hear the call…but someone had to keep the ranch running. Pay the bills.

Take care of Mom.

And sure, he'd been primally focused on getting their bucking bull line into the national limelight, but he'd taken their 9,000-acre ranch from the edge of bankruptcy to flush and more. But apparently, while he was digging the family out of the red, they'd abandoned him for greener pastures.

"Just one beer, bro. A little catch-up time. I need the dirt on this guy who Mom is dating."

Knox stared at him, his gut emptying. "What—?"

Tate's mouth opened a little. "Um…oh. She didn't tell you yet."

Perfect. Now Tate—tattooed, renegade, runaway Tate—knew more about their mother's life than the son she lived with.

"Who is he?"

Tate was pulling him toward the bar. Gestured to the busy guy behind the counter and held up a peace sign. He turned to Knox. "Hardwin Colt."

Aw, no… Knox grimaced. "He bought the Double Arrow from the Lindseys a few years ago. Really? Mom said she's *dating* him?"

Tate lifted a shoulder and turned to the bar to retrieve their drinks.

Knox was tired of standing on the sidelines, watching everyone else spread their wings. Live the life they'd dreamed about.

He cast another look at the bull machine.

His gaze snagged on a brunette standing at the bar. He might not have even noticed her—she wasn't necessarily trying to grab attention in her baggy jeans, Converse tennis shoes, an oversized gray shirt tucked into the front of her jeans. She wore her dark, shimmery hair back in a ponytail, a cap on her head, and no makeup. As if she might be in hiding.

Or worse, about to bolt. She wore the skittish look of a newborn calf as she tucked her lip between her teeth and eyed a couple cowboys leaning against the bar who'd noticed her too.

Knox didn't like the way their gazes ran over her, but he wasn't her keeper.

Still, he couldn't help but watch as she stepped up to the bar, nudging between the two men. One of them had a bright orange tattoo of flames that encircled his neck. She glanced at one, then the other, her mouth a tight line, then pulled out her wallet. The bartender retrieved a bag from along the back wall—ah, takeout of some kind.

"Here you go, bro," Tate said and handed Knox his beer. "Sorry to be the one to spill about Mom. She called to see if I was coming back for her big six-oh bash."

Right. She'd been peppering Knox about that party since her last birthday. "She's hoping Ford can get leave—"

"Do SEALs get time off?" Tate took a sip. "And Wyatt is in the middle of his schedule. And who knows where Ruby Jane is—last time I talked to her, she was headed to

Prague—"

Someone bumped him from behind, and he sloshed beer over his cup, onto Knox, who stepped back, avoiding a drenching.

"Don't touch me!"

The voice behind Tate caught Knox and he turned, finding the source.

The brunette. She was untangling herself from the grasp of one of the cowboys, her pale blue eyes wide, jerking away from him.

It ignited something primal and dark inside Knox, and he started toward her without thinking.

Tate grabbed him by the shirt— "Watch out!" He pointed to the scattering of greasy chicken wings soaking up the sawdusted floor of the tent.

And Knox wasn't certain what happened, but the climatic ending included her jerking hard away from the cowboy's grasp, turning, and fleeing through the crowd.

Knox met the eyes of her assailant, a man with gauged ears, an eyebrow bar and a port-wine stain curling up his neck, and Knox must have worn something dark in his expression because the man held up his hands. "She tripped. I caught her."

"I'll bet you did," Knox snapped, his gaze searching for her, but she'd vanished.

"She left her wallet," said the bartender, holding up the black clutch.

And before Cowboy could reach for it, Knox grabbed it.

Without a backward glance at Tate, he pushed through the crowd and out into the night.

Overhead, stars gathered like spectators to the balmy Texas night, the sounds of the nearby carnival in distant exhilaration, the tall Ferris wheel glimmering against the rodeo grounds. Neon green lit up the path that led to the red-splashed stock barn.

He spotted her, quick walking down the path.

"Stop! You dropped your wallet!"

She didn't turn. Instead, of all things, she took off in a run.

What the—

And he didn't think it through, just reacted, sprinting after her.

Maybe she hadn't heard him.

She cut a right at the path that ran between the stock barn and the massive beer tent, toward a parking lot filled with RVs, horse trailers, semis, and cargo trucks. The pathway, out of the splash way of lights, darkened, and he barely made out the shadows as she—

Ducked into the stock barn?

He hitched up his pace and entered at the far end of the building. The earthy smell of animal sweat, waste, and green hay swept over him as he stepped into the shadowed building. Pens for sheep lined one wall, and horses slept in open stalls that formed corridors throughout the building.

He angled toward the door where she'd entered—the bull pens. With heavy breathing, the bulk of the massive animals seemed to saturate the expanse as he quick walked down the aisle.

What was she doing in here?

His memory brought him down the aisle that held the Brafords. Specialized for the sport of bull riding, the monsters of the ring. Dangerous, even lethal.

And this aisle dead-ended at the most dangerous beast of them all, his own Hot Pete.

He spotted her against the far wall.

She turned, and even from here, saw her eyes widen as

they fell on him. She began to back up.

No. Knox held up his hand. "Don't move."

But before he could stop her, she landed at the gate. It rattled.

Movement stirred from the depths of the pen.

And the woman opened her mouth to scream.

Kelsey had just wanted something to eat. A calm night in the privacy of her tour bus, ratcheting down from the adrenaline of the stage.

A moment to step outside of the persona, the headlines, the woman on the posters, to be just a girl.

A girl without demons, without the crazy that threatened to possess her brain.

Problem was, she knew better than to go out into a crowd of strangers in a chaotic tent full of raucous cowboys. She'd broken nearly all of her rules...for what?

A Styrofoam container of buffalo wings?

She should have eaten the stale Cheetos in her trailer. Then she wouldn't have lost it when she'd stepped off the rail of the bar, fallen backward and into the hands of the tattooed cowboy next to her.

He hadn't meant to trigger the memories, to ignite the latent panic that always simmered inside her. Didn't deserve, really, the way she'd reacted, twisting away from him as if he might be committing a crime. Maybe he'd been trying to help...

She'd simply stopped thinking and reacted, despite the words of her counselor pinging through her—*Breathe. You're not in danger. Don't run.*

Except, that's exactly what she did. Her feet simply took off, a primal response, and before she knew it, she'd pushed through the crowd to the fresh outside air.

Her brain caught up then, slowed her down to a reasonably normal walk. She'd pressed her hand to her chest. *Breathe. You're safe*—and she might have successfully clamped down on the moment, wheeled her way past the self-recriminations—*Why can't you be normal? Don't make a scene!*—if it weren't for the voice that followed her out of the stupid tent and thundered in her wake.

"Stop!"

Hardly. And no, probably no one was going to hurt her, not anymore, but the rush of her pulse in her ears cut off any remaining thought, his words—even her sense of self-control—and she'd, well, *panicked*.

At least she hadn't screamed, hadn't melted down into a fetal puddle on the path.

Although her all-out sprint away from the voice, back toward the RV park certainly didn't seem *normal*.

Her stalker followed her down the shadowed valley between the tent and the next building, and—what if he followed her all the way back to her tour bus?

It wasn't as if Dixie or Gloria or even Carter would be around to...what? Protect her?

She knew better, *hello*. She could depend on no one but herself.

So Kelsey had ducked into the barn, hoping to lose the stalker in the shadows.

A gut reflex, born from old habits, but yeah, a stupid move. She should have made for the bustling carnival, although given the crowds, that might have been just as foolish.

She slowed, the redolence of farm animals, hay, dirt, and not a little feral trouble rising around her. She found herself lost, winding farther into the maze of pens and stables.

She turned down a row that looked like it might open

up—

No. A pen cordoned off the end, and she turned around.

Stalker came up behind her. Tall, over six feet, he wore a cowboy hat—she saw that outlined against the high windows of the barn that reflected the ambient carnival light. His face hung under shadow, however, and she couldn't help but back up, against the cold bars of the pen.

A scream pressed into her throat.

He held up his hand. "Don't—"

And that's when she felt a humid breath wash over her. Thick, foul, and—

She opened her mouth.

In two steps the cowboy advanced on her, slapping his hand over her scream. His voice careened into her ear, a low, guttural tenor. "Shh."

As if that might make it better. She clawed at his hand, yanking it from her mouth, but he grabbed her around the waist and pulled her away from the cage.

Then he released her so fast she didn't have time to push him away, to slap him, or even reach into her self-defense training and chop him in the neck, maybe disable him enough to get away.

He put his hands up, backing away from her. "I understand the urge, but screaming is only going to rile these animals up." His voice emerged quiet, but steady, and possessed an easy, almost languid western drawl, something weirdly soothing.

In the cage, some three feet away, the door rattled. A breath huffed out.

"That's Hot Pete," the man said. "He's a little high-strung."

On the tail end of his words, the door shook, as if something big had rammed against it.

She jumped.

He stepped between her and the beast, his voice now directed at the cage. "Hey there, Petey. Calm down. She didn't mean to mess with your beauty sleep." He'd changed his voice, modulated it to a soft timbre, almost a tune.

She looked over his shoulder, and her eyes had adjusted enough to see the dark, shiny eyes of a red, hairy bull, nearly six feet to its shoulders, its horns glinting against the bare light. It snorted, and she jerked.

But she didn't run. Although probably she should, with Cowboy's back turned to her, but it was the way he was still talking to the bull that tugged her in, glued her in place.

"There you go, buddy. See, we're all friends here." Then he launched into a song, the words nearly a whisper. "'Three-thirty in the morning, not a soul in sight...city's looking like a ghost town, on a moonless summer night...'"

The words rumbled through her. Wait—Garth Brooks.

"I know this song," she said.

Cowboy glanced at her, kept singing. "'Raindrops on the windshield—'"

"'The storm's rolling in...'" She caught the tune.

"'And the thunder rolls...'" The smallest of smiles tweaked up his face.

The bull shifted, moved away from the door, and the man reached in through the bars and patted the animal's body. Started in on the next verse of the song.

She hummed, listening to his low tenor, watching as the bull moved back into the shadows. The man's voice dropped away, and he turned, looked at her, and nodded with his head toward the door.

Like they might be creeping out of a sleeping child's room.

Her heartbeat had slowed to just a distant rush in her chest as he pointed their way out of the barn and onto the pathway that led to the carnival.

"You dropped this." He held out her wallet.

Her wallet. Not a gun. Not a knife, nothing that might actually harm her. And oh, please, let the ground open up and swallow her right now, here, and let her vanish forever.

"Thanks." She took the wallet.

"Are you hurt?"

She glanced up at him. For the first time, she got a good look at her pursuer-slash-hero. He wore a grim line to his mouth, surrounded by the stubble of cherry-brown whiskers and dark brown sideburns that, in the light of the carnival, seemed flecked with red. But his eyes, oh his eyes. Blue-green, the color of the forest, deep and penetrating. As if she could run into his gaze and happily disappear.

His voice threaded through her, as if it might be made of rawhide, designed not to break, to weather time and elements, as sturdy as the land he probably worked. Because yes, he wore cowboy like a second skin, the no-nonsense aura of hard work and get 'er done, and given the way he'd sung to his bull, he knew his way around animals.

He even stuck his thumbs in his belt buckle, letting his hands land there, nailing the cowboy persona down in spades. Probably used those wide shoulders to rope in culprits, to wrestle steer, and now her imagination had run away with her, but seriously, under that black T-shirt and jean jacket she guessed he might be all hard-work-hewn body, washboard abs, and powerful arms.

Which he now crossed over his chest, as if trying not to follow his question by skimming his hands over her body to check for broken bones. Instead, his eyes did it for him— and not in a way that would make her step back, but with concern etched into his hard jawline.

"Do I need to go back there and put some hurt on

anyone?"

He wasn't smiling, and she couldn't tell if he was serious—maybe. Which sort of unrooted her for a moment.

Um… "No. I tripped. There was this little ledge at the bar and I reached over for the container and…I don't know. Fell back. And my wings went flying, and I bumped into this guy and…" Now she just wanted to cover her face with her hands and slink away.

"You're okay, then?" He unwound his arms, glanced back at the beer tent. Waved his hand to someone standing outside on the pathway. The someone headed back into the tent.

She nodded. "I'm just…" Oh, who was she kidding? It wasn't like she could hide the craziness from him, not after he'd chased her down and kept her from being—what, *eaten*? maybe slimed—by a mad bull.

"I sometimes panic about…I have issues—"

"Like not wanting some strange man to grab you? That feels pretty normal to me."

And then he smiled, something soft, his mouth lifting up on one side, and it was so charming, the fist in her chest simply let go. Left her free to stand there in the semi-light, to smell the spring air, listen to the carnival music, and realize that maybe, right now, she was safe.

"Knox Marshall," Cowboy said and held out his hand.

"Kelsey. Jones." She slipped her hand into his. What she suspected—a working man's hand. Muscled, lean, and calloused.

She waited for a flicker of name recognition on his face, and when she got none, her chest unknotted a little more.

"Your dinner is in the dirt back in the tent." He gestured with his head toward the tent. "Can I get you something to eat?"

His suggestion raked up the savory redolence of fried cheese curds, french fries, cotton candy, and popcorn.

"I think their kitchen is closed," she said. "We'd ordered from the restaurant in the arena, but I had…um, plans, so I couldn't pick it up right away, so they left it out in the tent."

He didn't follow up her stutter on the word *plans*, and she didn't want to fill in the blanks.

It would only raise eyebrows, and besides, she'd changed her life. Tonight had simply been a fluke. A throwback response to old wounds.

"I could offer you some…fair food?" He glanced toward the carnival, and her stomach totally betrayed her, roaring to life at his suggestion. She pressed her hand against it and gave him a wry look.

"Maybe we could tame that beast with some high-calorie, bad-for-you cheese curds?"

She smiled then. "I'd sell everything I own for cheese curds."

He laughed, and it found her hollow spaces.

And then she was walking down the semi-shadowed path with a near stranger, evidence that yes, she had outrun her demons. *Really.*

The path led them into the carnival area, a midway filled with games, food, and thrill rides—a rollercoaster called the Comet, a whirly named the Enterprise, another ride aptly named Extreme, resembling a giant hammer with a carriage that spun in a circle while swinging around a massive arm. Blinking lights, screams, and the sense of carefree trouble gave the night a sweetly dangerous mix.

"I'd probably lose my lunch on any of these," Knox said, eyeing the rides.

At the very end of the grounds, a massive Ferris wheel rose, its glittering lights casting a glow over the entire fairgrounds and the city of San Antonio beyond.

Knox nodded toward a vendor stand and, before she could stop him, pulled out his wallet and purchased a basket of cheese curds. The smell alone could make her weep.

The last time she'd eaten, she might have downed a bag of chips as she and the girls had been rehearsing under the stage lights, trying to nail their new finale.

Tomorrow night everything could change for them in the space of the opening act.

Now, she popped a curd into her mouth, let the salty, cheesy goodness and the slight tang of the beer batter soothe the ragged edges of tonight's craziness. She held the basket out to Knox, and he took one.

He moaned a little as he savored the treat.

"I know, right? I'm from a little town on the border of Minnesota and Wisconsin that specializes in cheese curds. They win the cheese contest."

Down the row, country music wheedled out from a stage, and they wandered over to a band tucked into a side street, some locals trying to make a name for themselves. They'd gathered a small crowd.

She well remembered those days, playing for tips and the small but faithful audience. Still lived it, on a higher level, perhaps. She slid onto a bench, listening.

Knox sat next to her. Not too close, but enough to feel his presence.

"They're good," she said after the first song. "The lead singer knows how to work his audience." Tall, dark blond hair, wearing a pair of black Converse high tops, ripped jeans, and a baseball hat on backward, the crooner made eye contact with a few ladies and had them swooning.

To her recollection, Kelsey had never swooned over a man. Run from them, pushed them away, even feared them, but swooning?

She didn't have room for swooning. For charm or anything, really, beyond a basket of cheese curds under a starry sky.

Knox leaned back on the bench. "I guess so," he said in response to her comment. "I don't go to concerts."

"Do you listen to country music?" She didn't know why his answer caught her breath.

He lifted a shoulder. "Sometimes. I listen to whatever my mother has playing in the house."

His...mother?

He must have sensed her question because he looked over at her. "I run the family ranch, in western Montana, just outside the small town of Geraldine, south of Glacier National Park. Seems silly to build an entire house for just me."

Oh. Right. She offered him the last cheese curd, but he waved her off. She finished it and wiped her hands on a napkin. "So, I take it you knew that bull in the barn."

"Yeah. He's one of our stars. We breed bucking bulls—have a PBR champion named Gordo who's sired a number of other winners. Hot Pete is his best issue. He's four years old, and was a PBR Finals bull the last two years, a world champion. I'm working out his contract for the NBR-X."

She nodded, and maybe her face gave her away, because he raised an eyebrow. "What—?"

"I just... Isn't it cruel? To make them buck like that?"

"Make them...oh, you're thinking of the strap we put on around their hindquarters to make them buck."

She nodded. "I've...been to a few rodeos. Seen the protesters."

He shook his head. "I love my animals. They're valuable athletes just like the cowboys, and I wouldn't do anything to hurt them. The bulls wear a strap that adds pressure, but it doesn't hurt them. And I promise, it doesn't cut into their, um, sire abilities." He met her eyes again, and a streak of solid heat poured through her.

"People get killed riding bulls," she said.

"People can get killed taking a walk in the park."

Oh, she knew that. Too well.

"It's a sport that's been around since the 1930s. And every year it gets a little safer. But yeah, it's dangerous." He leaned forward, his muscled forearms on his legs. Thick, sinewed, and—

"Did you ever ride bulls?" She wasn't sure why she asked, but it just felt like maybe—

"A long time ago. Not anymore."

Something about his tone spoke just a little of wistfulness.

Then he looked at her, and a smile hitched up the side of his face. "You have to be young and a little crazy to get on the back of a bull like Hot Pete." He wore the smallest glint of dare in his eyes and for a second...

"You want to ride him, don't you?"

He frowned at her, then looked away. "No."

Except... "You do."

He considered her a moment, then, "Maybe. But those days are gone. I'm too..."

"Old?"

He drew up. "Practical. I haven't been on a bull for years. And I have a ranch to run. I don't have room in my life for..."

"Crazy?"

He seemed to stare through her. Nodded, slowly.

She looked away. Right. She didn't know why his response pinched. Except, it wasn't like she'd ever see him again. With any sort of luck, after tomorrow she'd have a permanent gig with NBR-X and be moving on to the next fairground, the next basket of cheese curds, maybe even another try at buffalo wings in the beer tent.

Without the debacle.

Because she just needed steady, safe, and consistent, and then maybe the demons would die for good.

"Are you here all weekend?" she asked, not sure why.

"Leaving tomorrow right after the rodeo."

Oh. Well, good.

"You?"

"After the show, tomorrow night." Really, it was the truth. "I'm just here with a couple girlfriends for the weekend." If she said anything more, he might hear hope in her voice. No, not hope…she'd put any ideas of romance long behind her. Who would want anyone with her wounds?

"Right," he said and got up. Stared down at her. "We probably need a ride on the Ferris wheel."

She raised an eyebrow, then glanced at the circle glimmering against the dark. "Really?"

He nodded, and those blue-green eyes made it seem like exactly the right idea.

He led the way and she followed, frustrated at her fluttering heart.

And why, when he climbed into the basket, she took his proffered hand. Sat next to him, under the stretch of his arm.

They ascended slowly, stopping for more passengers, and he said nothing beside her, not drawing her close, simply letting his arm linger behind her.

In case, perhaps, she got cold.

But the night air contained just enough warmth to keep a shiver at bay, and as they rose, the entirety of San Antonio spread out below them. The sparkling lights of the Grand

Hyatt, the spire of the Tower of the Americas, the bright orange tower of the Weston Centre behind the Crowne Plaza. Orange, red, gold, and below them, the midway, the screams and blinking lights of the rides adding festivity to the night.

"It's so pretty from up here," she said quietly.

"Yes," Knox said. Took a breath. "It's always good to get a different perspective. It changes your vision of things."

She glanced at him. He smelled good, the faintest hint of aftershave on his skin.

In fact, the man was dangerously attractive.

He met her eyes, smiled.

She swallowed, and then, because they were in the sky, in the vault of darkness, above the pull of the earth, far enough away for even her demons to be quieted, she leaned over and kissed his cheek.

He froze.

When she leaned away, he looked at her, his eyes wide. He blinked, and it seemed he held his breath.

"Thank you for…" She took a breath. "For being safe."

He frowned but nodded.

The Ferris wheel brought them to the bottom, and she hopped off. Knox followed her, and they walked out to the edge of the carnival grounds, toward the path that led to the RVs and her tour bus. The lights shone out from her rig, evidence that at least one of the girls had returned.

She turned to Knox.

He smiled down at her.

Her hand twitched, and she longed to press it to his chest, wanting suddenly to feel the timbre of his heart.

"I don't suppose…" he started.

She shook her head.

His mouth formed a tight line, and he drew in a breath. "It was nice to meet you Kelsey Jones." It looked like he wanted to say something more. Even reach out to her. Instead he shoved his hands into his pockets. "Stay safe."

"I promise," she said.

He smiled, and she didn't move as he left her there, disappearing into the chaos of the carnival crowd.

At least that's what she was trying to do.

2

Pretty Kelsey thought he was old. And safe.

Knox couldn't pry those two bullets from his brain as he stood in the private box overlooking the dusty arena where, in a few moments, Hot Pete would seal his deal with Rafe Noble and NBR-X.

Those days are gone. I'm too...

Old?

Thirty wasn't exactly old, but sometimes he felt ancient, so much of his life undone. The conversation with Kelsey had kept him awake all night, and he'd finally got up and stood at the ninth-floor window of his Hyatt hotel room, staring down at the carnival lights in the distance. The RV park was dark, but she was tucked away in some trailer.

He couldn't seem to shake her voice, or her smile, from his brain. The way the wind toyed with tendrils of her sable brown hair falling in tousles around her face. He'd wanted to reach out and run his fingers through it but made a point of keeping his hands to himself.

Especially after seeing the fear in her eyes when she'd stared him down in the stock barn. Jaw tight, ready, it seemed, to fight him.

It had unnerved him. That and her soft, almost apologetic, *I sometimes panic about...I have issues—*

He'd just had to save her, then. Maybe he didn't want to know, but whatever had happened to cause her to run—no, flee—from the beer tent had tightened his gut.

He'd thought about that far too long last night.

He knew about fear. And running.

Thank you for being safe.

As he stood at the window, his hand had gone to his cheek, where she'd kissed it. Safe. He was safe, and maybe he didn't mind that label so much.

But a small part of him wanted to add *young* and just a little *dangerous.*

Like Tate.

Except he didn't have Tate's charisma or Wyatt's superstar grin, Ford's die-hard warrior drive, not even Reuben's sheer courage.

He'd been gifted with the Marshall family brains. The wisdom to recognize a bull with the right genes to breed buckers. The steel-spine grit to negotiate a contract.

Shoot, he'd turned into his father. No, worse. At least his father had once been a hotshot, fighting wildfires in Montana.

Every one of you were put here for a reason. Find it. Live it.

His dad, in his head again, but this time alongside his own thoughts.

Old. Safe.

Please, let this not be his legacy.

"Good ride," said a voice, and he turned as Rafe Noble came up next to him.

Tall, rangy, and handsome, the former GetRowdy Bull Riding champion had once graced Times Square's glittering billboards with his whiskered face, when the bull-riding event landed at Madison Square Garden. Rafe then married a hotel heiress, moved to Texas, and started his own cattle ranch, following in the family business. He'd spent the past few years announcing for the PBR. He'd joined NBR-X on the board of directors, one of the founding organizers.

When Rafe reached out to Knox through his brother Reuben to contract Hot Pete, Knox hadn't wanted to mention the fact that once upon a time he'd wanted to be like Rafe. In fact, Rafe was only a few years older than Knox, and in his youth, Knox had dreamed of competing against the champion.

Rafe was referring to the young buck who'd just lasted 4.3 seconds on Windwhipper, a Brahma bull with a wicked body roll. The cowboy landed in the dirt and skedaddled to the rail while the cowboy clowns released the bull rope and directed the animal into the exit chute.

"Reminds me of PeeWee, the bull that killed my best friend," Rafe said quietly. He took a sip of his coffee. "They get a thirst for hurt and go after a cowboy."

"Hot Pete isn't that kind of bull. He isn't a killer. He just knows how to buck," Knox said.

"This is a family event, but we do want the best," Rafe said. "It's a fine line—thrilling the crowd but keeping our cowboys safe."

"Bull riding is hardly safe," Knox said. "But Hot Pete won't run a rider down."

Hopefully. Gordo had been that perfect mix of bull— feisty in the ring but amiable when the strap came off. "Hot Pete has a 4.52 average buckoff time and so far is unridden. That gives the audience enough of a thrill but keeps the stakes high. He's a hard bucker, often spins to the inside, but has a wicked back kick and will even twist. And he scores points for the riders—he's got an average of 41.5. The cowboys like him. But even more than that, he's smart. He can almost read a rider, know how to throw him."

Rafe was nodding, his gaze on the red 1,750-pound Braford bull as he lined up in the chute.

Massive, with a white stripe down his face and black eyes, the bull knew how to inspire terror.

Give a show.

Knox had raised him from a bottle. Trained him with a bucker and even once ridden him, back in the early days.

When he was younger, of course.

He was a good animal, and right now he might earn Knox enough cash to invest in a breeder cow named Calamity Jane that he had his eye on. He needed more champions if he wanted to…what? Grow the ranch?

Maybe.

Yes.

Because he'd been bequeathed the family legacy, and he had a responsibility.

The cowboy climbed into the chute. Next to Knox, Rafe drew in his breath.

Perhaps, like Knox, he was lost in history. Remembering winding the rope, sticky with resin, around the beast, of winding the rope around his wrist, knocking his fist tight, then wedging himself up against his bull rope. Knox had always slammed his free fist into his protective vest, just a couple times before breathing in and out hard, three successive breaths.

His lucky routine. Even now he blew out the breaths.

The cowboy yanked up his fringed chaps, then settled his full weight on the bull, his spurs ahead of the ropes.

Gripped the railing with his free gloved hand.

The crowd went deathly quiet.

He raised his hand, and the chute opened.

Hot Pete spun out of the enclosure, into the dirt, yanking the cowboy hard to the outside. The rider hung on like he might be on a carnival ride.

Then Pete jerked forward, his high quarters bucking up. The cowboy jerked forward, cracked his nose on the bull's head, and instinctively, Knox's hand went to his nose.

Broken a couple times on a bull's wide head before he'd been smart enough to ditch his cowboy hat for a helmet.

Blood spurted down the rider's face, but he had the grit to hang on despite what must be blinding pain.

Pete bucked again and this time twisted in midair.

The rider didn't have a chance. He flew off in the opposite direction, his grip breaking free of the bull rope. He landed hard, dazed, into the dirt as the clowns chased down Pete, herding him into the exit chute.

A medic had run into the arena, bending beside the young buck. But he came up on his knees, grabbed a proffered gauze pad, and waved to the crowd.

The audience exploded, cheering.

Rafe glanced over at Knox, grinned.

Deal.

"We'll email you the signed contract," Rafe said. "Although, are you sure I can't talk you into bringing Gordo out of retirement? For one epic ride?"

"What, are you going to ride him?"

He recognized the spark in Rafe's eyes as he grinned. Shrugged.

Knox shook his head. "You have a death wish, Noble."

Rafe laughed. "You sticking around for the show afterward?"

"The country music concert?"

"My wife's favorite band is playing. The Yankee Belles. They're auditioning for a permanent spot on the tour." Rafe glanced over to where his daughter, seven-year-old Victoria, sat with her mother, the beautiful Katherine—Kitty, as Rafe referred to her—Breckenridge Noble. New York socialite turned rancher's wife. But more than that, Katherine Noble had added her golden touch to the NBR-X, extricating the hard-rock edge the PBR thrived on and turning it family friendly and even into a charitable event, with their last-night donations at the door for wounded warriors. She wore her dark, sable-brown hair in a ponytail, a pair of jeans, and a pink NBR-X T-shirt that matched her daughter's.

"I can get you tickets if you and Tate want to go."

"I think Tate is working tonight. Security."

"Then come with us. Kitty has backstage passes—you can meet the Belles."

Oh, that was the last thing he wanted to do—meet the Spice Girls. What he really wanted to do was track down Kelsey, somewhere in this crowd, and show her that he wasn't quite as old as she made him out to be. For some reason, the cowboy in the ring had ignited something inside him.

The once-upon-a-times and might-have-beens. Maybe he'd go back to the beer tent and get on that mechanical bull, show those yahoos how it's done.

Or better yet—

You want to ride him, don't you?

His gaze turned to the final rider, watching as he fought to stay on the animal. He got flipped off after five point three seconds, landing and rolling in the dirt.

Knox's own gold championship buckle hung in his office back at the ranch.

"Ouch," Rafe said, making a face as he watched the rider limp off the dirt.

A group of riders on horses came out, riding bareback, doing tricks.

"Can I do that, Daddy?"

Knox looked down to where Victoria, her dark hair a mess of curls, pressed her hands on the glass.

Rafe crouched next to her, drew her into his embrace, between his knees. "Someday, Tori. But wouldn't you rather run barrels?"

She looked up at Rafe. "I want to ride bulls, like you, Daddy."

Knox laughed as Rafe made a face, glancing over his shoulder at his wife.

"That's what you get for being a champion," Knox said, the closest he could come to admitting hero worship. But what he wouldn't give for a son or daughter to look at him like that. A wife to grin at him, a twinkle in her pretty eyes.

He was so tired of standing on the sidelines of his life, feeling as if all his chances had passed him by. Tired of being the responsible one who did things *right* while others reached for their dreams.

Rafe got up as Kitty came up to him and slid her arm around his broad shoulders. "You sure you don't want to stick around for the concert? It's right here—in the back of the coliseum. The Yankee Belles are up-and-coming. And all very pretty." She winked.

Knox gave her a polite smile.

"And in the meantime, I'll talk you into joining the NBR-X as our Director of Livestock," Rafe said.

Knox looked at him. "What?"

"You have an eye for good breeding, Knox. You're developing a reputation in the business for your ability to find the right sires, for pairing them with the right cows. Five of your ranch's issues have gone on to the PBR finals, and if your new bulls are anything like Hot Pete, then I think they'll sell for top dollar. I'd like to see you bring that talent to NBR-X's selection of bulls."

Really?

The announcer listed off the winners, and the riders came out, waving their hats, collecting their applause. Knox was turning away when the ad for the upcoming concert flashed across the jumbotron.

He stilled, staring at it. Three girls standing, two blondes flanking the center brunette, who drew her straw cowboy hat down with one finger, staring into the screen. Her lips curved in a half smile, a twinkle in those pale blue eyes, and his heart stuttered.

Kelsey?

Except his Kelsey hadn't been the curvy, show-stopping country star with long black lashes and a look on her face that made his mouth a little dry. She'd been a girl from the Midwest who liked cheese curds and kissed him on the cheek and made him feel like her protector.

I'm just here with a couple girlfriends for the weekend.

The woman on the screen could have a lineup of cowboys offering up their hearts, not to mention their muscles, to keep her safe.

He didn't know what to think, what to say. But he couldn't unglue his gaze from the jumbo screen.

"That's the Yankee Belles," Katherine said quietly.

He looked at her, and she smiled, something glinting in her eyes. "You sure you don't want those backstage passes?"

Kelsey liked this version of herself. Too much, maybe, but the woman who looked back at her from the glimmering lights of the makeup mirror was not only beautiful, sexy, and strong, but she possessed a charisma and poise that Kelsey wanted to cling to.

Onstage, Kelsey became the person she wanted to be

offstage.

And tonight, she would rock it.

"Feathers?" The question, or rather, criticism came from Dixie Erikson, their fiddle player, who leaned over her shoulder and tugged on the duo of feathers fastened to Kelsey's long brown hair.

"You should talk—is that a tiara?" She turned, got a closer look at the glittery headband in the blonde's hair. Willowy and beautiful, Dixie usually turned heads first when she walked into a room, her Viking heritage in her blue eyes and long, braided hair. It was her family whom Kelsey had lived with back in high school, her family of country singers who had stirred Kelsey's love of music. She wore a leather jacket, ripped jeans, and black cowboy boots.

Although, in truth, Dixie wasn't her real name. But no country singer was named Donna, and Dixie had changed her moniker back in the days when they had a standing Saturday night gig at Rusty's Roadhouse in Chippewa Falls, Wisconsin.

Now, eight years later, Kelsey couldn't think of her as anyone but Dixie.

"Clearly, we all want this badly." This from Glo, who was sitting on a nearby sofa, plucking on her banjo, working on the chords of a song she was writing. She wore a strapless, one-piece body suit of leather, with red flowers painted up her shoulder and around her décolletage. Also blonde—although her hair was nearly white—and at five foot two, Glo was the shortest of the girl trio, but she had a soprano voice that could lift the rafters. With hazel-green eyes and curves, she was the sassy one, knew how to flirt with the crowd, and had managed to shuck off her highbrow Southern belle upbringing and embrace the country singer lifestyle. If it weren't for her living her high school years with her father in the small college town on the border of Minnesota and Wisconsin, the three would have never met.

Gloria Jackson was the harmonizer, the banjo, dobro, and guitar hero of their trio, the brassy one who made most of their decisions, thanks to her legal background. And frankly, downright unflappable, probably from all her years of training to be in the political limelight.

First Daughter.

Her mother's goal, not Glo's. If it was up to her mother, senator for the great state of Tennessee, she would come to her senses and start doing something respectable.

A knock at the door, then Carter stuck his head in. In his mid-fifties with graying dark hair, Carter had always reminded Kelsey of George Clooney with his cocky smile that could charm every radio station across the country.

The one time God had shown up, been on her side was the night Carter walked into the Double Buck in Nowheresville, Wisconsin, sat down at a table, and listened to their entire set. She always thought that maybe Dixie's dad might be to blame. God usually showed up when Uncle Dennis asked.

"Five minutes," Carter said, then smiled. "Knock 'em dead." He winked and shut the door, and for the first time, Kelsey felt her stomach clench.

Breathe.

But this wasn't the panic that had threaded through her and taken possession last night.

No, onstage, she owned the world. The crowd, cheering, singing along. She roused them to heights, brought them low with ballads, made them feel the soul woven into the music written by Glo and Dixie.

She was the entertainer of the group. The performer.

The lead singer.

And probably, the one person who should rightly be in hiding.

But she became a different person onstage, and it was this person who got up, high-fived Dixie and Glo, and headed out to the wings of the stage.

The arena smelled of dirt, horseflesh, and sweat, but props had laid down a floor over the dirt, and the crowd stirred, waiting in the semidarkness.

She loved their show. How they came onstage in the pitch black, their enchanting a cappella voices lifting together in perfect harmony, then the sudden crescendo as their drummer, Elijah Blue, brought the song to life. How the lights sparked and as one they dove into the song, a full video screen behind them. In that moment, she was part of something bigger than herself. Swept up in the lyrics, the music, the fervor of the performance. She knew it, relished it, and hungered for it.

Inside the orchestration of their performance, she was safe.

Glo came up behind her. "So, do you think he's out there?"

She glanced at her. "Who?"

"Tall, dark, and handsome," she said. "The guy who walked you home last night. Dixie saw him with you."

Kelsey's eyes widened "When?"

"At the carnival." Dixie winked. "I saw you on the Ferris wheel together. Who was he?"

The song piping through the arena was finishing its last notes.

"Just a cowboy. A rancher. A safe guy, but nobody."

Glo shook her head. "Right."

"What—"

But Dixie pushed her onstage, and they walked out in

darkness as a hush fell over the crowd.

She knew exactly the number of steps, found the shiny mic stand in the middle, gripped her hand around it. Cool. Solid. *Stay safe.*

Knox's voice rose inside her and she closed her eyes. Yes, out there the world came at her fast and hard, without rules, random and terrifying.

Not here.

She heard the tapping—Elijah at the drum, counting in their song. She took a breath, then eased into her voice, singing a cappella with Dixie and Glo...

Can you make me touch the sky
Can you give me a reason why
Don't leave me, don't make me cry...
Cowboy don't lie—Take me away and make me fly.

The harmonies died, and she grinned in the silence, a split second before the audience filled it with a thrumming cheer.

Then Elijah rolled in the beat, Glo added her banjo, and behind them, the bassist and keyboardist, two up-and-coming musicians Carter had hired in Nashville for this gig, joined in.

The lights came up, and for a second, Kelsey blinked against the brightness. But she grabbed the mic, raised her arms and took the lead.

It feels like yesterday when you gave me the moon
When you told me that you'd never let me go.
Ain't no way to understand why I let you
Tell me how you love me so...

Dixie stepped up with her fiddle, took the mic, and Kelsey hummed, her eyes closed, hearing the half-truth from last night.

I'm just here with a couple girlfriends for the weekend. Maybe she should have told him more. But there had been a magic in the evening, an anonymity, and she'd just wanted to be a girl with a cowboy.

She opened her eyes and grinned at the audience.

So sweet bull-doggin' man, take me home tonight
Sing me a song, pull the stars from the sky
Make me believe your words, that everything will be all right.
Cowboy don't lie—Take me away and make me fly.

The crowd erupted, and she glanced at Glo, then Dixie, then to the crowd and sent them a kiss. The applause filled her up, thick and rich in the hollow spaces.

She greeted the audience, introduced Glo and Dixie— the band would come later—and they launched into one of their hits, a song about trouble, Dear Johns, and broken hearts, and the crowd sang along.

She grabbed a tambourine and her mic and went to the front of the stage, grinned down at a couple of youngsters who just might be too young for their songs, but who waved to her. She winked at them and continued her walk across stage as behind her, Dixie did some fiddle magic.

She was just turning back to the center stage when she spotted him. Just inside the rim of visible lights, maybe three rows back and standing behind a little girl who sat on her father's shoulders, clapping. Tall, cowboy hat, dark hair with a touch of red, those magnetic eyes pinned to her.

Knox.

He was here, and he stared at her as if stymied, or

enthralled—yeah, she'd go with that. Surprised, for sure, and more than a little undone.

For a second, she nearly stopped singing, nearly hiccupped the lyrics, nearly tripped in front of the entire world.

But this was her world, her stage.

Her safe place.

So she grinned at him, and across the crowd, winked.

His mouth opened, and she didn't stay for more, turning back to center stage.

She finished the song, grinning at the Belles, then back out into the darkness as the audience erupted.

Stay safe.

At least he knew she was keeping her promise.

But she couldn't dislodge the idea of him standing out there in the crowd as she led them through the set. As she told the funny story about how the girls met—in high school, crushing over the same stupid boy, who would end up dissing them all. As she taught the crowd how to sing along to "Let Him Go, Go Go, Bye, Bye" and finally when she got quiet, the spotlight on her alone for her solo song, the one called "One True Heart," a ballad about young love, waiting for a happy ending, a soldier gone to war.

One of Glo's best, but she couldn't sing it without weeping, so Kelsey recorded it, and it had gone viral.

She met him on a night like any other
Dressed in white, the cape of a soldier
He said you're pretty, but I can't stay
She said I know, but I could love you anyway…

Kelsey knew how to work the song, her alto turning it husky and raw.

But you don't know if you don't start
So wait…for one true heart…one true heart…

She let the last notes linger, just her voice and the quiet auditorium, the sound haunting, the what-ifs lingering in the air.

They ended with their current finale— "Live It Up," an upbeat song about dancing, letting loose, and living rowdy.

Not that she—or any of them—did any of that, but it cemented the feeling she wanted to leave with the NBR-X audience.

They came back for an encore, their first hit with the banjo screaming, the fiddle burning, and a crazy tumble of lyrics that had her sweating under the lights.

She fell into the arms of Glo and Dixie backstage, breathing hard, part triumph, part exhaustion. Carter ran up and embraced them all.

"Hot, hot, hot! Listen to that crowd!" Indeed, they should probably have another encore, but Kelsey was ready to order room service and drop into a hot bath. Or rather, squeeze into the tiny bus shower and eat some cold pizza from today's takeout.

But by the look on Carter's face, they'd landed the gig. At least until, "One of the board members wants to meet you three. I'll go get him."

Oh. But she could put on her stage face for the brass if it meant they had regular gigs for the next six months.

Carter led them backstage to a meet and greet green room, then left to get the guest. She fished out a soda from the tub of ice. Pushed it to her forehead. She was drenched in a layer of heat, soggy right through to her bones.

The rest of the band had crowded into the room, and she high-fived Elijah, noticing how his gaze landed on Dixie.

Poor guy—Kelsey had a feeling he'd taken the gig to follow his heart...the one not attached to music. But the way Dixie glanced at him, too, maybe he had a chance.

He was certainly cute, with his long hair, pale green eyes, tight, martial arts frame. He reminded her of some ancient dark Viking warrior.

"Hey, Kelsey," Carter said. She turned and spotted him heading her direction. In front of him bounced a cute dark-haired little girl—maybe the one from the audience—grinning like she'd just seen a Disney princess.

Kelsey crouched to her height and held out her hand. "Oh my, did you know someone stole your front teeth?" She feigned shock.

The girl giggled, nodded. "The toof fairy!"

"Of course. Someone alert the sheriff." Kelsey winked at her.

"This is Tori Noble," Carter said. He gestured to a man and a woman standing beside him. "And these are her parents, Rafe and Katherine Noble. Rafe is on the board of NBR-X."

Kelsey stood up, wiped her sweaty hand on her jeans, and held it out for Rafe. Handsome, dark brown hair, muscled and lean, he bore the look of a man who knew his way around a rodeo. And his wife, Katherine, had the long dark hair and smile of a grown-up cowgirl, from her pink shirt to her skinny jeans and designer boots.

"Glad to meet you," Kelsey said, not sure what else she should add. Begging briefly shot through her mind, but she'd just given them her best. She wasn't sure what else she could offer.

Either they liked the Belles, or they didn't. She looked at Carter, searching for rescue.

And for the first time since she got offstage, a tremor ran

through her. What if—

"You were amazing."

The voice slid under her skin, landed in her bones, and her breath hiccupped as she turned to look for the source.

Knox had walked up, stood behind Katherine, grinning at Kelsey.

And just like that, Cowboy Marshall had the power to stop her world from spinning out from beneath her.

"Hi," she said softly, nothing of the stage in it, knocked away by the spell of his eyes.

Those dangerous blue-green eyes that held her, the language in them something rich, although a little confused.

"I...almost didn't recognize you."

Katherine had stepped aside, and Knox came up to Kelsey, his gaze taking in the feathers, the brown V-necked NBR-X T-shirt, cutoff jeans, and black tights that molded her legs, down to turquoise cowboy boots.

Okay, yeah, she looked a little different.

Whereas he looked exactly the same. Except for the suit coat over his black T-shirt.

Wait—was he on the board, too?

She drew in a breath, because...

The last thing NBR-X wanted was a crazy person, a troublemaker, someone who might crack at any moment, on their roster.

Or, probably, a liar. "I didn't want to...I..." She bit her lip, not sure what to say about her glaring omission last night.

He shook his head, grinned, saving her again. "It's okay. I get it. Sometimes a person just needs to eat cheese curds in anonymity."

Her mouth opened, closed. She nodded.

Shoot. Because this man had definite swooniness. "What are you doing...I mean, did you stay for the concert? Because you said you were leaving—"

"You two know each other?" Rafe Noble glanced at Knox.

"We met last night. She was picking up some wings at the beer tent," Knox said, not giving her up.

"I told little Miss Noble here that you'd sign a poster for her," Carter said, indicating Tori. She looked up at Kelsey, her eyes shining.

"Of course I will. You want to see my dressing room?"

Tori nodded, and Kelsey held out her hand, glancing for the okay from Katherine. "We'll be right back."

She waved her hand to Glo and Dixie, leaving them to mingle as she and Tori pushed through the crowded room. When they emerged to the hall, she noticed Knox had joined them. She met his eyes. "Really?"

"I want a signed poster too." He grinned then, and a strange warmth poured through her, touching her belly.

They wove their way to the back rooms, and she pushed open her door, a tiny room that held her costumes, makeup, and yes, that leftover pizza. She flicked on the lights.

Tori's eyes widened as her gaze fell on the rack of costumes dragged in from the bus. "You wear all these?"

"I couldn't decide what to wear." She let go of Tori's hand and looked at Knox, pitching her voice low. "I'm really sorry I didn't say anything."

His gaze turned warm and sweet. "It's not like we were sharing our deepest secrets. It's okay. And I meant it. You took my breath away up there."

She just didn't know what to do with this man.

And because she'd kept the truth from him before, she came clean. "The stage seems to be one place that's mine. It's where life makes sense. I'm safe, and yes, things go wrong, but it doesn't feel out of control."

He stared at her, those eyes reaching down with something like compassion. "Kelsey, what—"

The rumble started under her feet, a split second of warning. Knox's eyes widened, and he reached for her—

Then, the arena exploded in a blast of fire, smoke, and debris.

3

Knox felt his face to confirm that his eyes were open. Because in the pitch darkness, he couldn't even make out his hand before his face. He hadn't passed out—he remembered every second, almost in slow motion.

The floor had rippled, and he'd reached out to grab Kelsey, a move born of instinct as his arm curled around her.

In the same moment he looked at Tori, out of his reach, standing next to the makeup counter.

Then the boom resounded through the building, into his body, and the world emptied beneath him, simply crumbled with a great heave. He yanked Kelsey to himself even as screams lifted to mix with the thunder of the explosion.

He fell forever, clawing the air, the lights blinking out, debris raining down over him. Only his arm around Kelsey anchored him as chaos erupted. He landed hard, unable to brace himself, the air whooshing out of him.

Pain exploded through his leg, his arm, and Kelsey fell away in the ricochet of the impact.

He reached for her, but ended up pulling his legs tight to himself, his arms over his head as the debris pinged around him—metal, cement, furniture.

Smoke saturated the air, and he kept his face down, into a crack while the world careened to a stop.

Then everything was engulfed by an eerie, deep silence, as if time took a moment to simply catch its breath.

Him too. He took a gulp of dusty air, during which he heard his heart thunder in his ears.

What just happened?

Abruptly, a cacophony of sharp whinnies and groaning of stock animals erupted around him—clearly the destruction had torn into the stock pens below.

Yes, his eyes were still open. And he seemed largely unhurt, despite the bone-jarring crash. Dust embedded the hairs of his arms, clogged his nose, layered his face. He touched his chest, where his heart hammered, and tried to move.

Nothing felt broken.

He expected sparks, maybe flames with the odor of smoke, but nothing flickered against the all black, pitch darkness. It instantly swept into his pores, his bones.

Suffocating.

Only the whimpers nearby pulled him free. He reached out his hand, searching.

His grip closed around flesh, an arm. "Kelsey?"

No movement, but he did feel a pulse. He eased himself through the rubble, over cement and metal and wire, and scooted next to her. They seemed to be lying on the floor of the dressing room, but it had collapsed at an angle, so he had to climb toward her head.

He brailled his way up her arm, found her shoulder, her hair, brought his face to hers. "Kelsey, are you okay?"

A breath, harsh and fast, but she still didn't answer.

Kelsey wasn't the one whimpering. At least not audibly. "Tori?"

A hiccup of breath in answer, then a moan that turned into sobbing.

"Hang on. I'm coming, Tori." He hated the blackness. He put his hand toward the sound, but it hit something solid and metal.

Think, Knox. You're out on the range, in a blizzard, alone, with a truck that won't start. What do you do?

His father, showing up now to lecture him.

Except—yes. His phone still sat in his back pocket, and he wrestled it out in the darkness, pressed it on, and found his flashlight.

The app lit up their cave like the dawn of heaven illuminating the chaos of earth.

Thank You, God. He wasn't blind, even with his eyes open.

From what he could make out, the entire room had collapsed onto the floor below, one side falling farther than the other. The walls, too, caved in, detaching from their metal supports, and around them lay the debris of the room—broken mirror glass, light fixtures, the dismantled counter, and dissecting it all, one of the supporting ceiling beams that angled into the pit from its moorings above.

He aimed his phone to reveal where the joint met the wall and saw that the beam was cracked, the seam fractured. It could fall, crushing them at any moment.

"Help— please—"

Tori, and he wanted to weep with the pain in her voice. "Hang on, honey. I'm coming." He flashed the light on Kelsey.

She covered her face with her hands, her body trembling, and he made out a brutal scrape on her chin. She'd fallen away from him, her legs curled into her body. He pushed the hair back from her face, then checked her head for injury.

Nothing. "Kelsey?" He put his hand on her back, leaning over her in the small pocket of debris. "Kelsey?"

She wouldn't remove her hands, so he reached down and

pulled one away.

Her eyes were closed.

"Hey," he said. "Are you hurt?"

No answer, as if she hadn't heard him. "Kelsey!"

She stuttered in a breath, then, in a moment, opened her eyes.

But they didn't land on him, didn't recognize him.

As if—of course she was having a panic attack, or something close to it. "Kelsey, I have to get Tori."

Nothing.

"Help—"

He winced, but he had no choice but to turn the light toward the voice.

Tori lay under the remains of the makeup counter, trapped behind the ceiling joist. He climbed over Kelsey and shimmied under the joist, working his way down the space under the counter. It had fallen like a wedge over the top of Tori, and at first he let out a shudder of relief that she hadn't been seriously hurt.

Except, as he came closer, he saw how she gripped her leg, her whimpers turning to moans, then all-out tears as he moved the light over her.

Oh…no.

Her hand curled around a thin metal pipe, its jagged end embedded into her leg, in her lower thigh, right above her knee. Blood pooled around it, but it acted like a plug, keeping the leg from bleeding out.

"Hey, Tori," he said, fighting his voice. "I know you're hurt, but you can't pull that out, okay?"

Dust covered her hair and grimed her wet face, her eyes betraying terror, but she nodded.

He ran the light up the bar and saw that the angle ended at the broken joint of an electrical conduit that ran under the counter. It had broken off on one end and stabbed poor Tori when the counter fell.

"Stay still now," he said and reached over her to the joint. He held the conduit steady with one hand. With his other hand, he gave the metal connector that held the conduit to the wall a good wrench, and it broke free.

Tori cried out, but mostly from fear, as he hadn't moved the conduit. But now the conduit hung loose, two feet protruding from her leg.

He had to stabilize the impalement, keep it from ripping out of her leg before medical help came.

If it came.

Certainly, Rafe and Katherine knew where Tori had gone. They just had to hunker down and wait, right?

He flashed the phone around, and the light crested over the debris of the costume rack, tangled in metal and crushed under the cement. Reaching his hand through the opening, he yanked out a blouse.

This could work.

"Tori. This might hurt a little—" No, actually, a lot, but he didn't want to scare her. "I'm going to just wrap this around your leg, okay?"

Tori's wide eyes clung to him like he might be a superhero. But he felt like a villain as she cried out, as he wrapped her leg tight with the body of the shirt, cutting off some of the blood supply, then securing the bar with the arms, coiled twice, then also around her leg.

Please, let this hold. Because her breathing was shallow and fast, and she might be going into shock. He placed his big hand on her little cheek and bent his head close to hers. "I'm going to get us out of here. Just hang on, honey."

She nodded.

"I'll be right back."

He wanted to weep when she pressed her hand over his. But he scooted away and back to Kelsey. She had replaced her hand over her face, and he leaned to her ear. "Kelsey, I need you. Tori is really hurt. Wake up, please. Come back."

She didn't move, and he blew out a breath. Maybe she, too, was in shock. Which meant he had two people to rescue, and pronto.

He couldn't wait for the dogs or the SAR teams or whoever might be digging through the rubble to get to him sometime in the next twelve hours.

Knox shined the light up the falling ceiling joist to the floor above, then taking a breath, shimmied up alongside it so he could make out the damage.

When the joist fell, it had left a crawl space, and when he flickered his light into it, he made out the hallway. Beyond that, to his recollection, lay the expanse of the arena.

"Hello! We're in here!"

His voice echoed into the darkness.

He crouched back down. Closed his eyes.

Could use a little help here, Lord.

At least *he* wasn't hurt.

He took a look at Kelsey, then over to Tori.

Tori first.

He'd have to climb the ceiling joist. It was girded by smaller crisscrossed beams, almost like a ladder, but if he found a way to secure Tori, he could probably hoist her up to the next floor. Drag her out through the crawl space.

If the beam didn't collapse.

He crawled under it to Tori. Took her hand, his heart thumping.

"Okay, listen. You're so brave, Tori, and I need you to be braver. I'm going to get you out of here, but I need to figure it out, okay?" He needed a board, or something—

A scream filled the room and he jerked, slammed his head on the counter.

Kelsey.

She had begun to thrash, her screams ricocheting around the rubble. "No, no—"

He let go of Tori and scrambled back to Kelsey, not sure what to do—

He lay down beside her and pulled her back against him, his arms pinning her tight, his legs around hers, his mouth in her ear. "Kelsey, breathe. Breathe. You're okay. We're going to be okay."

He kept his voice low, like he had with Hot Pete, but mostly because he, too, wanted to scream, to unloose the coil of panic in his chest.

But if he did, he might never tuck it back inside. So instead, he began to rock her, to hum the first tune he could find...

She stopped screaming, as if listening, her breaths hitching, her body twitching in his embrace.

"Shh," he said. "You're going to be okay..."

Please, God, let us be okay.

———◆———

She wasn't lying in a bloody pile of soggy loam, the night lifting around her, leaving its moist tongue on her grimy skin. Wasn't broken, shattered, wounded, and violated. Her head wasn't spinning, throbbing, and coaxing her back into the sweet oblivion of unconsciousness.

Kelsey wasn't fourteen again, a victim of a terrible, random crime.

"Shh. You're going to be okay..." A low tenor slid over her, something familiar enough to reach in and tug away the confusion. To yank her back from the abyss, to silence the screaming inside.

The voice settled into her ear, her bones, and found the tremor inside. Clamped down on it. A hot, solid hand of safety that gripped her from the inside out.

Knox. Of course it was Knox—and now everything rushed back to her. The thunder that shook the building, him lunging at her, his arm snaking around her waist. Falling.

Then she was lying in the forgotten tangles of Central Park, fighting for every breath through cracked ribs, a broken wrist, her body torn, her blood saturating the earth. Trapped underneath the echo of her own screams.

Until Knox. Until he reached through the nightmares and pulled her against himself, solid, warm, safe, and held her body until she stopped shaking.

Shh.

She opened her eyes and looked up at him. Light splashed across a girder, the chaos of broken cement, glass, and debris.

"What—?" Her voice emerged weak, and the arms around her tightened.

She curled her hands around the forearms, thick and muscled, and the warmth of him holding her shucked away the last of her shaking.

"There was an explosion, I think." The arms loosened, and she just wanted to hang on for a moment longer, but he moved away. "Are you hurt?"

She lay for a moment, assessing. She hurt, but nothing deep and slicing, nothing fractured, and the pain throbbed low, as if her body might be rebounding from a body slam.

But she wasn't shattered. Wasn't wishing to die.

"I don't...I don't think so." Bruised, for sure, but she knew what *hurt* felt like.

No, definitely not.

He held a cell phone, the light flashing on the debris, then turned it up so it reflected down upon them.

Dirt layered his face, white eyes around grime. A fine layer of sweat slicked his brow, his eyes thick with concern as he met her eyes. He seemed to be testing her words.

And why not? Seconds ago, she'd been screaming, ungluing right before his eyes. If he didn't think she was crazy before, she couldn't imagine what he thought now.

It didn't matter what he thought of her.

Right now, she just needed to stay alive.

She cupped her hand around his wrist. "Are you hurt?"

He shook his head. "No. And I promise I'm going to get you out of this. But Tori is really hurt, and I need your help." He swallowed and glanced past her, then back to Kelsey. "She was impaled by an electrical conduit. I stabilized it, but we need to get her out of here before she goes into shock, or worse, starts to bleed out."

She let those words settle in, the worry in his tone painfully haunting.

"I know you're freaking out, and I get it, but…I need you to hold it together long enough to help me get her out. I need you to dig deep, Kelsey. I need you to be that girl I saw on stage. Can you do that for me?"

She didn't want to acknowledge any of his words—the fact that he probably knew that her nightmares had crawled into her brain to take hold. Or that he knew she was fighting the tug to sink back in.

Or even that he'd noticed that she became someone else onstage, someone who could probably keep it together. So, she took a breath, reaching out through the horror to nod.

You are more than you expect of yourself. Her counselor's words in her head, and Kelsey set them like a stone in her heart. Yes. Or she could be, right now.

"Where is she?"

He let her go and she untangled herself from his embrace. Followed the shine of his light.

Oh no. Tori lay in the shadows, crumpled, shaking. Broken, bloody from a metal rod protruding from her leg, her eyes huge with fear.

Breathe. Because the hand of memory had the power to scoop her up and yank her under.

"How are we going to get out of here?"

"The ceiling girder—we can climb it, as long as it holds. But we need something to carry her, like a table or a—"

"Guitar case?" She glanced over at him.

"Brilliant. But where—"

She grabbed his hand and directed the flashlight to Glo's backup guitar caught in the rubble near her costumes. Hard sided and made for rough handling, little Tori could probably fit in it.

"I'll get it." Kelsey didn't wait for him to respond, just took a breath, turned around, and climbed over the girder, heading toward the rubble.

Knox kept the light pointed in her direction, and she climbed over a chair, broken wood, and cement and found the case.

Miraculously intact. She grabbed the neck and wiggled it out free, pulling it onto herself, grabbing the handle, then unsnapping the latches. Glo's pretty mahogany Gibson lay inside. She pulled it out and left it in the wreckage, then closed the case and turned back to Knox, handing the case through the spaces.

He took it, then as he scooted to Tori, she climbed back to her space.

He laid it beside Tori, opened it. Considered it.

Then he took the two halves and yanked.

The hinges ripped from the case, first the ones at the neck, then at the back. He made a trough for Tori to lie inside, her body in the widest part, her legs along the neck. He ripped out the support for the neck to give Tori more room.

Kelsey shimmied under the girder and came out just as he bent to lift the little girl.

"No—no—" Tori gasped, both hands on her wound.

"Shh," Knox said in that same tone he'd used on Hot Pete. "I'm just going to lift you inside this case. I won't touch the pole, I promise."

"I'll get her shoulders," Kelsey said, and he looked up at her.

His eyes glistened, and he nodded, and her heart gave a lurch. This man.

But now wasn't the time to consider her wounds, the what-ifs and never-could-bes.

She gripped Tori's shoulders. So little, so breakable. Knox leaned over the guitar case to slip his arms under Tori's body.

"On three," he said and counted.

They moved her in one smooth transfer into the body of the case.

"We need to slide the case up the girder." Knox's gaze seemed to be calculating the how of his words.

"You could get on top, and I'll push her up to you?"

She wasn't sure where she'd dug up the words, but she nodded in the wake of them, as if trying to convince, well, herself.

He took a breath. "Okay. Help me get her on the girder. I'll climb up with her, and you push. Stabilize." He shined his light on the angled supports that braced the inside of the girder, then on a hinge at the top of the girder.

It hung half torn from its bracing.

She got up, considered the ten-foot rise to the next floor. "Maybe—"

"She could go into shock. We can't wait for help."

That's not what she was going to say. And the suggestion that she climb the girder nearly escaped anyway. But he had already moved the case into the girder, balancing it as he stepped onto one of the spokes.

It groaned, and she straddled the girder, securing the case. "Go."

He climbed fast, threw his leg over the top of the girder, turned to look down at them, and started to inch his way up, climbing backward as he tugged her up.

It was working. Kelsey stretched out, climbed up on the spokes, and tried to ignore the shuddering of the girder.

"I'm almost…there," Knox said, his hand white-gripping the case as he reached out for something above him in the darkness.

The metal groaned. "Hurry!" Kelsey shouted.

He slid onto the lip of the floor above, turned, and lay on his stomach, grabbing for the case.

In a second, he'd pulled Tori up and into the darkness beside him.

Voices echoed above, and she heard Knox shout back.

"Over here!"

They'd found them. She closed her eyes.

And in a moment, the past rushed up, light scraping over her body, nearly frozen through, a dog barking, warm hands on her. Someone draping a coat—

"Kelsey, c'mon!"

Knox was holding out his hand to her, lying on his stomach. She started to climb, hooking her feet on the spokes.

The metal shook, twisting with her exertions.

"Knox—?"

She reached out for his hand, brushed it.

The metal snapped off its mooring and in a second, she was falling, her footing sliding free.

A scream cut through her and she wanted to brace herself for impact—

Except a hand clamped onto her wrist. A vise that halted her midair as the world crashed around her. She dangled there, looked up.

Knox held her, his jaw tight, eyes in hers. "I got ya. I told you, I'm going to get you out of this."

4

The ambulance lights splashed the parking lot blood red, and Tate just wanted to hit something. To add a little pain and violence to the chaos inside.

Please, just give him something to do. Something productive, something that might stop him from unraveling.

He'd nearly lost his brother. And that thought had Tate by the throat, nearly suffocating him since the moment Tate had watched the back of the arena crumble under the shock of the explosion.

He'd been working security near the far exit, far away from the impact. Thankfully, the damage centered on just the area backstage, probably one particularly placed explosive. Why, he hadn't a clue, but he'd left his cohorts to control the screaming masses pushing to exit the auditorium and ran toward the smoke, flame, and cloud of debris.

Tate had sprinted through the center of the arena, leaping onstage and barreling to the back where other grounds security were already gathering, calling in for help. People had switched on their cell phones, tiny spotlights skittering over the wreckage of the explosion.

Miraculously, the explosion hadn't taken out the entire back area, hadn't left people with sheared limbs, burned and shattered.

From what Tate could tell, the explosion occurred a level below, caving in the mezzanine level, specifically the dressing rooms.

The sprinklers had switched on and bathed everything in a soggy wash. Smoke billowed up from a tangle of metal, cement, and debris.

From the first moment, he knew Knox had been buried. Because big bro had sent him a text telling him he was going backstage to meet the pretty Yankee Belles, that they'd catch up later.

And stupid him, he'd actually been jealous. Knox got all the good stuff—the reputation, the girl, even everything their father owned.

Knox was the Midas boy. Everything he touched turned to gold.

By the time Tate reached the backstage rubble, a crowd had gathered, some holding each other, crying. Others had started to move debris, and he joined a man on his knees, peering into the darkness of the crater.

"My daughter is in there somewhere," he said as he glanced at Tate, eyes reddened in horror.

It just took a second—it would have been faster without the smoke and screaming—but yeah, Rafe Noble, PBR champion, worked beside Tate to rip away the cement debris that crushed his daughter. Tate had seen him perform on television, back in the day when Knox rode in the juniors.

Rafe was on his knees, feeding his phone light into the darkness, when a shout lifted from deep in the bowels of the rubble.

"That's Knox!" Tate said and dropped down next to Rafe.

More lights, voices, and Tate got on his stomach, trying to dissect a way through the mess.

But he didn't have to. More hands appeared, digging at the rubble, reassured by Knox's voice.

Which, frankly, was normal. Knox knew how to reach out and hold people together.

Even when they didn't deserve it.

Maybe that's why Tate barreled into the wreckage, pulling out twisted metal, lugging out cement blocks, and finally unearthing a passage inside. Why he pushed Rafe back, got on his belly, and shimmied inside, a flashlight clamped between his teeth.

Why he nearly wept when he called out and Knox answered.

Because Tate simply couldn't lose the one person who never gave up on him.

Now he stood outside in the parking lot, pacing as the medics gave Knox a twice over. He'd sliced his arm diving over the edge of the platform, grabbing onto the brunette from the Yankee Belles. Had hauled her up as if she weighed nearly nothing, holding in a grunt and saying nothing about his wound until he climbed out after her.

Blood saturated his shirt, and Tate had taken off his own shirt to wrap it. Knox must have nicked an artery, because blood pumped out in a rhythm high under his arm. Tate had hooked his arm around his brother's shoulder and despite his protests, hauled Knox outside.

He heard Knox growling at the EMT, demanding something stupid like they give him a Band-Aid so he could—

"I'll find her," Tate said, stalking up to him, more than a little leftover adrenaline in his voice. "What's her name?"

Knox still wore the grime of his imprisonment on his face, his jaw scraped, his shirt sopping with the blood. Definitely hospital-bound, and they should take a good look at his head while they were at it, because what was his no-fun brother doing attending a girl band concert, and more—hanging out backstage with one of the singers?

Although, yeah, well done, bro. It was time for Knox to get a life.

So, "What does she look like?"

"She's the brunette. Long brown hair with a feather in it, brown T-shirt, turquoise boots."

Oh, that one. Yeah, Tate had seen her picture on the screen only about a billion and a half times over the past weekend. Pretty pale blue eyes, a smile that could make a man forget his name. Other men. Not Knox.

Big bro hadn't gone out with a girl since Chelsea had dropped him like a brick and headed out of town.

He could have told Knox that Chelsea was trouble. The girl lived a few different lives—the cheerleader version that Reuben fell in love with—poor guy. The girl-failing-calculus who went after Knox for his brains. Knox had been so over the moon with the most gorgeous girl in school, he hadn't stopped to think through what stealing Reuben's girlfriend might mean for the family.

And then there was the version Tate knew. The party girl who showed up with a smile for any guy with a six-pack of Budweiser. Neither brother knew, probably, that she didn't know the meaning of the word *exclusive*. Tate couldn't count how many times he'd watched Chelsea climb into the back of a pickup with one of his buddies.

Not him. He wasn't stupid. Reuben could take him out with one punch.

Then.

Now, they'd have a decent go-round, thanks to the moves Yuri had taught him. After three years working on Yuri Malovich's "security" crew, Tate might actually stand a chance against his smokejumper, tough-as-nails big brother, but the lessons learned watching Chelsea stuck in his brain.

Girls were trouble. Sometimes a good kind of trouble, but not worth the time and energy that came with chasing them down for date *numero dos*.

But Knox didn't think that way, which meant that he'd probably done something stupid like given this girl his heart. Probably the moment they shook hands.

"Her name's Kelsey. I need to know if she's okay," Knox said as the tech took his blood pressure.

Tate didn't want to stick around for the expression on the EMT's face when those results came in. He patted Knox on the shoulder. "I got this, bro."

Keep it light, no problem, but his throat was thick as he moved away into the grouping of rescue vehicles. Fire engines, ambulances, rescue trucks, and so many police cars they clogged the parking lot. He spied Rafe Noble standing with his arms crossed as he watched his little girl being loaded into one of the rigs.

He ran over. "How is she?"

Rafe's wife climbed in beside her daughter, holding her hand. Rafe's face betrayed the wreckage of his fear. "It didn't hit a major artery or vein, so—" He lifted a shoulder, glanced at Tate. "Knox is your brother?"

Tate nodded.

"Tell him that if he needs anything, anytime…" He swallowed. "He saved my daughter's life tonight." He pressed his hand over his mouth, shook his head as the EMT tech closed the door. Turned away and jogged, then sprinted over to a truck parked under tall lights.

The ambulance pulled away, sirens screaming.

Tate turned to scan the area for Kelsey. Surely she was in one of the other ambulances—although she'd seemed okay as she scrambled free.

He spotted a blonde standing in front of a closed ambulance, doing something on her smartphone, and jogged over to her.

A spur of recognition—yeah, she was one of the Belles. "Hey," he said.

She looked up, a tiny pinch of annoyance to her mouth. Her pretty mouth. And hazel-green eyes that raked over him, assessing.

"I'm looking for someone named Kelsey Jones?"

She put the phone in her pocket. "Why?"

He frowned. "I want to talk to her. To see if she's okay."

The blonde studied him, head to toe, then shook her head. "I don't think so, pal."

Now he studied her. Short, but with curves and white-blonde hair. She wore a sleeveless leather number, and a red tattoo curled from her shoulder, around her front, a tangle of flowers. Except the stress of the past few hours had smudged the tattoo, so probably paint.

But it gave her a sort of war-torn toughness, all that leather and blonde hair and sass and the way she looked him over…

He suddenly felt like the thug he had been, maybe still was. And that's when he realized he wasn't wearing his shirt. He'd whipped it off, wrapped it around Knox's wounded arm. He folded his hands over his chest, feeling a little, weirdly, naked.

"Why not?"

"Seriously?" She cocked her head. "I've seen it all, buddy, so if you think a little"—she gestured with a flick of her wrist to his naked chest—"eye candy is going to get you past me to get dirt on Kelsey, you've got another thing coming."

He blinked at her.

"Oh, don't bat those blue eyes at me, honey. I've been

around the block a few times. I know exactly what you're after."

Honey? And he thought he was the king of phony endearments. He unlatched his arms. "Claws in, *sweetheart*. I haven't a clue what you're talking about—"

"Really. What's this then?" She flicked the security pass around his neck. "You need to try a little harder."

He grabbed the pass. Frowned. "What are you *talking* about?"

Her guard dog demeanor dropped for just a second, and a flash of confusion turned her suddenly vulnerable. As if behind all that tough girl and sass might be someone he'd like to start over with, get to know.

To mean it when he said, "I promise, sugar, whatever you're thinking, I'm actually harmless."

She drew in a breath. "You're not…" She met his eyes then, nothing of weakness in her gaze. "You're not paparazzi, here to steal a front-page picture of Kelsey for some rag, right?"

He held up his hands. "No camera." Then he grinned, put all of his charm into it, lowered his voice. "You can search me."

Her mouth opened, closed. She cocked her head, as if suddenly he might be interesting.

Finally. For a minute there, he thought he might be losing his touch. He softened his voice. "Listen. I'm not paparazzi. Far from it—I'm security here. And I helped pull her out of the rubble."

She was listening now, her gaze roaming over him with a sort of wary smile.

Better, much better.

"And, most importantly, I was sent to find Kelsey by my brother Knox."

He waited, hoping that might ring a bell, but she didn't move.

"Knox Marshall? The guy who was trapped with her? Tall, cowboy type?"

A tiny smile tugged up her mouth. "Mr. Safe. Right."

That sounded like Knox. "He's got a wicked cut—I think they're taking him to the hospital for some stitches, so he sent me out to find her. He's worried about her."

She crossed her arms as if assessing his words.

And then he dropped the flirt, added a little raw emotion. "Listen. I get it too. I'd do anything for Knox. But whatever you're trying to protect her from, it's not me. Tate Marshall. Good guy. I promise."

She raised an eyebrow, her eyes going to his shoulders, the tatted right sleeve. He had the strangest urge to do something like flex. Instead he stuck his hands in his pockets and added a smile, something authentic.

But all this had his radar on high. Sure, the Yankee Belles were pretty, a little popular, but they weren't the Rolling Stones, for crying out loud.

"Okay. She's inside. But you'd better not be lying, champ. If I see one hint of a camera, even a phone, you're—"

Enough with the nicknames, already. But he held up his hands and nodded.

"Fine." She turned and opened one of the back doors, then the other.

Stilled. "What—?"

Empty. Except for the EMT who sat on a bench filling out something on his iPad. He looked up.

"Where's Kelsey?"

"She took off."

"She was in an *explosion*!"

He set down the iPad. "And she refused medical services.

Left a few minutes ago." He nodded to the open driver's door.

"Perfect," the blonde said. She turned to Tate. Sighed. "Thanks a lot."

He blinked at her, stymied. "What did I do?"

She narrowed her eyes, gave him another once-over, and now he stood there, letting her take a good look because really, this was silly.

"You're really in security."

"Really."

"Do any personal protection?"

"Some." He didn't particularly want to dig out that résumé, however.

"Hmm," she said, as if she were trying to decide on an order off a menu. "Okay. I guess you'll do. For now." She held out her hand. "Glo. Jackson. Come with me, tough guy."

Huh? But when she stalked away, he followed her.

And not just for Knox.

He'd do? Oh, he'd see about that.

⬥

Yeah, okay, Glo *may* have been a smidgen of a jerk to the tall, tattooed, half-naked so-called bodyguard following her through the jammed cars and roped off security of the arena toward the RV parking area.

But Glo knew Kelsey better than almost anyone, except Dixie, and no one from the press was going to get a good look at what might be going down in that ambulance. Kelsey had lived through enough trauma in her life not to have her grimy, traumatized face hit the front pages. Again.

And sure, it was a gigantic, Texas-sized leap to think that—what was his name? Tate—might be working for TMZ or some Nashville-based rag, but she had personal experience with what the media would do to get a story. Reporters camping out on the front lawn of her house, sleeping in their cars, posing as pizza delivery, bike messengers, even once as a security guard. So yeah, a man sniffing around with concern in his eyes, wanting to find Kelsey, had ignited her radar.

Although, she'd never seen the shirtless approach. For a second, it wiped a response from her brain, distracted by the script that wound up his thick bicep and over that sculpted shoulder. It made her want to linger, try to read the words. Which would only give Mr. I-Think-I'm-a-Charmer the exact wrong idea.

Even if he wasn't a reporter, she wasn't going to fall for his white smile, those blue eyes, or even the hint of raw vulnerability that flashed on his face when she'd accused him of running Kelsey off.

What did I do?

Maybe nothing. But it was very possible that Kelsey took one look at Tough Guy through the window and every tucked-away nightmare had woken and chased her out into the night.

Please, no.

Which meant that making Tate help her find Kelsey might be a wretchedly bad idea, but frankly, the flip side was that Kelsey and, honestly, the rest of them were rattled.

Might do them good to have someone with her as she searched for Kelsey.

Maybe even put a tough guy on payroll who could assure their safety if they were to keep touring.

First things first— "Kelsey probably ran back to the bus." She glanced over at Tate, who had pulled out his phone, texting as he walked.

"Who are you texting?"

"Knox. I told him to go to the hospital, that Kelsey was all right." He shoved the phone into the pocket of his dark suit pants. The ensemble of his bared, tattooed chest with his dirty dress pants and scuffed shoes made for an interesting combination. Part trouble, part Mr. Safe and Sound. She didn't know which one to believe.

Glo ignored the stir of something forbidden inside her and headed toward the RV section. The beer tent was quiet, the flaps closed. Down the path, the carnival had also shut down. The tall Ferris wheel glowed, unmoving against the night sky.

She cut through the shadowed path of the stock barn, and it came to her that if Tate were trouble, she'd just led him down the perfect path to assault her. Her hand closed around her phone.

But he walked with his hands in his pockets, as if he might be aware of her tension. "Where are we going?"

"The tour bus. And…thanks."

He glanced at her, raised an eyebrow. "For what?"

"Coming with me. It was a…" She swallowed. "A little tense back there." She looked away but felt his gaze on her. "We're all pretty shaken up."

"You don't seem shaken up."

She lifted a shoulder. "Years of training."

"What, are you with the CIA?"

She tucked a smile away. "Close. My mother is a senator. Years of bodyguards and press prowling around our house."

"Ah, that's where the claws came from."

"Ouch."

"Sorry. But I might need medical attention."

She glanced at him—oh, bad idea. The shadows and moonlight turned the planes of his body into a work of art. But he shot her a grin.

She swallowed, looked away. "Sorry. I was just…"

"Why does your friend need protecting?"

She shook her head. "It's not my story to tell. We just need to figure out what's going on. If someone is trying to hurt us."

"Why do you think it's about you? Could be a political statement, or even someone angry at NBR-X."

"Probably, but…" She took a breath. "Okay, listen. If you are a reporter and you betray me, I will personally find you and kill you in your sleep."

He blinked at her, his mouth opening. "Really?"

"I'm kidding." She shook her head. "I just—"

"You can trust me, Glo."

And it was his low tone that found her bones, as if a warm hand curled around her. Hmm.

"Okay, so, Kelsey has a reason to think someone might want to hurt her. A history. And maybe that's just paranoia talking—probably it is, but if I were Kelsey, that's the first thing I'd be thinking. And that's why maybe having someone around who could give her a sense that she isn't on her own might keep her from…"

She paused.

"From…?"

They came out of the path and headed toward the RV park. Their tour bus wasn't fancy—an old 1992 remodeled Greyhound that now hosted six bunks in the back, a tiny kitchen, a couple sofas, a television, and a storage area for their equipment. They'd pooled their cash and bought it for $40K.

Her mother hated it. Which was yet another selling point.

"Kelsey has the occasional, um, panic attack."

He raised an eyebrow.

"She's amazing onstage. Turns into this confident,

breathtaking performer—I'm sure she's the reason we're still getting gigs. But offstage, crowds freak her out, and she's been known to—"

"Run?"

She glanced over. Frowned.

"She was in the beer tent last night. Sort of had a weird altercation with this guy who grabbed her—"

She stopped, turned to him, and touched his arm.

Okay, the man really needed a shirt, but, "A strange man *grabbed* her?"

"Not...well, she fell, and he sort of caught her." Tate looked at her hand on his arm, then back to her. Oh, those eyes. She pulled her hand away but let him continue. "But she freaked out and took off. She dropped her wallet, and Knox chased after her to return it."

Mr. Safe. Interesting.

"So, you think she's panicked?"

"And maybe she's hiding in the bus, but if she's not, we need to find her."

Tate nodded, as if this might be something normal. "Got it. Let's go."

Oh. She liked a man who got on board that easily. She headed toward the bus, noted the dark windows, and un-locked the door.

Climbed aboard. "Kelsey?"

Light from the parking lot filtered in through the privacy curtains, striping the gray velour sofa, the white Formica counter in the mini-kitchen. She glanced at Tate, who climbed up the stairs behind her. "Stay here."

He cocked his head, argument on his face.

"If she's here, let's not freak her out more."

He nodded then, and she crept into the bunk area. All the bunks came with a curtain to pull, and she noted with dismay that Kelsey's curtain, on the bottom bunk, was cracked open. She pulled it aside anyway and flicked on the tiny light in the cubby.

No lead singer.

She turned around.

"Check the bathroom," Tate said, still on the stairs.

Good idea. She knocked, then opened the door to the tiny bathroom/shower room. Empty.

She closed it and came back through the bus, shot a look at Tate standing there, one arm holding the upper grab bar, then turned and moved to the back where they kept their suitcases. *Sorry, Elijah.* She stole one of his shirts lying on the top of his clean wad of clothing and tossed it to Tate.

He grabbed it with one hand, glanced at her, then said nothing and pulled it over his head.

Oh, Elijah might kill her—it was his well-worn black Rascal Flatts concert tee. But it looked dangerously hot melded against Tate's physique.

"So, where would she go?" Tate asked as she closed up the bus.

She pulled out her phone, checked her texts, then sent one to Kelsey. Glanced back at Tate.

Now that he wasn't exuding all that raw maleness, she considered him. Short dark brown hair, a thick five-o'clock shadow, and a scar along his jaw as if he'd been nicked during a fight.

Probably a few fights, the way he held himself, just a little tight and alert. Yeah, the guy had ready-to-protect written all over him.

It eased the knot in her gut she hadn't realized was there.

"I don't know. She doesn't usually leave the bus, so—"

"What about the stock barn?"

Glo frowned at him. "Why on earth would she go to the

stock barn?"

He held up a hand. "Step back there, Columbo. I saw her come out of there last night. Maybe when she took off last night, she ended up there?" He lifted a shoulder.

She glanced at the barn. Back at Tate. "I don't want to waste our time—"

"We're wasting time standing here arguing." He turned, as if he didn't care if she followed him, and stalked back toward the barn.

Fine. She caught up to him and walked in silence to the barn.

The side door was unlocked, and Tate took out his phone and flicked on the flashlight. They'd entered at the far end of the barn, where they kept the bulls, and the odor of bovine flesh, manure, and the earthy scent of hay and straw rose around her.

"Reminds me of my grandfather's place," she said quietly.

"Farmer?"

"Owner. Thoroughbreds. In Tennessee."

He glanced at her, gave her a look she couldn't read. "Really."

"Yes. Listen, Dr. Phil, there are too many layers here for you to dissect, so don't try. Let's just find my friend."

His eyes narrowed, as if he might be up for the challenge, and shoot, but that little stir of something forbidden only took hold.

No. Tate Marshall was absolutely the last, very last person she should let into her life.

But oh, her mother would hate him.

"It smells like our barn too. My brother breeds bucking bulls for the Marshall Triple M. In fact, one of our bulls was in the arena tonight." He was shining his light into the stalls. A few thousand-pound-plus bulls lay in repose, hulking bodies heaving in slumber. A few raised horned heads and considered them with glassy eyes.

A handful of the pens were empty but filled with fresh straw.

He stopped at an intersection. "Hot Pete is housed down here." He shot his light down to the end of the row.

A door stood open, and the light landed on a figure sitting in the fresh straw, her legs drawn up, her head in her arms.

"Kelsey," Glo said and touched Tate's arm. "Stay here."

"Aye, aye, boss."

She ignored him and headed down the aisle. She noticed he didn't exactly obey her, coming up behind her to shine the light on Kelsey.

Who raised her head, her eyes wide. Her gaze flickered past Glo to Tate, then back.

"Hey," Glo said softly, crouching. "How're you doing? I was worried."

Kelsey leaned her head back against the wooden slats of the pen. "Sorry. I just had to get out of there. So much…"

"I get it." Glo came into the pen, searched for a cow pie, but found the straw fresh. She kneeled before Kelsey.

"I don't know why I came here. I used to go to the barn when…well, before. When I was a kid, and it was just instinct, I guess."

"Tate said you came here last night."

Kelsey glanced at him standing a few feet away, holding the light down to puddle on the dirt floor. "Tate?"

"Knox's brother. He was working security. Helped pull you out tonight?"

"Right." She nodded at him. "Hey."

He lifted his head in return, his mouth a tight line.

"Knox was worried about you," Glo said. "And sent Tate

to find you."

Kelsey closed her eyes. Shook her head. "I can't bear to see him again. It was awful, Glo. I just…I completely freaked out. You'd think I hadn't had a minute of counseling. I was fourteen, stuck—"

Glo touched her arm. "Don't. You're fine. Safe."

Kelsey slid her hand over Glo's.

"But it's also completely normal to be shaken up when a freakin' building blows up around you!"

Kelsey met her eyes. Swallowed. Nodded.

"But you're okay, right?"

Kelsey kept nodding. "I wouldn't be if Knox hadn't caught me, but—how is he? He was cut—"

"He'll be fine," Tate said and took another step closer. "He's on his way to the hospital, but he wanted to see you."

"No." She made a wry face. "No. I'm too…" She looked at Glo. "We need to get back on the road. To our next gig."

"It's a week away. I think we can take our time—even cancel."

"No!"

Glo jerked at her response.

Kelsey held up her hand. "Sorry. We just…let's just get out of here. Put this behind us."

Run. The word pulsed in Glo's head, but she didn't voice it. Because maybe yes, for tonight, go. Get someplace safe.

Then they could all take a breath, figure out their next move.

"Listen, I hate to butt in, but really, Knox needs to know you're okay—" Tate came up to the stall. "He's really worried."

"I know. I'm sorry, but…" Kelsey looked at Tate now, pushing herself up. "Knox was amazing. Sweet and yeah, I've been sitting here for the last hour remembering him singing to Hot Pete. It helped. He probably saved my life tonight." She reached up and pulled the feathers, now stripped and grimy, from her hair. She dropped them into the stall. "But he's just a reminder of…" She shook her head and met Glo's eyes. "I just need to forget this entire weekend."

"Okay," Glo said, taking Kelsey's hand.

Kelsey turned to Tate. "I'm sorry, Tate. I don't want to see him. But tell him thank you."

She squeezed Glo's hand, then let go and headed out of the stall, past Tate.

Glo followed her but stopped in front of Tate. "Thanks—"

He touched her arm, softly, but with enough strength in it for her to hear him. "Let me help. I don't know what's going on, but I'm pretty good at reading people, and your friend—and you—are probably suffering from a little PTSD. I could run security for you, make sure that nothing like this happens again."

She raised an eyebrow. "That's a pretty bold statement—"

"I mean it. I used to protect some fairly important people with targets on their backs, and they're still alive, so…I'd like to help."

Something sarcastic, along the lines of *I'll bet you would,* entered her brain, but the earnestness in his blue eyes simply shut it down.

And she fought the crazy urge to nod.

Especially when he added, "I'm good at what I do. Ask around. Look me up, Glo."

Not honey, not sweetheart. Her name on his lips found its way under her skin, held her hostage for a long moment.

Then, "Okay, Kevin Costner, give me your number. We'll see if you're as good as you say."

He let her go, but smiled, something dangerous entering

his expression. "That'll do. For now."

———————◆———————

Kelsey *wasn't* okay, and no amount of texts from Tate was going to convince Knox otherwise.

Knox lay on a gurney at Methodist Hospital, bare chested, his right arm up over his head while some third-year female intern stitched up the slice that had cut into his artery. The flash of dark, bone-deep pain had rendered him a little light-headed for a bit as Kelsey hung from his grip between floors.

But he wasn't going to let go, no matter how many shadows crossed his vision.

I'm going to get you out of this. Knox had made that promise, and now it practically thundered in his head, a drumbeat keeping time with his pulse.

He checked his phone again. He'd texted Tate back, a voice-to-text that came out awkwardly spelled and said something like *Tell her I'm gonna finer.*

Close enough. Because the second he got off this table, he was headed back to the arena to track down her tour bus.

Then he was going to pull her into his arms and tell her that she was safe. That he would make sure of it. Because he'd seen the look on her face—the one after the world had erupted. Knew in that moment what he was asking of her when he'd begged for her help.

Knox remembered how it felt to have something sit inside you, a darkness waiting to tug you down, pull you from your foundations. The panic when it had its way with you.

He also knew what it took to climb out of that darkness, find yourself, and care about the people around you.

Kelsey had no doubt reached way past herself to help him get little Tori to safety.

Or maybe she'd simply put on a mask, like the one she wore while performing.

And because Knox couldn't go anywhere, because he was trapped under the ministrations of the dark-haired intern trying to sew him back together, Knox closed his eyes and allowed himself a minute to remember Kelsey onstage.

Let himself sink into the way she'd reached into his heart and sparked to life something he thought he'd long buried. Intrigue, admiration, maybe even desire.

He might not have recognized the woman he'd met the night before except for her sweet ballad. She possessed a Karen Carpenter kind of alto, something deep and honest that wheedled inside him, made a home. Especially when she'd wrapped her hands around the mic, stared out into the audience as if finding just one, and poured out her heart.

He'd wanted to believe she might be singing just to him. *I'm too young to fall in love again, but he said try...*

Under the lights, her long sable hair had shone, exotic with the twin feathers, and in her cutoff shorts, her long shapely legs clad in black hosiery, the brown v-necked NBR-X T-shirt, she looked like a hometown girl who might say yes to a ride in his truck. Or maybe on Duncan, his old quarter horse.

Yeah, Knox fooled himself into that fantasy as he watched her sing, almost gave in to a crazy urge to tear up as her song ended.

So wait...for one true heart...one true heart...

Yes, the Kelsey he'd seen onstage had rocked his world.

And coupled with the Kelsey he rode with on the Ferris wheel last night at the carnival... Knox had walked backstage with the intent of sticking around, seeing if he could earn more than a *Thank you for being safe.*

Safe and...well, not *old*.

"Just a couple more, Mr. Marshall," the intern said. She wore the name S. Garcia on her badge.

They were in a cubicle with hanging cloth walls, other survivors of the explosion who needed attention in the stalls beside him. Just a handful.

They'd been remarkably lucky. Knox was still trying to puzzle it all together—how Tate had found him, how no one else had been seriously hurt. *Thank You, God.*

In his gut Knox knew—like he knew how to spot a good bucker, knew when the weather would shift, when a cow would birth, and when his brothers got in over their heads—that Kelsey wasn't okay.

No matter what Tate said.

Garcia, the intern, took out a gauze pad and affixed it to the wound. Was cutting off tape when the curtain slid back.

Honestly, Knox expected Tate. So the sight of two men in suits had him frowning. They glanced at the woman, and one flashed a badge.

Local PD investigators.

"Knox Marshall?" said one of the men, a real cowboy type, lean and wearing a white Stetson, the Lone Ranger with dark hair and a tough cut of his jaw.

"Yeah," Knox said, starting to sit up.

"Hey, hey, I'm not done yet," Garcia said and put a hand on his chest. "Almost. Just settle down."

Knox lay back down.

"Detective Torres," said Lone Ranger. "We're just here to see if you can identify a man we think might be connected to tonight's events."

"The bomber?"

The man behind Torres held up his hand, a blond with wide shoulders and wearing a tie. "Not necessarily, but we were wondering if you might have seen him backstage,

79

perhaps right before the incident?"

"You mean the *explosion*? Was anyone seriously hurt?"

"No," Torres said. "Just some animals."

Animals.

But Knox didn't have time to consider further because Torres pulled out his phone. Held up a picture on the screen. "You recognize this man?"

Knox took the phone. Stared at the photo, clearly from some security camera, of a balding man standing near two other men at a bar in the arena.

"No," he said.

"Look closely. He was one of the rodeo clowns. Didn't show up for the final show."

"So, maybe he was sick, or injured—"

"He was seen by one of our security guards entering the lower level a few minutes before the blast went off."

"Maybe he was checking on the stock." Knox took another look.

Stopped. *Wait.* He widened the picture, scrolled over. One man, with gauged ears, stood with his back to the camera, but a port-wine stain extended out of his collar, wound around his neck. Knox scrolled to the other one. He stood beside his friend, slightly turned, looking over at the suspect.

If he looked closely, the shadow of a tattoo, maybe. Flames.

"I don't know him, but this one is familiar," he said, handing the phone back. "I saw him last night in the beer tent."

"We are questioning them. But they're just a couple cowboys. One of them is the son of the local mayor."

"What are they doing talking to the bomber?"

"Not the bomber," said Blondie.

Garcia finished wrapping his arm. "Take it easy with

this," she said as she helped Knox sit up.

The world turned a little wobbly, and he gripped the side of the gurney. Took a breath.

He met Blondie's gaze. "Maybe. But maybe they know something about him."

Torres took his phone, examined the picture. "It doesn't look like they're with him."

"Whatever. Listen, can I go?" Knox made to slide off the gurney.

His legs buckled.

He grabbed the table. Torres grabbed his other arm.

"You okay there, pal?"

Oh. Now he felt like an idiot. He shook Torres off. "Long night."

The intern had come around the table and now pressed him back onto the gurney. Grabbed the blood pressure cuff. "Let's just take a look."

"We'll be in touch if we have any more questions," Torres said and turned to go.

"Wait—you really think that's the guy?" Knox said as the intern strapped his arm.

Torres stopped at the curtain, looked at Knox. "That would sure be easy, wouldn't it?" He left as the intern finished taking his pressure.

"It's a little low, Mr. Marshall. I'm going to ask you to stick around. Would hate to have you pass out and wreck all my stitches." She smiled, winked.

Hello…flirting. At least, if he were reading her right.

Maybe he wasn't quite as old as Kelsey made him out to be.

But now he was back to worrying about Kelsey, and he pulled out his phone. Voice-texted Tate. "Where are you?"

"I'm going to get you some orange juice," Garcia said.

She patted his leg and left him alone in the bay.

The text came back. *On my way.*

Knox hoped that meant with Kelsey. Maybe she was actually here, and he should just get up and—

Yeah. Enough sitting around like some pansy. He sat up, and his head didn't swim. Stood.

See, he was just fine.

He cast back the curtain.

Nearly smacked full into Tate.

"Whoa—!" Tate said. "Hey there." Tate grabbed him by the shoulders. "Bro. What's going on?" He pushed Knox back into the room.

Knox noticed his brother had donned a new shirt, something a couple sizes too small. Of course. "Did you find Kelsey?"

"Absolutely," Tate said. He guided him to the gurney. "Take a load off."

Knox brushed Tate's hand away. "I'm fine."

"Yeah you are. You look like you've been trampled by a bull. How much blood did you lose?"

"Not that much. I'm fine. Let's get out of here—I want to see Kelsey." Knox made to push past Tate, but his brother stiff-armed him.

"Rein it in, Knox. Just…"

And then Tate looked away.

Oh, he could read his brother like he could the sky. "What?"

He made a face as he glanced back to Knox. "She doesn't want to see you."

Knox tried to process that information. "No. What? *Why?*"

Tate's shoulders rose and fell. "She's pretty upset about what went down tonight. I'm not exactly sure what she meant, but she said something about completely freaking out—"

"We were nearly buried to death. We were *all* freaking out!"

But Tate held up his hands as if he had nothing to add.

"That's just stupid," Knox said and again tried to push past Tate. And would have if, yeah, he hadn't lost a pint or two of blood. And maybe Tate had filled out a bit over the past couple years, apparently taking seriously his gig as a security for some Vegas casino.

"No," Tate said and met his eyes.

Still, in that moment, Knox gave serious consideration to taking his little brother down. Except he probably would open a stitch or two, and who knew if he would be the one getting back up.

Instead he took a breath and slumped onto the gurney. "I don't get it. I just—"

"Want to help? Yeah, bro, you did that. You got her out of there. I tried to tell her that you wanted to see her, but she was pretty gung ho about leaving town, pronto."

"She's leaving town?"

"Sorry. I think they're all just trying to figure out what to do next. Probably suffering from a little PTSD—"

"Which is why I want to see her!"

"C'mon, bro. You can't fix her."

"I promised that I'd keep her safe. Get her out of this mess."

"And you did. She called you sweet. Said you saved her. But also that you're just a reminder of the explosion."

Oh. And then he got it.

She was embarrassed. Stupidly, unnecessarily embarrassed.

He closed his eyes. And he was a reminder to her of

whatever had her running.

So much for being safe.

The steps sounded behind Tate, and he looked up, expecting to see Garcia.

Rafe Noble appeared. His face was drawn, his eyes reddened.

"Rafe!" Knox's voice turned Tate around. "How's Tori?"

Rafe came in, breathed out hard. Shook his head, and his eyes filled despite his gritted jaw.

And for a moment, Knox's gut dropped. No—

"Alive, thanks to you, Knox." Rafe held out his hand, his eyes fierce on Knox's.

Knox took it, but Rafe pulled him into a hug, his voice a little ragged. "Thank you."

Knox's own eyes burned. He leaned back from Rafe, slapped him on the shoulder, took a breath. "She in surgery?"

"They were able to close the wound in the ER. She's with Katherine, eating a Popsicle." Rafe turned away, ran a thumb under his eye. Swallowed when he turned back to Knox. "And actually, I'm here for another reason too." His mouth tightened, and he glanced at Tate, then back to Knox.

And Knox knew it even before Rafe said it. Had the foresight to reach back to the gurney and brace himself even as the solemn words issued from Rafe's mouth.

"I'm so sorry, Knox, but I got a call from the stock manager at the arena." He put his hand on Knox's shoulder. "The explosion..." He shook his head. "Hot Pete is dead."

5

If Kelsey didn't go on tonight, she might never take the stage again.

At least that's what the voices whispered, both in Kelsey's head and in Glo's and Dixie's low tones as they'd stood outside her partially open door to her dressing room in the Rodeo Opry center in Oklahoma City.

The historic building was embedded with the soul sounds of the likes of Reba McEntire and even recently, Josh Turner. Its ornate carvings, the smell of history in the carpets, and even the coziness of the stage, flanked by deep red velour curtains, should have conspired to instill inside her the sense of safety.

Who would bomb the Rodeo Opry?

Kelsey sat at the wooden dressing table, staring at the amount of black she'd circled around her eyes, the way she'd pulled the top half of her hair up into a messy bun, let the rest fall in dark waves. She'd even added extensions for a dramatic effect. She wore a white sleeveless bandeau lace top, a thick leather belt, a flouncy brown skirt, and her favorite turquoise boots.

She picked up the hot rose lipstick, noticed her hand shook, and set it back down.

She glanced at her phone. Ten minutes before showtime.

I know you're freaking out, and I get it, but...I need you to hold it together...

She didn't know why she let Knox roam around her head, but somehow his voice inside helped her clamp down, find an anchor.

Mostly.

It would help if the explosion hadn't followed her from San Antonio. If a group of reporters hadn't camped out, waiting for her bus to arrive in Oklahoma City with probing questions about how she might be handling yet another tragic event. And was Kelsey feeling that—

That she would never really escape the random terror of life? The fact that at anytime, anywhere, tragedy could hit.

Even onstage.

Um, yes.

She pressed her hand to her mouth, staring into her own blackened eyes as she remembered the catastrophe during today's rehearsal. When they'd started to work on it before San Antonio, she'd wanted to craft a different number for their finale, something that would let the audience take a small piece of the Yankee Belles home with them. A rousing sing-along, maybe. Kelsey envisioned the lights going down, having them leave the stage in darkness, the way they came on.

Which of course had been exactly the problem. The darkness.

But before the darkness happened, one of the overhead light pots dropped from the rafters onto the stage. Just one pot, but it somehow detached and shattered right behind Kelsey.

She'd been at the mic, sinking into the song, the twang of Dixie's fiddle, Glo's banjo brilliance, and was about to lead the would-be crowd in the sing-along portion, her hands clapping over her head, when the explosion sounded behind her.

Glass shattered, the boom shook the stage, and her note morphed into a full-out scream as she dropped to her knees, her hands over her head.

Even Dixie and Glo screamed, but she'd been the one who'd watched, almost numbly, as the road crew cleaned up the mess, as the stage manager checked the rest of the lights.

Just a random fluke. The rest of the pots were fine, and she'd forced herself to run the song again, her gut in knots as she enacted a smile, glancing at Glo, her fingers crazy on the fingerboard.

Kelsey raised her arms, started clapping through the bridge, cast first to Glo, then to Dixie, who lit her fiddle on fire. Then the song swung back to her, and Kelsey dove into the repeated chorus.

So, when life doesn't make sense
when you want to run away
When the songs seem over
and you ain't got nothing to say,
Stick around, boy, and give us a chance.
Take my hands…and let's just dance!

She sang the chorus once, twice—then, just like that, the lights cut off, leaving only the starlight of a giant disco ball twirling overhead and at the very last moment, an explosion of silvery confetti.

They were supposed to sneak off stage, leaving the band playing, then quieting as the crowd took over. End the night hearing their own voices, letting the dance fill their souls.

She wanted them to remember the Yankee Belles, a band who reached into the dark places and eased the pain, at least for the space of a set.

But it hadn't quite happened as she'd scripted.

The lights flashed, died.

At once, the darkness poured over her like thick tar. Seeping into her pores. Choking, hot, and paralyzing.

She stood, gripping the mic, unable to move.

"Kelsey!" Glo's voice had hissed behind her, but it faded, and only Kelsey's cascading breaths filled her ears, looping over each other, faster and faster—

Her legs collapsed.

"Kelsey!"

The lights burst back on, turning the world a bright red through her closed eyes. Then an arm went around her back, another tucked under her legs, and she fell against a thick, warm, broad chest.

Knox.

No, *not* Knox—and silly her to even let that thought find her—because as she reached out and fisted her hand in her rescuer's shirt, she opened her eyes to find their new security lead, Tate, cradling her to his chest.

She wanted to close her eyes, grit her teeth, to muster something from deep within that might make her push him away. Not cover her face with her hands, not start to shake.

Not fall apart as Tate had carried her all the way to her dressing room.

He'd settled her on the worn red sofa in the room, crouching in front of her. He wore a black Yankee Belles T-shirt, a pair of jeans, and spoke into his mouth piece. "We're in the dressing room."

Not that he needed to alert anyone, really, because seconds later Glo appeared, her short blonde hair under a baseball cap, dressed in a pair of black jeans and a sleeveless shirt with the Belle's pink logo on the front.

"Thanks, Tate." She glanced at him, and he moved back, a solid presence, his arms folded across his muscled chest.

Not that Kelsey had noticed, but the man reminded her of his brother Knox, a problem she didn't foresee when Glo had talked Carter into hiring him for their road security.

She briefly wondered what else Glo had been thinking with her recommendation, but that thought left her as Glo joined her on the sofa. "What's going on, Kels?"

Her hands shook, and she folded them together. "Nothing. Just...I'm fine."

"You're *not* fine," Tate had said, almost under his breath, and Glo shot him a glare.

Then Dixie strode into the room. Stopped in front of Kelsey, such an enigmatic look on her face Kelsey had to ask. "What——?"

She shook her head. "We should be canceling."

"This is Rodeo Opry! This chance isn't going to come around again. We can't cancel——"

Dixie held up her hand. "Fine. But we go back to our regular finale. All the lights on—no theatrics. No confetti——"

"No. I am not..." Kelsey held up her hands, closed them into fists. "I'm not going to...let him win."

And oh, she didn't want to bring her past into this moment, but...yeah. It was right there, hovering like a shadow ever since the explosion had freed *him* to roam her brain.

"Let who win?" Tate said. "Because they think the bomber is dead, Kelsey."

She didn't look at him, just closed her eyes.

Glo got up. "C'mon, Superman. We need to give her some air."

Kelsey opened her eyes to watch Tate frown, then follow Glo from the room. Dixie stayed standing nearby. Took a breath.

"We *could* cancel, Kelsey. The chance will come again."

"I'm fine—"

"You're not sleeping, you're wired—even I can see that. And yeah, the stage is your preferred addiction, but it could destroy you."

She met Dixie's eyes. "It's all I have, Dixie, and you know it. It's my safe place. Or it was... I just need to keep moving, figuring it out. I'll be fine tonight."

Dixie's mouth made a tight line.

A knock came at the door, and Kelsey tore her gaze from Dixie to see Carter standing in the threshold. "Can I talk to Kelsey for a minute?"

Dixie nodded but walked over to Kelsey and pressed a kiss on the top of her head. "No one thinks you're weak," she said quietly. "But no one would blame you, either, if you wanted to hit pause."

Kelsey touched Dixie's hand but let her go.

Carter walked into the room. Leaned against the counter. Folded his arms over his dress shirt. Concerned Clooney. "So, at what point are we going to talk about it?"

She stiffened. Met his gray eyes. Tried an easy tone. "Talk about what? The explosion?"

His mouth made a tight line. Then he shook his head. "You know I care about you, Kelsey. When Dennis asked me to be your manager, I knew he was really asking that I watch over you girls. You're like daughters to me. Okay, more like kid sisters." He smiled, but it quickly faded. "When are we going to talk about the letter you got from the New York Department of Corrections?"

Her breath caught. Oh. "You saw that?"

"I get all the mail. Yes." He took a breath. "So, did they parole Russell?"

Her throat thickened with the question, and she found

herself nodding. "Good behavior."

He let the silence stretch out, then took a breath. "It wasn't him, at the stadium in Texas. You know that, right?"

She nodded, drew up her knees.

"Vince Russell won't get to you. And more importantly, he won't hurt you. We won't let him."

She nodded, her eyes turning scratchy. She couldn't look at Carter.

"Okay." He leaned up. "You're not going onstage tonight."

"What—?"

He held up his hand. "You heard me. Listen, one night for you to get it together. I got this. Just…enjoy the show."

"Carter—"

But he was already walking out the door.

And she had let him go, weighing his words for the next three hours.

Except, if she didn't lead the group, who would? Not that Glo or Dixie couldn't handle the crowd, but…okay, she wanted to be the headliner.

It's all I have, Dixie. It's my safe place.

The words found soil, dug in.

She was going onstage, so help her.

Vince Russell and his gang of thugs weren't going to make her break her promises to herself.

She added lipstick, stood, and gave herself a once-over in the mirror. She was tough enough to keep the nightmares quiet for an hour, at least.

The Opry had booked a local band to open, and as she walked backstage, she heard their final song fading, the audience robust as they finished. She spotted Carter standing in the wings. He was talking with another man, his back to Kelsey. Glo and Dixie looked up from where they were fine-tuning their instruments.

Something about Glo's glance at Carter put a fist in her gut.

Aw, what sort of wannabe newcomer did Carter get to fill in for her tonight?

Sorry, but this was her band, her spotlight. She walked up to the duo, not a little hot.

"Carter, I'm not sure who—"

And then she simply stopped talking as country superstar Benjamin King, recent Entertainer of the Year, platinum artist, and all-around icon, turned and smiled down at her.

"Hey," he said. "How are you doing, Kelsey?"

She'd met Benjamin King once, about a year ago at an awards show. Carter had scored them tickets, and somehow she ended up in the bathroom with Ben's wife, Kacey. Who'd actually heard of her and their one star-studded song, "One True Heart." Practically grabbed her and forced her to meet Ben.

Handsome, broad-shouldered, with a smile that could make a girl forget her name—which Kelsey nearly did when he shook her hand, when he told her that if she ever needed anything, to give him a shout.

Apparently, Carter had shouted.

She stared up at him, then at Carter, back to Ben. "What…what are you doing here?"

Ben's mouth tightened, and he glanced at Carter, raised an eyebrow. "Um—"

"He's in town for a concert tomorrow night at the Chesapeake Arena, and I told him a bit about our situation…"

Their *situation*? She might be ill, right here, backstage—

"Everybody is glad you and the Yankee Belles are okay, Kelsey. And frankly, the fact you have a show tonight is pretty gutsy. So, yeah, when Carter called and said your voice was shot, I thought…maybe I could help."

She wanted to kiss Carter. Okay, right after she slugged him, but she smiled at Ben. "Our fans are going to go crazy for you."

He bent and gave her a kiss on the cheek. "Kacey will be jealous. She likes you. Come to Montana sometime and see us."

She might turn into a fan puddle on the spot. Until she watched the stage go dark and Glo and Dixie take the stage.

Carter's hand curled around her arm. "They've got this."

She watched from the sidelines as they raised their voices, just a little empty without her. And then Ben walked out to join them, his smoky tenor filling in her gap.

"How does he know our music?" she said.

"Said he was a fan," Carter said into her ear. "And we're playing a few of his hits, too."

Of course.

The career she'd worked so hard to build, slipping away in the space of an hour.

Yeah, she was going to get herself together. Because she liked Benjamin King.

But this would never happen again.

———◆———

Again, Knox dove over the edge of the floor, leaping for her.

Again, he caught her wrist.

Again, he heard himself make promises. *I got ya. I told you, I'm going to get you out of this.*

And then Knox watched as her hand slipped away from his, the grip turning clammy, his strength ebbing. She stared up at him with those big pale blue eyes, her mouth open.

Fell.

Screamed.

Knox sat straight up in his bed, his heart a fist against his ribs, beating to escape. His entire body slicked with sweat, and he ran his hands through his hair, gripped his head.

The moon hung low, the night waning, and beams of soft light glazed his wooden floor, across the rug, and his knotted covers.

He kicked them off, set his feet on the floor, then got up and reached for a pair of faded jeans draped over his nearby easy chair.

Outside, the starlight turned the yard to silver. He leaned on the window frame, his gaze on the barn. Maybe he'd check on Daisy Duke and see if she was near delivery. Hot Pete's first—and now only—issue. The thought pumped a knot into his throat.

He grabbed a T-shirt and pulled it on, stopped by the bathroom to splash water on his face, chase away the dream, and brush his teeth. Then he headed downstairs. Flicked on the overhead light in his mother's expansive kitchen. Granite countertops, new stainless steel appliances. The kitchen his father had always wanted to give her. Knox had it remodeled last year for her 59th birthday.

This year, he hoped they could afford a cake.

No, they weren't that broke, and with the insurance on Hot Pete, he'd be able to buy Calamity Jane, add the pedigreed cow to his stock of breeding cows. But he'd counted on Hot Pete's ongoing purse, and later his straws, to grow and strengthen their line.

He poured in grounds to make coffee and glanced at the clock. Four a.m.

While the coffee brewed, he wandered into his office, just off the kitchen. No, his father's office. The family Christmas picture taken the summer of Reuben's senior year still sat on the worn oak desk. The entire family sat in front of the soaring stone fireplace in the great room—

Everyone smile, when I tell you to—that means you too, Knox. Tate, enough with the bunny ears—Ford, scoot over. I'm going in next to you. Rube! Stop laughing! Oh Wyatt, seriously, you had to show up in your hockey jersey?

Ruby Jane's bossiness as she set up the timer on her Nikon.

Even now, the motley picture made him laugh—his big brother, Reuben, looking fierce and bold in an ugly Christmas sweater. And yeah, Wyatt, two years younger than Tate and just starting to contend for his place on a serious hockey team, wore his favorite jersey—the Minnesota Blue Ox. Ford and Ruby Jane, fraternal twins who wore the same mischievous smile. He always thought they could read each other's mind. And right in the middle, Troublemaker Tate. His hand was caught mid-sabotage over Knox's head.

Flanking them on one side, Gerri and Orrin Marshall. His father always reminded him of Tom Selleck, with a full head of black hair and a mustache. Big hands, a hearty laugh, and the kind of faith that seemed embedded in his bones.

Wow, Knox missed him. Especially when he sat in the faded leather desk chair. Or traced his name written in the top of the desk, an early crime with a pocket knife. Funny that his dad had never sanded it off.

Knox had changed little when he took over the office. Kept the furniture, the Charles Russell print hanging on the far wall, his father's complete collection of Louis L'Amour in the bookcase. Had even reinforced the note his dad had taped to his desk, handwritten lyrics from his favorite hymn.

Be Thou my Vision, O Lord of my heart;
Naught be all else to me, save that Thou art;

Thou my best Thought, by day or by night;
Waking or sleeping, Thy presence my light.

He was trying, oh, Knox was trying.

He reached for his computer and opened it, the light illuminating the entire room. The news article about the NBR-X bombing came up, and he read it again, although he knew every line.

Arnie Gibbs, from Lubbock, Texas. Deceased at age 41. Body found in the rubble of the bombing. Investigators had found the ingredients for a bomb at his house, but even Knox had fertilizer in his barn. It didn't make him a terrorist. Of course, Knox wouldn't think of mixing the ammonium nitrate with fuel oil, boosting it with C-4, and adding a blasting cap. Gibbs had wrapped it all in a plastic bag and dropped it into an empty water bucket in the temporary stock holding area in the arena.

Only the fact that one of the stock handlers had moved it over to the dumpster area protected the arena from more lethal devastation. The blast had been localized to one area, secured inside what effectively acted as a cement bunker.

No one had answers to what Gibbs had been doing in the stock area, lingering for his own demise, a glitch Knox simply couldn't get out of his brain.

But it wasn't his puzzle to solve. Nor was figuring out who the two cowboys were in the picture, and what connection they might have to Gibbs. He'd called Torres, but the man gave him a total of two-point-three seconds, just short of hanging up on him.

Yeah, so maybe he should just let it go.

Except every night Kelsey kept slipping out of his hands. And every night he heard himself say, *I told you, I'm going to get you out of this.*

And he had, *hello*.

It had been *her* decision to walk away from him. And why not? It wasn't like they had a passionate, torrid romance.

Not with Safe, and Old, Knox.

Aw, that wasn't fair. He *was* older than her.

And safe.

Shoot, he needed coffee.

Knox was closing the computer when he heard a knock at the door.

His mother walked in, her curly brown hair pulled back in a headband, dressed in an oversized flannel shirt and a pair of yoga pants. She was carrying two mugs of coffee and set one on the desk.

"Early start," she said, blowing on her coffee.

"You too."

She slid into a leather cigar chair in front of the desk. "Your father couldn't sleep, either, when he was worried." She raised an eyebrow.

Tall, willowy, and strong, Gerri Marshall seemed to be able to see right through him. He always felt thirteen under her scrutiny.

"I'm not—"

"I heard you set up an appointment at the bank." She took a sip of the coffee. "Are we in trouble?"

Seriously. He couldn't jaywalk in the small ranching town of Geraldine without it getting back to his mother. "How did you hear that?"

She lifted a shoulder. Then, a smile. "Hardwin Colt is the bank president."

Oh. Which, by the way, "Tate told me you two were seeing each other." He ran his thumb along the handle of his mug. "When did that happen?"

She drew in a breath. "We're not really *seeing* each other.

He came to one of my watercolor classes at the library, and we struck up a conversation. He took me out for dinner a couple times."

A couple times— "Ma. Listen. We don't know anything about Hardwin. He just moved here—"

"Don't get your knickers in a knot, son. He's lived here for five years, so he's not exactly new in town. But he's just a nice man who lost his wife a few years ago. We have a lot in common is all. Besides, I get lonely sometimes."

Lonely. "You have me."

She gave him a look.

And that felt a little weird, so he didn't chase it.

She took another sip of coffee. "So, if it's not the ranch, is it what happened in Texas? Tate called to tell me about it."

Clearly Tate was trying to mend his demolished fences.

"No. I'm fine. I'm just…"

"Something is eating at you. A mother knows, and I hear you roaming around this house in the wee hours of the night." She leaned forward. "Thank the Lord that no one other than the suspect was killed—" She held up her hand. "No other human being was killed. I know you're upset about Hot Pete."

"Hot Pete could have landed in the NBR-X championships. Again. He pays—paid—the mortgage on this ranch."

She went silent. "And you raised him from a calf."

He drew in a breath, looked out the window. The moon had fallen, leaving a gray-red wash upon their land, undulating over pasture, coulee, and ridge, all the way until it reached the Garnet Mountains, still snowcapped and jagged in the distance.

"I think you just need to put this horrible tragedy behind you."

He looked back at her. "Yes. Absolutely. It's behind me."

She narrowed her eyes at him. Sighed. "I was thinking… maybe we should think about renting out the land." She leaned back. "Hardwin's looking to expand his herd and could use more grazing land."

"We need our grazing land for our herd."

"The herd is half of what is was when your father—"

"That's because we're breeders now, Ma. Of champion bucking bulls."

He didn't mean to raise his voice, especially when she tightened her mouth. "Knox. I know you mean well. And I do trust you. You have your father's instincts, and more. You took a gamble with Gordo and it paid off. But my family has run cattle just as long as the Marshall family has, and I know a few things about ranching. And I know we don't need all this land for twelve hundred head of cattle, even if we keep one section fallow and one section for fescue and one for alfalfa. One cow calf only needs two acres of forage land a year. That's less than three thousand acres. We can afford to lease one section—"

"Okay!"

She recoiled.

Oh, he hadn't meant for his voice to emerge with so much edge. "I'm sorry, Ma." He ran his hand over his jaw— he needed to shave. "I'm just…yeah, you're probably right… It's just that Dad never had to lease the land and…"

Now he sounded pitiful and thirteen. He took a sip of coffee, unable to look at his mother.

"Knox. You are not a failure. Not by a long shot. Your father would be so proud—"

He met her eyes, and she drew in a breath.

"You need to stop wondering if you were the right one to take over the ranch," his mother said quietly.

"It doesn't matter. We didn't really have a choice, did we?

I gotta check on Daisy. She's about to birth." He finished his coffee. Got up. "Thanks for the coffee."

She nodded, her mouth a tight line, and she wore the same look she had when Reuben told her he was leaving.

He might not be a failure, but if he'd stuck around, then Dad wouldn't be gone, would he?

Just another person he'd let down.

He pulled on a lined flannel shirt and his work boots, then exited the house and followed the trail to the barn. He'd spent three summers re-siding the barn, installing pens for the bulls, and creating a corral where he might train them. It wasn't a science—the breeding or training—as most bucking bulls simply possessed the genes to throw off a cowboy. But he could add to their Pavlovian response by training them to buck when they felt the pressure of a dummy.

More of a remote-controlled box than the form of a rider, the twenty-or-so-pound dummy was harnessed to the youngster bull. When the bull bucked especially hard or jumped high, Knox released the dummy. The practice wasn't widely heralded, but he'd used it on Hot Pete...

Knox drew in a breath at the stab. Swallowed down the memory of him singing to the animal that last night in the stock barns.

And of course, Kelsey's voice sneaked in beside his.

He'd found her album online, downloaded it, and even sang along to a couple songs.

Cowboy, don't lie—Take me away and make me fly.

Once, he'd turned it on in the barn when he was mucking out a pen with his hired man. Fell into the memory of her at the concert when her lonely ballad came up.

But you don't know if you don't start
So wait...for one true heart...one true heart...

He eased open the door and flicked on the overhead light to the barn. Gordo glanced over at Knox with big brown eyes, his big white leathery Brahma bull body shifting in his pen.

"Hey there, Buck," he said. Gordo turned, shoving his bony snout between the bars of the gate. Knox reached into his pocket and pulled out a baggie of old apple slices, now browned. Opened the bag and pulled out one, feeding it into Gordo's mouth.

Gordo's long tongue drew it in, chomping it, and Knox ran his hand between his eyes. Scrubbed his nose. "You're going to have to give me a few more champions, buddy."

He fed the bull another slice, then headed down to where Daisy stood, heavy with calf. He checked her udder, found it to be swelling, the same for her birth canal. Her pelvic bones had started to loosen, but so far she hadn't seemed uncomfortable. He ran his hand over her face, those long-lashed eyes blinking at him. "Hey, sweetheart. Give me a good bull, okay?"

The four two-years-olds were asleep in the pens in the back of the barn, their red bodies rising and falling with slumber.

The Marshall Triple M would be just fine. He'd purchase Calamity Jane, breed her with Gordo, and hopefully produce another monster in the ring.

They'd land back on their feet, no problem.

He wasn't going to drop anything. Or anyone.

Knox fed the cattle, both in the barn and the calves and cows in the nearby breeding pen, and by the time he returned inside, the sun bit into the cool morning air, burning off the chill, leaving glistening teardrops on the grassy pastures around the house.

Three generations ago, Great-Grandfather Marshall had headed West, built the Triple M for his three sons, including the homestead cabin still tucked below the ridge, which was protection against the elements.

Two left, one for Texas, the other for Minnesota.

One stayed. The two-story log home was built by Knox's grandfather, Joseph, in the fifties, and his own father, Orrin, had inherited it when Joseph died too young at the age of forty-six. Knox loved this house, this land, ripe with the husk of earth, cattle, prairie grasses. He loved sitting on the front porch, watching the sunset burn through the land, and in the winter, playing a mean game of Sorry! with his family in front of the hand-hewn rock fireplace that soared two stories in the family room. Even loved their annual re-chinking, where they filled in gaps in the hand-cut logs, inside and out. The second story bordered the family room area with a balcony edge, the bedrooms off the walkway. He remembered sneaking out of his bedroom as a child to dangle his feet between the spindles, watching *Magnum, P.I.* on the television below through the slats.

He still slept in the bedroom he'd shared with Reuben, although he'd replaced the twin beds with a king.

And, now, just like for as long as he remembered, the smell of bacon and eggs greeted him as he came in from chores in the morning. That and the sight of his mother, her hair pulled back, wearing her blue-checked apron, cooking bacon as savory smoke rose from her cast iron pan on her gas stove.

As usual a plate of buttered, homemade wheat bread sat on the counter.

She looked up and smiled at him as he came in. "There's coffee left."

He came over to her, put his arm around her, and kissed

her cheek. "I love you, Ma."

She swallowed, nodded, and he hated that he'd hurt her.

"Listen," he said as he slid onto a stool. "I know what I'm going to get you for your sixtieth birthday."

She put a plate of bacon, soaking into paper towels, on the counter. He stole a piece.

"A new set of paints?"

He raised an eyebrow. "Really, do you need—"

"No! You've given me that every year for the past four years."

Oh. He didn't realize he was so boring. Add that to Old. And Safe.

She ladled eggs onto a plate. Set it in front of him. "Which is fine. But…what?"

He added bacon to the plate. "I'm going to make sure every one of my siblings is here."

She stilled. Looked at him. "You…how? Even Ford?"

"I'm going to give it my best shot."

She sat on the stool next to him. "You are a good son."

He let the words heal the wound between them.

She turned on the news and they watched it in silence, eating their eggs.

A report of the bombing came up, a wrap of the events as investigators closed the case. He said nothing. But a tiny hum lingered in the back of his head. *Cowboy, don't lie—Take me away and make me fly.*

"Good," his mother said as the report ended. "It's over. You can put it behind you."

He nodded, finished eating, and washed his plate. "I'm going to shower."

Then he filled another cup of coffee and headed across the great room, up the stairs, with the dawn gilding the smooth pine floors, and into his room.

He set the cup of coffee on his bedside stand. Walked over to his closet. Opened it and considered the contents.

Inside, pictures of the bombing, taken from the internet—aerial shots, layouts of the arena, crowd photos, anything he could find—were tacked to the back wall, along with news articles with highlighted and circled data. He'd included the entire roster of cowboys, stock animals—with the deceased underlined—and a rough timeline of events.

He'd even run down a list of Kelsey's crew, although they seemed unlikely culprits, as well as the security staff, thank you, Tate.

In the center of the array was the picture of the two cowboys he'd seen, sketched out from memory. A bad sketch, but he'd inherited some of his mother's skill. And on top of it all, he'd posted yellow notes with questions, along with a phone number to the private investigator he'd hired down in San Antonio. Probably not the wisest of expenses, but he just needed names. Somewhere to start to answer the questions he couldn't escape.

The most important being—why would a cowboy clown from Lubbock, Texas, want to bomb a rodeo?

No, this wasn't over. And he wasn't putting anything behind him.

I told you, I'm going to get you out of this.

Tate didn't know how to protect Kelsey. Not since she'd turned into a zombie. Or at least part of the walking dead, because every day she seemed to fade. Sure, she gave a rather gallant attempt at showing up for practice. Especially since they were opening this weekend in the city of Lincoln, Nebraska, for Brett Young, a country singer out of Nashville. Carter had nabbed them the fill-in gig when Young's warm-up act had bailed.

Kelsey wore her game face during the day, rehearsing the finale she'd orchestrated as they practiced onstage at the Bourbon Theatre, another historic venue, a 1930s renovated movie theater. Tate had watched from the wings as she powered through her song, refusing to let the darkness own her as she walked offstage with Glo and Dixie.

The woman had the steel-edged spine of a warrior.

Reminded him a little of his sister, Ruby Jane. She would have joined the SEALs right alongside her twin, Ford, if the Navy would have allowed it.

Instead, Ruby Jane traveled the globe as a travel agent/interpreter. The woman was fluent in five languages.

In fact, all his siblings had scraped out spectacular lives. Knox, the legendary breeder; Wyatt, with his superstar career as goalie for the Minnesota Blue Ox; Ford, kicking down doors and saving lives as a SEAL; and even big brother Reuben, jumping out of planes like he might be a superhero, into a flaming forest.

While he, middle-child Tate, managed to—what?—well, he'd emerged from his years working security for a Russian casino boss in Vegas alive. That counted for something. But while he liked hanging around the Belles, managing their security seemed at best low-end babysitting. Other than Kelsey's midnight strolls, he hadn't a clue why Glo had hired him.

Maybe for moments like this, when Kelsey slipped out of the tour bus for a midnight stroll. They'd given him a sofa on the bus while they figured out the last few weeks of their tour, and he hadn't hated it. Sort of liked listening to the breathing of the three ladies, not to mention the snores of Elijah Blue. It reminded him of bunking with Wyatt and Ford back at the ranch.

Wow, he missed those guys.

Not that he'd let on, but yeah, every time Ma brought up coming home for her birthday, he wanted to ask—*Will Wyatt and Ford be home?* Not that he didn't want to see Reuben and Knox, and especially Ruby Jane, but he'd never related to his older two brothers.

At least Wyatt and Ford looked up to him. Then.

And Ruby Jane thought he hung the moon.

Yep, he missed that. But as long as he'd committed to trailing after Kelsey and her midnight strolls, he would miss the big event.

Better to be employed, perhaps. *Sorry, Ma.*

He waited for Kelsey to tiptoe by him and open the door before he got up, grabbed his shirt, and followed her out.

He gave her a long leash. They'd arrived a few days early, so although Glo had voted for a hotel, Kelsey insisted they park the bus at a place outside town, the venue being locked in the concrete jungle. Elijah Blue and Dixie opted for a nearby hotel, which left him, Glo, and Kelsey to spread out in the bus. It also meant that he didn't stress out when Kelsey went on her walkabout.

Most of the time she simply wandered the long tree-lined campground. Once, she sat at the edge of a river, staring into the swaying moonlit grasses.

He stayed back, in the shadows, her silent sentry.

But her restlessness shimmered off her. A very present wariness, as if at any time her world could drop out beneath her.

PTSD. Ben King had nailed it at the concert. Apparently, Ben's wife, Kasey, suffered from occasional issues with PTSD from her time in Afghanistan. But a person didn't have to be a soldier to be stressed out and traumatized.

He guessed that more people walked around with PTSD

than they realized.

He hung back and watched as she headed down to the kiddie park that contained a slide, a couple swings, and a merry-go-round.

Kelsey sat on one of the swings, dragging her feet along the ground.

And Tate's heart went out to her. He knew what it felt like to be alone, the night pressing in, no one to turn to. Maybe that's what propelled him forward, out of the shadows, to stroll up to her.

"Only took you five nights," she said without looking up at him.

Oh. Maybe that's why she so freely roamed the premises—because she knew he was her shadow. He said nothing and sat on the swing next to her.

She leaned back and pushed off, back. When it reached the apex, she leaned back on the metal chains, her legs out, and began to pump in an easy playground rhythm.

A springtime night breeze rolled across the prairie, stirring up the smells of earth and cattle, and it reminded him very much of a sultry, starry night in Montana.

"I know you think I'm going to lose it onstage," she said as she gained speed.

"I do," he said softly, hating—but needing her to hear—the truth. "You think you're fine now, but next time you're on stage, with all those people watching—"

"You're wrong. The stage is the one place where I'm safe," she said. "Nothing touches me there."

He said nothing, pushed off next to her.

"Okay, until yeah, my stage blew up, so there's that."

He let a tiny smile find his mouth. Started to pump, catching up.

The night deepened around them as they climbed toward

the sky. The moon came out to watch.

"Kelsey, what did you mean when you said you weren't going *to let him win*?" Tate didn't look at her, hoping to make it easier.

For a long time, he didn't think she'd answer.

Finally, "When I was fourteen, I was attacked in New York City, in Central Park. I was with my parents, who were both murdered, and I was beaten and left for dead."

He stopped pumping, dragging his feet on the ground, almost halting himself cold.

What—?

His throat filled, bile in his chest. Her cool, almost reporter voice had left him bereft.

Well done, Tate. Make her bring that up.

She kept pumping, as if refusing to be halted by his shock. Then again, she'd lived with that reality for…what, twelve years?

No wonder the woman had PTSD.

"I'm so sorry, Kelsey."

She dragged her feet on the ground, kicking up dirt. "Life is tragic and random. At best, we all have to learn to survive it."

"And you did."

She stopped and now stared at him. "I was found by a jogger and his dog, nearly frozen, nearly bled out, and I spent almost two months in the hospital. When I got out, I went to live with my mother's cousin in Wisconsin. Dixie's dad."

She held the chains of the swing, her whitened hands the only evidence of stress, her voice easy, conversational.

"No one in my school knew what happened. It might have made the news, but I think the papers tried to protect my name. I determined to put it behind me. A couple years later, Glo showed up. She has her own tale of tragedy, and we sort of bonded. Dixie's family played bluegrass, and I liked to sing. And Glo was ready to do anything that would annoy her mother, so we started the Yankee Belles."

So much in that explanation to unpack, but Tate focused on the one thing that mattered. "Kelsey, I know you don't want to hear this, but I think you have a little PTSD. You need a break."

She looked at him. Sighed. Shook her head. "You have to get it, Tate. The band is all I have. I went to college for a couple years, and it was a disaster. Singing—the stage—makes me feel like I'm, if not normal, then in control."

"And, to use your own words, 'my stage blew up, so there's that.'"

Her mouth tightened.

"Listen. Carter talked to me. He told me he can cancel the opening act with Brett Young, and I agree."

"What? Why would you do that?" She pushed off the swing, rounding on him.

He held up his hand. "Because I'm trying to help."

"Then don't interfere. I thought maybe if you heard the story, maybe you'd be on my side—"

"I am on your side!"

She shook her head. "What is it with you Marshalls that make you think you can chase me down, stick your nose into my world—"

"Hey. You pay me to stick my nose in your world."

"Fine. You're fired!" She turned and stalked away.

"I don't think so." He caught up to her, grabbed her arm. "Listen. I *do* understand." He ground his jaw, then, "I understand, more than you realize, the need to prove yourself. To show yourself that you're not afraid, not the person who is going to run. But if you don't face this now, in a year you might not have anything left to give."

She pulled away from him. Met his eyes. "And if I quit now, I might never get back onstage. And if you can get on board with that, you can stick around." She unlatched her arm from his grip and strode away.

Oh yeah, he had a real charm with women. He blew out a breath and made to follow after her as she took the path back to the bus, her frame already under the park lights.

"Tate."

The voice stilled him, and he turned.

What, did every Belle go out for midnight strolls? Glo stood just outside the perimeter of the kiddie park. She wore a bulky sweatshirt, pajama pants, and flip-flops, her short blonde hair captured in a hairband. The look only accentuated her high cheekbones, those luminous, now angry, hazel-green eyes.

Maybe he should quit while he still had his skin. He shoved his hands into his pockets, frowned at her. "What are you doing out here?"

She came up to him. Glanced at Kelsey.

"Were you following her?"

"You, actually. Both of you."

"Still trying to figure out if you can trust me."

He wasn't kidding, but a tiny smile tipped her lips. "Maybe."

Super. "I don't know why I'm even here, Glo. Kelsey told me about her past. Tragic and yes, she has a right to be jumpy, but I don't seriously think she's in any danger—"

"What about me?"

He stared at her. "What about you? Do you have a stalker I need to know about?"

Something flickered in her eyes and for a second—wait—*what*—?

But then it vanished, and she shook her head. "No. I don't. But she didn't tell you everything."

He cocked his head.

"I probably shouldn't tell you this, but she was also raped. She was fourteen. Her assailant also promised to find her when he got out of prison and do it again. And this time finish the job."

Oh. He felt sick.

Glo only made it worse when she said, quietly, "She found out just before the bombing that Russell, the man who hurt her, is out on parole."

He had nothing then, his lungs so tight he couldn't breathe. Finally, "Which might mean he's walking around in New York with an ankle bracelet, but just as easily might mean that they signed him into a halfway house and he's really in Indiana, flooring it to Nebraska."

Right.

"You should have told me sooner, Glo."

She looked away. "Yeah. I thought they found the bomber, and it wasn't Russell. And at first, I didn't hire you to keep us safe as much as to make her *feel* safe. Make us all feel safe." And there went the flicker of something again. "But most of us don't have nightmares that come to life and try to kill us, and I guess I should have taken that more seriously."

"Okay. Then let me do my job. Let me get you all out of here and to someplace safe while I figure out if this guy *is* after Kelsey."

"Where?" Glo seemed to be actually considering his words. Which he took as progress.

Anything other than Glo belittling him with nicknames felt like progress.

"My family's ranch. In Montana. It's remote enough for us to catch our breath and for me to do some digging into this Russell guy."

Glo cocked her head. "Do you have a barn?"

Huh? "Yes. Of course. And horses. And maybe a few kittens…"

She rolled her eyes. "Okay, Farmer John. I'll see if I can talk Kelsey into saying yes."

Farmer John?

But then she touched his arm, gave his bicep a little squeeze, and walked past him. "Good idea."

And shoot, but he nearly, stupidly, flexed his farmer's muscles.

6

With every mile, Kelsey's future slipped from her grip. "I'm a hostage here, just so we're clear." She sat on the step between the front driver's seat and the back of the bus, staring out the massive front windshield as Tate maneuvered the bus through the foothills and twisted curves of the Garnet Range, east of Helena, Montana.

Montana.

Talk about hiding away. They'd been driving for the better part of two days since leaving Lincoln, her show, and her spectacular finale, yet unseen, after the showdown of the century in the RV village.

What do you mean you pulled us from the show?

Her words to Carter, not quiet in the least, and even she could figure out that she was unraveling. She didn't need Dixie to take her by the shoulders, look her in the eyes, and tell her that she didn't want to be onstage when she had a meltdown.

She'd wanted to rip herself away from Dixie's gaze, and then from Glo, who put her arm around her and essentially betrayed her with an agreeing nod.

A couple of Benedict Arnolds the way they sided with Carter—and her new warden, Tate Marshall. "Two weeks off—that's all I'm asking for," Tate had said, shooting a glance at Carter, who'd folded his arms across his chest, nodding. "Enough for us all to take a breath and figure out if Kelsey is really in any danger."

And oh, perfect, her past had shown up to wreak havoc on everyone's lives. She didn't know who had ratted her out, but the news about Russell's parole had found Tate's ears, and suddenly the man had decided to earn his paycheck. But no one seemed to be complaining about the hijacking of their show as they disbanded, briefly, half the band heading for the airport—Dixie to Minneapolis, Elijah Blue back to Austin, Texas, Carter to his office in Nashville.

Except, of course, Glo and Kelsey. Now, Kelsey sat on the steps of the bus watching as her world went from city to farmland to mountainscape.

And okay, it *might* be a little breathtaking, the way the rustic green foothills, speared with deep green pine, edged the hazy-blue snowcapped mountains in the distance. Tufted white clouds against an impossibly blue sky hung over the horizon for as far as she could see.

A girl could probably stand in the middle of a field and scream and not be heard for miles.

In fact, a rather large part of her wanted to try it.

Just run off the bus into one of those wildflower fields, drop to her knees, and release the roil of frustration inside.

Except, then Glo and Tate might decide she didn't just need two weeks off, but perhaps a little white jacket to go with it.

"What, exactly, am I going to do for the next two weeks?" Kelsey said, mostly to no one.

Tate sat in the driver's seat, dressed in a blue T-shirt, a pair of jeans, and cowboy boots. He hadn't shaved since they left Lincoln, and now a deep brown scrub of whiskers covered his face. He wore a baseball hat backward on his head and a pair of aviator sunglasses. "You could…pet the cats."

"I'm allergic to cats."

"Feed the chickens, gather eggs."

She shook her head.

"We have baby goats."

"Really?" This from Glo who sat on the sofa behind them, her feet up, dressed in a pair of yoga pants and a hot-pink tee. She was reading something on her tablet. "I love baby goats."

"Do you like horses?" Tate asked, and Kelsey wasn't sure to whom, but she answered anyway.

"We used to have a horse on the farm, back when I was a little girl. We'd try and saddle him, and he'd blow out his stomach so that we couldn't cinch down the saddle. Then, we'd be in the middle of a field and he'd let out his breath. The saddle would fall right off, and us with it. Then he'd leave us stranded there and head back to the barn. I hate horses."

Tate glanced over his shoulder at her. "Wow. Who's us, by the way? Sister? Brother?"

"Half brother. Hamilton Jones. He's from Dad's first marriage. About ten years older than me. A SEAL. I haven't seen him in years."

She drew up her knees, crossed her arms on them, and propped her chin on top. "I suppose I could work on the new album. Maybe write a couple songs." She looked at Glo through the rearview mirror. "What do you think, Glo?"

"Mmmhmm," Glo said.

"We have to do *something*."

"You could just *relax*," Tate said as he touched the brakes. "Maybe try to get a decent night's sleep?"

He turned onto a dirt road, stopped, and opened the

door of the bus. "Stay here."

Where, really, was she going to go? Because as far as she could see was rolling green pastureland dotted with dark humps of cattle, rough-edged gullies, and the occasional tumbleweed. A real mecca of activity.

Tate unlatched the gate under the soaring log braces of a grand entrance with the words Marshall Triple M Ranch cast in iron hanging from the crossbar.

He got back on the bus.

"Are we here?" she asked.

"Almost. Another mile up the road." He eased the bus through, then got back out and closed the gate. Returned.

But before he started, he turned, one arm on the steering wheel. "Listen. My mom can be a little...friendly. She doesn't mean to, but she'll get into your business, and...anyway, just brace yourself."

"Your mom is here?" Kelsey asked, and something stirred inside her.

Wait, huh—

But he had nodded and turned back to the road.

His family's ranch...oh no, she should have...wait, *wait*—

But what could she say? Turn the bus around?

Maybe Knox didn't even live here—maybe she was simply doing what she did best—conjuring up a worst-case scenario. How terrible, really...

Oh, the last thing she wanted was to relive the memory of her dreadful panic. She simply couldn't bear the pity in his eyes.

The ranch house came into view and for a moment, everything else dropped away. "This is your home? It looks like a freakin' resort!"

A main ranch house was situated at the foot of a hill studded with lodgepole pine. The craggy hill fell to a groomed front yard cordoned off with pale, faded hitching rail fencing. In the middle of the yard at the apex of a curved drive, sat a dark log-sided, two-story home with a stone front porch, complete with rocking chairs, of course, and a dark red door. A basket of flowers sat on a bench near the door.

Charming.

"My grandfather built the house. Hand-sawed the logs, cleaned, and stripped them. The house was just a simple box until my dad added on the wing with the kitchen and great room in the back. You should see the fireplace. We hauled in those stones one at a time."

He pulled up in front of a four-stall garage. To the right, a gambrel roof barn painted green completed the aura of ranch life. She very much expected a cowboy to walk out of those big wide doors.

Probably one that looked a lot like Knox Marshall. Tall, ruddy brown hair, a cowboy hat. Maybe even wearing chaps and leading a horse named Silver.

Yeah, okay, so she'd built him up a little in her mind. It didn't mean she wanted to see him. To have to apologize in person.

Frankly, she was too afraid to ask if Knox might be here. Too afraid that she might just climb into her back bunk and pull the curtain.

Refuse to come out.

In truth, she almost didn't move when Tate opened the door, got up, and reached out his hand. Helping her up, maybe, but she had a sneakin' suspicion he remembered what she'd said to him nearly two weeks ago.

I'm sorry, Tate. I don't want to see him. But tell him thank you.

Jerk.

She ignored his hand and stepped past him, out of the bus.

The glorious scent of pine and aspen, of wide-open spaces, and yeah, a working cattle ranch, swept through her.

She took another sniff and wanted to cry, a crazy lump filling her chest.

Glo landed behind her. "Oh my gosh, this is amazing." She grabbed Kelsey's hand, gave it a squeeze. "Listen to all that...nothing."

Nothing was right. No traffic, no honky-tonk band in the background, no buzz of parking lot lights.

It felt almost empty. As if, without the buzz, she might actually hear herself.

See, she should have said no, dug her feet into the safety of the rich Nebraska soil.

Tate led them around the bus, and Glo didn't release Kelsey's hand, holding her hostage as she dragged her after Tate.

A woman had come out to stand on the porch. She wore her brown hair back in a headband, a curly mess springing out like it was trying to escape, a brown flannel shirt, a pair of cargo pants, a green T-shirt, and gardening gloves, which she now took off and set on the bench by the door. Only then did Kelsey notice the pots, the bags of dirt, and the geraniums in baskets, ready to be repotted for summer.

"Tate? Are you kidding me?" The woman came off the stone porch, arms open, and practically flew down a worn stone path to the dirt drive.

She dove into Tate's arms, and he swung her around, and it did something crazy in Kelsey's chest to see a grown man love on his mother. The woman let him go, but cupped his face, grinning, a glisten in her eyes.

Sweet.

He kissed her forehead, then put his arm around her as he turned her. "Ma, this is Kelsey and Glo. They're with the

Yankee Belles. We need a little…timeout from touring."

"Oh, that's wonderful." She grinned at them, her eyes so warm Kelsey had to look away, out into the jagged horizon where the snowcapped mountains burred the skyline.

"I'm Gerri," she said and didn't stop to ask permission before she gathered Glo into a hug. Glo grinned at Kelsey over her shoulder, waggling her eyebrows.

Kelsey submitted to a hug, too, and then Tate's explanation of their band and how they lived through the attack in Texas.

"I've been watching the news on that. Terrible, terrible. I'm so glad you're all putting it behind you."

Or, trying.

"Let's get your stuff. We have plenty of room."

Tate turned into a porter and retrieved their packed duffel bags, bringing them into the house.

Kelsey stood inside for a long moment, drinking in the polished logs, the stacked stone fireplace, the beautiful kitchen, the round table with the leather chairs, the overstuffed leather sofas, and most of all, the view.

The view. In the backyard, the land stretched out across emerald pastures, then fell into a valley rimmed with dark green fir. A river ran a silver finger through the hills, winding lazily to a small town in the distance.

She was on the Ponderosa, from *Bonanza* fame. Her father's favorite show and she'd been plunked into the middle.

She'd met Hoss, the thug, aka Tate. And of course, Knox would be handsome Adam Cartwright. All she needed was a Little Joe.

"I'll put you girls upstairs in Ruby Jane and Coco's room."

Gerri led them up a wide staircase, then along a balcony to a room with twin beds with curved leather headboards, dressed in western blankets, thick white comforters, and enough pillows to bury herself under, head to toe. Water-colors of white columbine and purple irises hung over each bed, and sheer linen curtains framed the windows.

The room was airy, warm, and embracive, and she barely refrained from leaping onto one of the beds and climbing under the covers.

Except, of course, for the sleeping part.

"Will this work?"

"I just might stay forever," Glo said.

Gerri laughed as Tate put the duffel bags on the floor.

Kelsey walked to the window. Stared out at the barn.

"I'm going to make elevenses in a bit here. Make yourself at home, wander around. I think there might be a couple baby goats to find."

What was it with the Marshalls and baby goats? But after Gerri and Tate left, after Glo collapsed on the bed feigning tears of joy, Kelsey followed her inner nudge and headed outside.

To the barn.

The smaller side door hung open, and she stepped inside. The soaring rafters smelled of hay and fresh straw, of horseflesh and dirt, and she wrapped her arms around herself.

A goat mewed at her, and sure enough, baby goats scampered around in the pen, skin and bones, their hides rough. She rubbed one between its not-yet-horns.

She stepped back and spied a massive Brahma bull staring at her, a chew of hay in its mouth. Dark eyes raked over her, and she remembered Hot Pete's cool gaze. He was probably bucking off cowboys somewhere in Texas.

On the other side of the barn, the four pens were empty, the straw matted, used and soiled with cow pies.

A moan, something big and in distress at the far end of

the barn drew her, and she followed the sound. Stopped as she watched a man, dressed in a pair of jeans, a T-shirt, a grimy gimme cap, and a pair of long plastic gloves, gripping the hooves of what looked like a baby calf emerging from its mother's body.

The mother lay on her side, grunting, her massive body heaving.

"C'mon, Daisy, work with me," he said.

The voice was soft, gentle, and solid, and she'd recognize it anywhere. *I told you, I'm going to get you out of this.*

Knox.

Kelsey didn't breathe a word as she watched the calf emerge slowly, its red face with a white stripe wrapped in sheer, sticky caul. The body fell onto the thick fluffy straw, and Knox began to massage it, clearing the sack from its head.

A long pink tongue curled around his hand. He laughed, and the deep resonance of it, like the jagged beauty of the mountains, filled Kelsey to her bones.

Thank you for being safe.

"Good job, Daisy," he said as the cow got up suddenly, moved around to lick her baby. The calf's dark red coat was thick with spit and mucus, but it looked up, its ears velvety and pink as they stuck out around its face, big brown eyes blinking against the ministrations.

The sight of it drew Kelsey forward, and she crouched at the edge of the pen, watching, a strange cotton in her chest.

Silence from the man standing behind the calf until he too, crouched inside the pen. Put his now ungloved hand on the railing. Gripped it, not unlike he'd gripped her arm to keep her from falling.

"Did you know cows have feelings?" His voice hardly betrayed a hint of surprise, a casual Montana drawl that settled her racing heart. "I had a mama cow once follow her calf down the road a half mile after we weaned it and separated it into another pasture. She bellowed for hours until my brother Ford couldn't take it anymore and put them back together."

He followed with a low chuckle.

And just like that, she'd always belonged here, at the ranch, always known this man, always felt safe.

She leaned into it, desperately needing to hold on. "My dad had a cow named Harriet that had an amazing memory. She would chase me out of the field whenever I took a shortcut through it."

"You lived on a farm?"

She nodded, looked up at him. He had the same warm, blue-green eyes that she remembered, and now she found herself wishing— "I'm sorry I didn't—"

His hand touched hers. "What's important is that you're okay. And here." He scratched behind Daisy's ears. "Welcome to my home."

She reached through the bars and put her hand on the velvety, stout ear of the calf and said the only thing that made sense since she'd left Texas. "I'm glad to be here."

◆

"Don't get me wrong, bro. I'm glad the Belles are here, but what is going on?"

Knox had followed Tate into the pantry, just off the kitchen, his voice cut low as he blocked his brother from escaping the tiny walk-in closet where Tate had chased his late-night stomach growl in search of chips, or rather—yeah, a couple of their mother's homemade cookies.

Tate stuck a chocolate chip cookie into his mouth. "Whaddya mean?"

"Kelsey. She looks pretty rough. Dark circles under her eyes. And what in the world are *you* doing with her?" And he didn't mean for it to sound harsh, or even full of blame, but hello, one minute Knox was sending his brother on a search and rescue mission, the next he was telling him that Kelsey didn't want to have anything to do with him.

Then he shows up with her two weeks later? In their tour bus?

For a second, as she'd walked into the barn, stopped at the stall and watched him birth Daisy's calf, he'd thought he might be hallucinating.

But no. Yes, *thank You, God,* he still possessed all his faculties. And apparently the Almighty was still in the miracle business too, because in his wildest dreams, Knox turned and saw Kelsey standing in his barn, her long brown hair down around her shoulders, smiling at him, her eyes free of fear.

She could stay for the rest of her life if she wanted. But still, he couldn't quite figure out how she'd ended up here, the beautiful realization of all his hopes.

"I'm their bodyguard." Tate finished his cookie, grabbed a bag of pretzels.

"Right. And I'm Prince William—"

"No, seriously, Your Highness." Tate shouldered past Knox and headed into the kitchen. The late hour pressed into the windows, the night velvety and sweet, the stars hanging overhead so close they could eavesdrop. Tate grabbed a glass and filled it with ice from the pull-out ice box in the fridge. "There are things you don't know."

"Then give me a sit-rep."

Tate filled his glass with water from the sink. Turned, one hip against the counter. He'd apparently dug into his old clothes and pulled out an orange Geraldine Bulls T-shirt.

Again, two sizes too small. "I can't."

Knox considered him a moment then, "Yeah, actually, you can. Why does Kelsey look like she hasn't slept in weeks?"

"Because she hasn't." Tate reached for the pretzel bag, pulled out a couple knots. "She's a zombie since we left Texas. Nearly had a breakdown onstage—"

"What—?"

"Total meltdown during the rehearsal for their new finale. Had to bring in—get this—country singer Benjamin King."

"*Benjamin King?*"

"Nice guy. He's the one who suggested I get her out of the limelight for a while. Said she could have PTSD."

That made sense.

"So, she's not sleeping. What else?"

Tate dropped the pretzel in his mouth, crunched, shook his head. "Takes these little midnight strolls around the bus, but otherwise stays in her bunk."

"You're sleeping in the bus?"

"Where else am I going to sleep—the luggage compartment?"

Knox said nothing, but he couldn't help but glance upstairs to Ruby Jane and Coco's room, where Kelsey and her bandmate—Glo?—now slept. Shoot, he wasn't jealous, was he?

He schooled his voice. "Okay. So she needed to get away. And you thought of here?"

Tate lifted a shoulder. "Seemed like the right place."

Except that Kelsey had said she didn't want to see Knox. Not that he was complaining, but, okay. He could work with this.

"Stick around for Ma's birthday, okay?"

"That's sorta the plan."

Knox nodded. Opened the fridge to grab the container of orange juice. Reached for a glass in the cupboard.

"Did Daisy give birth to a bull today?"

"Yeah," Knox said, pouring a cup. "Out of one of Hot Pete's straws."

"Think he'll be a bucker?"

"Counting on it," Knox said. "Goodnight, Tate." He left his brother there and headed into the den off the great room, the former family room before the addition. Now, it had turned into a place to put his stockinged feet on the worn coffee table, settle back into the ancient leather sofa, and watch football. Or, this time of year, hockey.

Knox picked up the remote and scanned the channels. Maybe he could catch a Blue Ox game, watch his brother Wyatt catch pucks between the goalposts.

Knox had left at least three messages for his superstar brother but hadn't yet gotten a return call. He'd left the same message for Ruby Jane and emailed Ford, hoping he wasn't aboard a ship in the Middle East or wherever Team 2 deployed.

As for Reuben, yeah, he was just starting his preseason training for a hot wildfire season up north in Ember, but his big brother had been the first to text his RSVP. With his fiancée—cute, petite redhead pilot Gilly Priest.

Knox just might be able to keep his spur-of-the-moment, impossible promise to his mother.

He found a Canucks versus Blue Ox game and forgave his brother a little when he saw the score. Oh, that was rough—3-0, third period.

Knox settled back with his orange juice and tried not to think about Kelsey, unable to sleep. Kelsey, the way she looked as she'd crouched in front of Daisy today, something forlorn and rattled on her face.

He'd wanted to reach out and save her all over again.

It had taken him a couple hours to clean up the birthing pen, then he'd driven his pickup into the back field to see if any more cows might be birthing. His hired man, Lemuel, had pulled a few of the near-to-delivery mamas back to the barn, and was watching them, but Knox didn't want any animal forgotten and in distress.

The sun had hung high, the day beautiful and warm, the snow glinting off Black Mountain to the east, the Garnet Range ahead of him. He loved this pocket of land where he could see all the way down into the valley, to the little town of Geraldine.

He didn't really want to leave the ranch. Probably.

But Knox *had* fought a spark of heat when he came in later, grimy, sweaty, tired, and found Tate lounging on the leather couch, playing a hand of rummy with the other bandmate, Glo.

And Kelsey in the kitchen with their mother, helping with the cookies.

Someone had to run the place.

He'd showered, changed, and come down for dinner.

Kelsey was painfully quiet, picking at her mashed potatoes. She retired right after the cookies and ice-cream portion of the night.

Oh, how he hoped she was sleeping.

"Hey."

The voice made him look over and, shoot, nope. Kelsey stood in the doorway, dressed in her yoga pants and a pink Belles Are Made for Singing shirt. Her dark hair was down, freshly washed, with darker strands still wet amidst the drier tousles.

She didn't wear any makeup, which made her look about twenty-one, and came in and sat on the recliner. "What are you watching?"

"Hockey. My brother Wyatt plays goalie. For the Blue Ox, the guys in blue."

"Seriously?" She leaned forward, hands between her knees, watching the screen. "It looks like...oh, they're losing."

"Yeah. But they don't have a terrible record this year. They lost one of their players to injury—Max Sharpe—and that has left a big hole in their offense. But they have good coaching, and usually Wyatt is on his game. Not sure what's going on with him."

"So you have a superstar brother. Cool."

Knox lifted a shoulder. Refrained from saying something that sounded small, like, *Actually they're all superstars. While I stay home and play midwife.*

But he had birthed a *bull* today. With Hot Pete's face.

Hopefully, with the late bull's genes for bucking, too.

She leaned back in the recliner. "I have to admit, when I saw this place...I can see why you don't want to leave it."

"It's not that I don't want to leave it. I really...I can't."

He wasn't sure why he said that, because given the choice...except he *hadn't* been given a choice. He didn't have the option to hit the road with an all-girl band and play bodyguard-slash-plaything. Not when people were counting on him to keep a legacy alive.

"You can't?"

"When my father died, I was the only one he'd trained to run it. My big brother, Reuben, had left a few years earlier to be a smokejumper, and Tate was also gone. Wyatt was on his way to the juniors, so that left Ford, but he had this dream of being a SEAL—"

"You have a brother who is a Navy SEAL? And another one who is a smokejumper?"

He supposed this conversation was inevitable. "Yes."

"And Tate is a bodyguard."

"I wouldn't exactly call him—"

"Oh, trust me. He's bossy and shadowy and knows what he's doing. He has Kevin Costner written all over him."

"Kevin Costner?"

"That old movie, with Whitney Houston? He's her body-guard and falls for her?"

And that might be the last thing Knox wanted to hear. Because yes, Kelsey would be so very easy to fall for, with her sweet smile, those beautiful pale blue eyes. He drew in a breath. "Tate does know his way around a brawl, that's for sure."

"We haven't had any of those, but…" She sighed. "He did rescue me when I sort of…" She met his eyes. "I freaked out onstage, and everybody is completely overreacting. They canceled our shows, and Tate and Carter practically coerced Dix and Glo to mutiny. They refused to go onstage with me until I started feeling like myself again, but …I'm best *onstage.*"

He liked her with this much passion. It reminded him of the woman he'd watched singing under the spotlight. "You are pretty amazing onstage."

She smiled, tucked her hair behind her ear.

"But you're also pretty amazing offstage."

She looked away, as if his words hurt.

Shoot. "Maybe Tate's right. Maybe you just need a few days off. Get your feet back under you." He went out on a limb. "I'm a safe guy, remember? And this is a safe place."

She smiled. "I remember."

He let the memory linger between them, a view from a Ferris wheel.

"Your barn reminds me of the farm where I grew up in

Minnesota. Dad was a dairy farmer."

"Hence your love for cheese curds."

She laughed. "Yeah. I really missed the farm after..."
Her face turned solemn. "My parents were murdered in
New York City when I was fourteen."

He stilled but didn't move his gaze from her face.

She, however, looked down at her hands. "You're the
second Marshall I've told that to."

He tried to ignore the spur inside him. Nice. So Tate
knew more about her than he did. But he said nothing, just
nodded.

"I don't know why, but the explosion has sort of brought
all of it back to the surface."

"The loss of your parents?"

She looked up at him. "And the fact that now I've nearly
been killed twice. Randomly."

He frowned.

She wrapped her arms around her legs drawn up on the
chair. "I was with my parents when they were murdered. We
had gone to New York City for my birthday to see *The Lion
King* on Broadway and decided to talk a walk through Central
Park after the show. They came out of nowhere. Just—one
minute we're walking under a bridge, the next a thug has his
arms around my mother and is demanding money from my
dad." She looked out the window. "He would have given
them anything, but then my mom broke free and took off.
The guy pushed her, and she slammed into a rock on the
path and just..." She sighed. "Anyway, my dad jumped one
of them and told me to run. All I remember is my dad shouting at me, hands grabbing me, then the horror of listening
to the fight—fists on bone, him swearing and grunting and
shouting my name as they beat him."

"They?"

She let out a shaky breath. "Three men. But there was a leader—a man named Vince Russell. They were all caught, and no one could determine who was the actual murderer, but one of the other gang members testified against him so he got twenty years. He only served twelve."

"That's not enough."

"I agree." She leaned back against the chair. "Especially since they beat me and left me for dead."

His entire body went still, her words a punch dead center in his chest. He tried not to gulp for air, but really, he couldn't breathe. Just stared at her.

No, don't do that. He tore his gaze away, his throat tightening.

She drew her sleeves down over her hands. "A jogger's dog found me."

He moaned. "Oh, Kelsey. I'm so sorry." His voice came out soft, and it took everything inside him not to crouch before her and pull her into his arms, mostly for himself.

Because the crazy, inane urge to do *something* charged through him, turned him edgy and hot.

She looked up at him. "I'm okay. But that's why sometimes I get freaked out. And why I wanted to just put everything behind me. Like the explosion."

Right.

Because he didn't know how he would live with the emotions, the rage, the frustration simmering inside him but to walk away.

"And that included me," he said gently. "I really did get it, you know. The need to walk away."

She studied him for a moment. "Who are you, Knox Marshall, that you're so nice to me?"

He blinked at her, not understanding, really, the question. "I'm not...I just..." He wasn't kind. He was just...well, of course, and why not? The easy answer was because he wanted to. But that sounded lame and even a little desperate.

And even worse was…because he liked to see her smile. Oh brother.

But as if she might be confirming his unspoken answer, she turned to him, her eyes soft, a slight smile tipping her lips. "Okay. You don't have to answer. But…thanks for being so nice."

Nice.

Old. Safe. And now Nice.

He didn't have anything of nice in him at the moment as he thought of her—fourteen years old—beaten…yeah, he needed to get outside and hit something.

She turned to the television screen, draping her legs over the padded arm of the recliner.

They watched the rest of the game in silence, not one moment of his attention on the game.

One minute before the buzzer, the Blue Ox scored. It barely registered, but he tried to cover it up, turning to her for a high-five.

Her eyes were closed, her body rising and falling in the rhythm of deep slumber.

He watched for a moment, a little forbidden pleasure of seeing her pretty lashes on her face, the slightest smattering of freckles on her nose. The pretty mouth. He got up and grabbed the gold knitted afghan from the end of the sofa and draped it over her.

Old. Safe. Nice.

Whatever. He sighed. Then he pumped down the volume, turned off the light, and slowly crept from the room.

But for the first time in a decade, Knox decided that Tate the troublemaker had done something right.

7

Apparently, Kelsey could be healed with a glass of fresh milk, homemade cookies, late-night hockey, and the endless landscape of western Montana. By days filled with nothing but wide-open spaces redolent with the smell of lavender, fescue and even cattle. Massive beasts that looked at her under heavy-lashed eyes.

Who knew? She could have saved thousands in counseling.

Over the past three days, she'd spent more than a little time in the barn, watching Knox bottle-feed the bull calf.

No, watching Knox.

He talked about the ranch and his brothers, his sisters, one actually a foster sister from Russia, named Coco. Introduced her to Gordo, Hot Pete's sire.

Told her the sad news about Hot Pete.

At night, after the house became quiet, she wandered downstairs to join him for late-night television. Usually hockey, but after last night's game, he flipped to the Cowboy Channel.

Wouldn't you know it, Hoss, Little Joe, and Adam walked onto the screen like they'd been expecting her. She fell asleep to Ben Cartwright's wise voice.

And Knox's steady presence. He tiptoed out every night, sometime after he covered her with the gold afghan, left the television light on, the sound muted, as if he knew she might be afraid of the dark.

She had never slept so hard as she did in the recliner. After the first night, she tilted it back, found it to be worn in all the right places, the velour cozy and soft and…oh, who was she kidding?

Knox was the reason she dropped off to oblivion without a whimper.

Safe. Nice. Knox.

Although why she'd called him old, she didn't know. It had stuck out in her mind, despite being a casual remark. Maybe she'd meant…safe. Or responsible. Because he wasn't old—only four years older than herself, something she discovered when she asked Glo how old Tate was and did the math. According to her calculations, Knox was barely 30 to Tate's 28.

Which meant he wasn't old at all, a fact confirmed when she saw him yesterday wearing a sleeveless white T-shirt as he tagged and vaccinated new calves in the yard behind the house.

His muscled chest stretched out his shirt, and he was strong and agile when he chased calves down, separated them from the cows, and pushed the mamas out of the way when they bellowed.

She liked how he knew his way around animals without hurting them.

She'd add noble to her list, probably.

She sat on the rail while he talked about the different aspects of their ranch, from the cow-calf business, to the beef business, to the bucking business. Clearly, he possessed the mind of a man who had breathed ranching his entire life.

But definitely not old.

And he smelled good—husky and clean—when he'd arrived at the dinner table.

She'd found herself in the kitchen, helping Gerri with dinner, the kind her mother used to serve. Baked potatoes, pot roast, chili, homemade cornbread, pie.

She had probably gained ten pounds in three days. And didn't care.

Now, she sat on the back porch, the view silencing her. Jagged, gray, white-capped mountains framed the horizon to the northwest, and down inside a bowl surrounded by rolling green hills sat the tiny town Knox said was named after his great-grandmother. Geraldine.

Romantic, if you asked her. For a man to name an entire town after the woman he loved. She'd seen a picture of Jacob Marshall, the patriarch from the early 1900s, and decided Knox looked a little like him. Bold cheekbones, a square jaw, pensive, but kind, eyes. And a rare smile that could fill her entire body with heat and light and…

No. She could not fall in love with him.

She was just here short term. To breathe and heal and rest.

And eat cookies, apparently, because the door opened and Gerri walked out, a tempting plate of browned goodies in hand. "You have to try these," she said as she sat down in the rocking chair next to Kelsey. "They're my grandmother's peanut butter recipe, but I added molasses to it, and…what do you think?"

Kelsey took a proffered cookie still radiating warmth from its recent escape from the oven.

It practically dissolved in her mouth, and she let out a groan.

"Oh good," Gerri said. "I'm going to serve them for the

birthday party."

Kelsey took another bite of the cookie. "Knox says it's a big one."

"The big six-oh." Gerri set the plate down and looked over at her. She wore a floral-patterned scarf in her hair, an oversized sweatshirt, and leggings, her feet bare. "You want to know a secret?"

Kelsey glanced over.

"I could care less about turning sixty. It's just a number. I'm hoping to give my kiddos an excuse to show up. They haven't all seen each other since…well, for a few years. I managed to get them all home one Labor Day a few years ago, right before Ford left for basic. Knox is beating himself up one side and down the other for not keeping the family together, and I wanted to show them that we can be together and still be off on our own journeys."

She grabbed a peanut butter cookie, tore off an edge. "Might help him let me go a little."

Kelsey frowned.

"I met a man." She smiled, wagged her eyebrows. "He has a motorcycle."

Kelsey couldn't help but smile at the twinkle in Gerri's eyes. "Is that bad?"

"Not in the least," Gerri said. "In fact, Hardwin reminds me, in a way, of Orrin. Safe, sturdy, smart. But under all that is a man who might as well be seventeen, ready for adventure."

She sighed. "Don't get me wrong. I loved Knox's father with everything inside me. I still ache with missing him— he's everywhere here. He proposed to me right there—" She pointed to a knoll at the far edge of the property.

She dropped off into silence, as if remembering. "After he died, I'd go out there sometimes. Sit and listen."

"To…what?"

Gerri glanced at her. "To the Lord. His voice, in the wind. In my heart. I'd pour out my grief. 'From the ends of the earth, I cry to you for help when my heart is overwhelmed. Lead me to the towering rock of safety, for you are my safe refuge.' And He was my safe place, every day. He gave me just enough grace for that day to keep going on with my life."

She sighed. "Of course, I don't know what I would have done without Knox. Poor man. He had dreams of making it big in the PBR, but I couldn't run this ranch alone, and he knew it. Came out without a word and went to work. I handed him the reins and he took a chance on the bulls and it's paid off. He's got his father's head for business, my creativity, and his own brand of get 'er done."

"I'll never forget the way he caught me in the arena, when I was falling," Kelsey said quietly. "He's amazingly strong."

Gerri glanced at her. "He didn't mention that."

"Hmm. Let's just say he refused to let me fall."

Gerri nodded. "He refuses to let *any* of us fall. I just worry about what it costs him."

"What it costs him?"

"He's so hard on himself. Driven. Focused. But I think he spends so much time working he never gets a chance to breathe. He's told himself that he must be as good, if not better, than his father and doesn't see that it's strangling him. Not that he could with his head down, always driving forward. I don't think he's ever even let himself cry for his father."

Kelsey looked out. "Maybe it's the only way he can hold himself together."

"That's the problem. He doesn't need to. Not all the time. There's a time to just let Jesus take the wheel, as Carrie Underwood would say. Hey, do you know her?"

Kelsey laughed, shook her head. "But Benjamin King sang a few nights ago with the Yankee Belles."

"Benjamin King. Wow. My son Reuben has a friend, Pete, who knows him."

"He's a nice guy."

Gerri stood up. "I'll leave the cookies with you."

"Not if you love me."

The words just tumbled out, easy, as if—

"I do love you, sweetie. That's why the cookies are staying."

Gerri winked at her, her smile sweet, as if she didn't even notice that Kelsey's heart was suddenly hanging on the outside of her body.

She opened the door but paused in the threshold. "There's a path to the high place, if you're interested." She pointed to a thin, worn trail. "A little change in perspective always helps."

The door closed behind her.

Kelsey listened to the wind whispering, then got up. Grabbed a couple cookies and headed off the porch, through the grasses up to the ridge, climbing a hidden trail cut out of the rocks like stepping stones.

Scrub pine and cluster grasses cluttered the top of the ridge, but she followed the trail farther through the maze and found at the end a small wooden bench. She slid onto it, her breath catching.

The ridge overlooked a winding river, the same one that led down to Geraldine, but here, she could make out a breathtaking waterfall that fell from a high mountain ledge into the pine-edged lake below, frothy white, a mist rising from the cascade like a veil.

It dropped into a moraine lake, then down into the valley in a river that widened as it hit the valley floor, meandering around granite cliffs and steep, green mountainside until it emerged into the flat land, spent.

"My father proposed to my mother up here."

"I know." Kelsey turned and shielded her eyes to find Knox standing behind her. A pretty quarter horse grazed with dropped reins not far away. "She sent me up here."

He took off his hat and settled it on her head. "Can I join you?"

She adjusted the hat and patted the seat, feeling a little like she was in high school. Although she'd never once had a handsome cowboy—or any guy, really—pay attention to her in high school. Or if they did, she—or more aptly, Glo—ran him off.

Knox sat far enough away for her not to run. But close enough for her to see a day's whisker growth in his beard, which glinted copper in the sunlight. He wore a denim work shirt, the cuffs rolled up around his forearms, a pair of canvas work pants, and his scuffed cowboy boots. A pair of gloves hung on his belt.

"It's beautiful," he said. "And you'd never know the waterfall was here unless you went looking."

"I love this place," Kelsey said, the words just spilling out of her.

He gave a low chuckle, and she could feast on it every day of her life. "Yeah. It sort of gets into your bones. But don't be fooled—ranch life is dangerous, hard work."

She had no doubt, but something… "I know it's none of my business, but…would you tell me how your dad died?"

He went silent for a moment. "Are those my mom's cookies?"

"She's tweaking an old recipe."

"Sure she is," he said as she held out the napkin. He took a cookie. "She thinks cookies are life's answer to every problem." He took a bite, made a humming sound. "Maybe."

She laughed and sort of hated that she'd asked—

"He had a heart attack. In one of the back fields. He was riding fence all alone and he couldn't get to the radio in time. Ma got worried when he didn't come back before dark and sent out the hired man and a few other guys we had working for us at the time. They found him about four hours later."

He finished the cookie, brushed off his hands. "I should have been there. I was off competing in a rodeo that weekend. I won, but...we always rode fence together and if I'd been home..."

She longed to reach out, to touch his arm, tell him exactly what his mother had said. "You're too hard on yourself."

Oh. Whoops, she hadn't exactly meant for it to slide out, but he looked at her. Frowned.

"Sorry. I just think...well, I know what it feels like to be driven by the need to do something, anything, to get your head out of the grief. To see your past in your rearview mirror and your destination in front of you and never feel like you really move forward. It's exhausting."

He was simply staring at her. Then, slowly he nodded. "Yes, it is."

She smiled, and he smiled back, his beautiful eyes in hers, holding her—willingly—a little hostage. Her heart gave another tug, something powerful, as if adjusting for room inside.

"Would you...would you like to have some...fun?" He made a smile, almost a grimace, as if it might be a terrible idea.

And she didn't help with her surprised, *"Fun?"*

"With me?"

"With you?" What was wrong with her? She'd suddenly lost her ability to comprehend, apparently.

"What? Is that such a crazy idea, to go out with an old, safe, nice guy and expect some fun?"

Now she really had no idea what he was talking about. "Uh…no. Yes, I mean—" She made a face, tipped his hat down over her eyes. "I'd love some fun, cowboy."

He grinned then, his eyes twinkling, something almost… mischievous? in them. And she had the first sense that maybe Knox Marshall wasn't quite as safe as she thought.

At least not to her heart.

Would you like to have some…fun? Knox's own stupid words rang in his ears as he sat in the Bulldog Saloon, wishing he could slink out and floor it back to the Triple M. What on earth had he been thinking?

Kelsey didn't like crowds. So what did he do? Bring Kelsey to the only packed hot spot in all of Geraldine. Dancers jammed the wooden floor in front of the stage, swinging and two-stepping to a cover of a Brad Paisley song. The entire place was alive, buzzing with shouts from the guys playing pool behind him, people cheering the hockey game playing on the flat-screen televisions over the bar.

And in the middle of the chaos, Kelsey sat beside him and nursed a lemonade, her expression suggesting she was parked a million miles from Geraldine, Montana.

Worse, he wasn't helping. Because apparently, he *had* forgotten how to have fun. Knox sat on the winged bar chair like he'd suddenly entered a foreign world, never smelled the tangy craft beers, the sizzling steaks, never heard country music in his life. Forgotten how to talk around a pretty woman.

Although in his defense, Kelsey had pretty much swept his breath from his chest tonight when she showed up wearing a short black V-necked dress, her turquoise boots, her hair down and tousled, shiny and smelling like something floral. It was all he could do to keep his eyes on the road as he drove them into town, Tate and Glo in the back seat.

Frankly, his neck was so stiff it would probably shatter if the crooner on stage hit a high note.

C'mon, Knox, loosen up.

He'd thought the old watering hole in town might be the perfect place for them to relax, sink into the music, comforting eats, and anonymity of a small-town crowd.

Except he forgot Kelsey was a country music star—or on her way. She probably thought this was small town and provincial compared to the raucous stadiums where she played.

And all that pressure had glued him to the bar seat at the table. Which only confirmed that he was not only Safe and Nice but Small Town, and if he summed it all up...Boring, with a capital B, all exclamation points.

I'd love some fun, cowboy.

Knox would give about anything to have Tate's easygoing, nothing-hit-him demeanor. His brother sat across the table, his chair turned backward, leaning on the back, nursing a long-necked beer.

Glo sat next to him, bobbing her head to the music.

Shoot. Knox did know how to have fun. Maybe too much fun, once upon a time. But still, of *course* he knew how to break loose, let go...

Okay, maybe it had been a serious while since he'd hung out at the Bulldog Saloon. Hadn't even realized the former owners had sold out to new management. The century-old watering hole had undergone a makeover, including a new speaker system for the stage in front. New ironwork lighting hung from weathered beams, and the makeover had opened the walls to the copper brewery tanks now housed in the former livery stable. Tufted leather high chairs replaced the previous tractor seat barstools and were now pushed up to the freshly stained and polished oak bar.

The new owners had kept the aged mirror over the back of the bar, but now flanked it with two flat-screen televisions. Tonight, a baseball game—a local feed of the Helena Brewers—played on one screen; a hockey game —not the Blue Ox, Knox noticed—played on the other, both with the sound off.

The makeover had included a fresh polish of the floor, and a few locals had enticed their dates out for a dance. Knox recognized the guy at the mic as Turner Berry, the foreman at the Stinson ranch. He'd also seen the man at church a couple times with his beautiful cowgirl wife and their son.

"Make a hole, guys. Nachos coming in, nine o'clock."

Knox looked up and spotted Tannie Bower holding a massive plate of chicken nachos. Glo and Tate moved their drinks, along with Kelsey's lemonade and Knox's boring lemon-infused water, and Tannie set the plate of nachos in the middle. Knox wanted to order a beer, but he was the keeper of the car keys tonight.

"Long time no see, Knox," Tannie said. She wore her bleached blonde hair in a high ponytail, pretty and young, and he could hardly believe Chelsea's kid sister had grown into such a beauty. He remembered her as a bony-kneed ten-year-old when he'd dated Chelsea. If "dated" was the right word. More like a clandestine affair that was high on his list of regrets.

Her gaze flickered to Glo, then Kelsey. Finally, back to Knox, just a hint of the past in her eyes. No doubt she blamed him for her big sister's departure from Geraldine. He did too, frankly.

He should have steered clear of the Bulldog. But his other option for grub and a dance floor was the fine dining at Granite Ridge Lodge, twenty miles west.

Tannie tucked her tray under her arm, hung her hand on it. "How's your brother?"

Which one? The question tipped Knox's lips when Tate piped up. "Somewhere overseas, saving us from terrorists."

Oh, *Ford. Of course* Tannie would have an eye for his handsome, charming youngest brother.

"I'll pray he gets home safely. It seems all the best ones leave town. Anything else I can get you guys?"

Tate shook his head, and Knox ignored the barb and turned his attention on Kelsey.

She took a plate from Glo and dragged a couple chips onto her plate.

Onstage, Turner started with a song about broken hearts and letting go, and Knox couldn't help himself.

"You okay, Kelsey?"

She glanced up at him. Pale blue eyes, and they looked at him for a second, empty before they focused on him.

"So, not really at all, huh?"

She gave him a small smile. "No. I was thinking that this song is a Brett Young cover. 'Mercy.' We're supposed to be opening for him tonight."

"Let it go, Kels," Glo said, filling her own plate. "Have some fun."

"Speaking of—how about a dance, Glo?" Tate was sliding up from his chair and holding out his hand.

Glo looked up, her eyes big, then smiled—and if only it were that easy. Knox shook his head as Tate took her hand and weaved through the crowd to the dance floor.

Glo came up to his shoulder, but he bent a little and took her into his arms.

Kelsey turned back to her nachos. "I think Glo likes him."

"I think the feelings are mutual. I haven't seen Tate quite so smiley since…okay, maybe I don't know. He left town not long after he left the military, and hasn't been around much since then."

"Why?" She let a piece of long cheese dangle into her mouth and wrapped her tongue around it, grinning as she slurped it in. "Oops."

Something happened to his stomach with the sight of her sudden smile.

"Oh, it's a long story. I lost my cool…got him in trouble with my Dad. He and dad had it out, and Tate took off."

She raised an eyebrow. "You…lost your cool? I don't see that."

"Not now, maybe, but I had my dark days. Wild, angry… It wasn't a good season." And frankly, he'd spent quite a lot of it here. He hadn't realized how many ghosts still lingered, despite the makeover.

"Your mom said you wanted to be a professional bull rider."

He rolled his eyes. "What didn't my mom tell you?"

"She didn't tell me if you could dance." She met his eyes, tucked her lower lip between her teeth.

Oh. Really. He glanced at Tate, who picked that moment to meet his gaze and raise an eyebrow.

Mentally, Knox wrapped his hands around the bull rope, knocked himself in the chest a couple times. Then he got up from the chair, and held out his hand. "Yeah, I can dance."

She smiled, the distance leaving her gaze.

And when she wiped her hand and took his, something sweet curled through him.

Just because he'd etched a few bad memories into the

walls of the Bulldog didn't mean he couldn't carve out a few new good ones.

And in case anyone in this small town thought he wasn't over Chelsea Bower and her windy exit from his life...

He swung Kelsey into his arms. He took her left hand and put it on his shoulder. Then he took her other hand. "Hold on to me and let me lead. I got this."

She looked up at him, just a little hint of question in her gaze. He leaned his mouth to her ear. "Quick, quick, slow..."

He moved with his words, and she caught on quick, probably already knew the two-step. But she hung onto him and in a moment, they'd joined the other dancers circling around the floor.

Her hand curled around his neck, those pale blue eyes in his, and he had that sense of the girl he'd met on the Ferris wheel, her heart right there, offered up for someone to claim it.

A strange emotion simply swelled through him, the sense that maybe no, he wasn't Tate, wasn't the guy who could charm a girl into her forgetting her name. But he was the guy who'd show up and catch her heart. Keep it from hitting the ground.

Turner ended the song and slowed the next one down. A love song that had Tate and Glo exiting the dance floor, but Knox curled his arm around Kelsey's waist and let out a tiny, long-forgotten piece of himself. "Stay here and dance with me."

He drew her in close, aware of how perfectly she fit against him, and began to sway with the music. A Florida Georgia Line song about dark days and broken hearts.

You're an angel, tell me you're never leaving
'Cause you're the first thing I know I can believe in...

She was mouthing the words as Turner sang, her eyes holding Knox's, and he could hardly breathe.

What was happening here?

Then she laid her head on his chest, and he nearly closed his eyes with the strange effect it had on him, suffusing his cells with an overwhelming tenderness, the nearly frightening sense that he would do nearly anything for this woman.

No, this wasn't fun.

This was a little bit of heaven.

The song ended, and he could have sworn that Turner was conspiring against him when he rolled into an old Elvis remake.

Wise men say only fools rush in
But I can't help falling in love with you...

Yeah. But...shoot.

What was he thinking? Kelsey had a big life. His was here, on the ranch.

Yet, when the music died out and Turner suggested a break, Knox found his throat so thick he had no words. Just stood like an idiot on the dance floor as Kelsey slipped out of his arms.

She smiled, and the trust in her eyes shot through him, took a hold of his brain.

"Wanna get some air?"

She nodded, and he wove his fingers between hers, glancing over at Tate who was finishing off his beer and laughing at something Glo said. He led Kelsey through the bar all the way to the entrance.

The stars hung high, scattered pixie dust across the arc of the Montana sky. To the west, the Garnet Mountains rose in a dark, jagged outline. A breeze raked up the scent of the ranchland around them. Kelsey shivered.

Aw, shoot, maybe he should have…

"I saw a blanket in your truck," she said, glancing up at him.

Right. "Yeah. Uh. Ma keeps it there in case…uh…the weather can be unpredictable in Montana…"

Way to go, Knox. Bring your mother into the conversation.

He headed for the truck, however, and pulled out the ancient fringed stadium blanket. Wrapped it around her shoulders. She leaned against the truck, looking at the stars, and almost on reflex he went around to the back and opened the tailgate. Then he climbed onto the back and held out his hand.

She cocked her head for a moment, then took his hand. He lifted her up, catching the blanket before it fell. She dropped the blanket on the bed and sat on it, leaning back on her hands.

He considered for a moment and then took a chance, settled down behind her, tucking her between his legs, his arms around her shoulders, and pulled her back against his chest.

She sighed and hung her hands on his forearms.

"Still cold?" he asked.

"Not so much."

Oh, he wanted to kiss her. Could hardly believe, however, that he'd somehow ended up with her in his arms.

And then she started to hum. The vibration tunneled through him, the song light in the breeze. He recognized it.

But you don't know if you don't start

He heard the words in his head.

So wait...for one true heart...one true heart...

Her hair tangled in the wind, and he couldn't help it—he caught it and pulled it away from her face, tucked it behind her ear. Which left her neck open for him to kiss.

He'd almost talked himself into it when she said, "Glo wrote that song."

Huh? Oh. "Really?"

"Yeah. It was after her first—only—true love died overseas. He was a soldier. It hurts too much for her to sing it, so I do. But it was our first big hit. Our only big hit..."

"You'll have more."

"I wish I could write songs like Glo, or even Dixie. I guess it takes a sort of vulnerability and poetry I don't have."

"You have it onstage. There's a poetry to the way you woo people. You're a showman, for sure, but...you draw the crowd in. That takes a special kind of vulnerability."

"People compare us to the Dixie Chicks, but I don't want to wear their label. We need our own voice, something authentic..."

"I liked what I heard at the concert."

She glanced up at him. "I nearly forgot the words when I saw you standing in the audience."

"You saw me?"

"You're hard to miss, Knox Marshall. All shining knight with a little Marshal Dillon thrown in."

"You know *Gunsmoke*?"

"Used to watch the reruns with my dad in our basement. He had this scratchy old sofa in his den, and I'd lay across the top while he lay on the sofa, and we'd watch Festus and Miss Kitty and Marshal Dillon round up the bad guys." She cocked her head. "You do sort of remind me of him. Tall, stern…"

"I was hoping for handsome. Maybe a little tough guy."

She smiled, turning to look up at him. "That too."

Really? And he didn't know why, but something simply lit inside him, something fierce and bold and—

He kissed her.

Maybe he should have asked, but he lost himself a moment there as he touched his hand to her face, drew it to himself, and…

Shoot, it wasn't a gentle, tentative, boring kiss either, but something long banked, a feeling he'd been harboring for a few weeks now.

He wanted her to belong to him. It felt primal and cowboyish and he knew that, but the way she'd sunk against him on the dance floor, and even the quiet surrender of her spirit as she sang—

He wanted to hold on to Kelsey and never let her go. To protect her and pull her into his world and curl every bit of himself around her and never let the world touch her.

And heaven help him, but he poured all of that into his kiss, holding her to himself, and yeah, losing himself a little into her touch.

She hesitated only a moment, and that's when the thought hit him—*definitely* he should have asked.

He drew back. "Kelsey, I'm sorry. I—"

She met his eyes, her breath caught. "It's okay," she whispered.

Yes. Then she leaned into him, her arm curling around his neck, and when he kissed her again, her lips softened. Surrendering.

As if she wanted to belong here, in his arms, to him, too.

He wanted to slow himself, wanted to take a breath and just savor. But her hair tangled around him, through his fingers, and she smelled of the spring night, sweet and mysterious and tugging him in.

He almost didn't realize it when he'd turned her, settled her back on the blanket, stretching out beside her, cradling her in his arms.

Almost didn't realize it when he tucked one arm under her head, the other around her waist, deepening his kiss, molding her body to his.

But he was very aware that her arms curled under his shoulders, pulling him closer.

Oh, she tasted of the sweet lemonade, his mouth drinking her in. And for the first time in years, something ignited inside him, something powerful and alive and not at all safe. Or boring. Or perhaps even nice.

Because suddenly, the ghost of the guy he'd been woke up. Began to haunt him.

The guy who'd taken something that hadn't belonged to him. He wasn't that guy. Never again.

He pulled away, breathing hard.

Breathe, Knox.

Safe.

Her eyes were wide in his.

"Kelsey. I…" He swallowed, met her eyes. "I…" What? Loved her?

No, but…he could. Or…shoot. He was probably already on his way, conjuring up happy endings and a life for them on the ranch.

Right?

"I'm sorry. I didn't mean to get carried away there. I just…"

Wanted to kiss her again. *Nice. Safe.* His eyes went to her lips, roamed back to her gaze for permission.

But she caught her lip between her teeth. "Knox. I…"

She touched his chest, right on his too-fast beating heart, then pushed. "I'm sorry. This was a mistake."

He rolled away, back, not sure what to do when she sat up.

Then, with what looked like a wretched look on her face, she scrambled off the truck and fled for the saloon.

———————◆———————

Tate was going to be a problem. A big one, if Glo let the man's charm any further inside.

Shoot, the man had moves. And yes, she should have figured that out when he'd all but thrown the gauntlet down back in Texas, challenging her to not let him under her skin, in response to her own challenge, *We'll see if you're as good as you say.*

Apparently, he was.

Because she stood in the bathroom, staring at herself in the mirror, pretty sure if she went back out to the dance floor she'd let the man kiss her.

If she didn't lay one on him first.

Way to go, Glo, fall for the bad boy. No, she wasn't falling for Tate. Just a little woozy from his charm, maybe the Killian's Irish Red she'd consumed, and the power of being in his arms.

His amazing, muscled, bodyguard-thick arms. And it wasn't just the dancing either, which was particularly amazing because he sort of bent and pulled her close, but the two-stepping too.

The man had moves. He spun her fast, pulled her close, twirled her back out, twisted them into a pretzel, his blue eyes catching hers, then unwound them and caught her, his strong arm behind her back, all the while keeping them in perfect step.

Was there nothing the man couldn't do?

Never mind his cutthroat abilities at gin rummy. And he hadn't lied about the stupid baby goats. Painfully cute, especially when he caught one and held it in his arms for her to pet.

He'd shown her around the ranch, told her about his brothers, his sister, Ruby Jane, and even the foster girl, Coco, whom her parents helped raise, so much love in his voice for his family, it could make a girl like her, with sharp fragments that comprised the word family, believe in the impossible.

It would help if he wasn't downright hot. Short dark brown hair under a baseball cap, the smattering of brown whiskers on his chin, dressed to kill tonight in a royal blue button-down, the sleeves rolled up, a pair of ripped and faded blue jeans sneaking a peek of knee, and cowboy boots to round out the Montana bad boy aura.

How about a dance, Glo? She'd practically leapt from her chair.

Get a hold of yourself, Glo. Because Tate was the exact opposite of the person she was supposed to fall for.

Which probably made him all that more enticing.

Except for the fact that something lingered behind Tate's eyes. Something haunted and hidden, something that came out only when he talked about his brothers.

She recognized the look of shame and couldn't chase it.

Not if she really didn't want him to get into her heart. Because then she'd try to fix it, and...start really caring.

And then it would come to her telling him about *her* past, and nobody really wanted to open that can of darkness.

So, she was hiding in the bathroom, trying to pour water on the flames stupid Tate had stirred to life inside her when Kelsey came barreling in.

Crying?

"What the—" Glo grabbed her by the hand and pulled her into the roomy handicapped stall, closed the door behind them.

Took her friend by the shoulders and pulled her tight. "Shh. What's the matter? Was it Knox?" She pushed Kelsey away from her, met her eyes. "What did he do? I'll kill him—I'll have Tate kill him—"

Kelsey put her hand to her mouth, shook her head. "No—he's..." She closed her eyes and ran her fingers over her cheeks, catching the escaping tears. Drew in a breath before she opened her eyes again. "He's amazing. I think...I think I love him."

Oh. Uh. Glo just blinked at her.

"It's horrible." Kelsey pressed her hand to her mouth, her eyes wide. "He kissed me, and it was amazing, then... Oh, Glo, it was Danny Mueller all over again! I just...freaked out. I *ran* away from him. Like..."

"Like a woman who's been through a trauma and isn't sure how to sort out the good from the bad?"

"But I do...I mean...I feel safe with Knox. He's..." She drew in a breath and leaned back against the stall. "He just surprised me, and I didn't think—I just reacted."

"What did you do?"

"I kissed him back!" She stared wide-eyed at Glo. "I just wrapped myself around him and hung on and *kissed him back.*"

"Good!" Glo laughed, caught her hands.

"But...what does that make me?" Kelsey looked at her. Swallowed.

"Kelsey, with the exception of Danny Mueller, who I don't count, Knox was your first real kiss. It's supposed to be amazing and freak you out and leave you wondering how to put yourself back together again. Unless, of course, he scared you."

She shook her head. "No. I feel…"

"Knox is a good guy," Glo said. "And the fact you kissed him back makes you nothing but a woman who liked being in his arms. That's a good thing…and seriously, it's about time you had a real kiss."

Kelsey gave her a tentative smile and it made Glo want to march out and grab Tate and…

Nope. *Nope.*

Then Kelsey's smile fell, something of horror in her eyes. "I probably need to tell him—"

"You don't have tell him anything. Listen, you have nothing to be ashamed of. The past is behind you—way behind you—"

"It feels a lot closer," Kelsey said quietly. "Especially right now." She pressed her hand to her mouth, her eyes still filling. "I hate Vince Russell."

"Me too," Glo said quietly, then pulled Kelsey into her arms. "I wish I knew how to fix this."

Kelsey held on. "I'll be okay. I think I want to go home, though."

Yes. Good. But shoot. "Okay. I'll get Tate."

"I'll meet you by the door."

They exited the bathroom, and Glo wound her way back to the table.

Tate sat straddled on his chair, and when he saw her, his eyes brightened, and her stupid heart did a sort of backflip.

Get over him. She reached for her jean jacket. "We gotta go."

"What? Why?" Tate stood up, however.

"It's Kelsey. She's…she's tired."

He glanced past her, toward the door. "She looks upset."

Glo pursed her lips together.

Tate's expression turned thunderous. "Wait. She went outside with Knox. What happened?"

"Nothing."

Tate pushed past her.

"Tate!"

He wove through the crowd, Glo following.

And as bad timing would have it, met Knox just coming inside. Where Kelsey stood by the door.

"What's going on?" Tate said, nearly charging Knox.

Glo caught up in time to see poor Knox's confused expression.

"What are you talking about?"

"What did you do to her?"

Knox's eyes widened. "Nothing—"

"Then why was she *crying*?"

And now Knox looked gut punched. Turned his attention on Kelsey. "What—"

She pushed past him out the door.

Knox turned, hot on her tail. "Kelsey?"

"Leave her alone, Knox!" Tate came up on him fast.

Knox whirled around and stiff-armed. "Step back, bro. I think you've had too much to drink."

Tate swiped his hand away. "All I know is that Kelsey was just fine before she went outside with you."

And if he'd hit Knox, it probably couldn't have affected him more. His jaw tightened, and a person would have to be blind to see how Tate's veiled accusation stripped him.

"He didn't do anything," Kelsey said suddenly, standing a few feet away from them, her arms around herself. "I'm just tired. And…" Her gaze flickered to Knox, then Tate. She shrugged.

And Glo wanted to weep for her.

She walked up to Tate, put a hand on his arm. "Come

on, tough guy. Your brother really doesn't have anything to do with this. I promise."

Tate looked down at her, blinking into her eyes. Then back at Knox. And she could nearly feel the anger shudder out of him.

Knox, however, stared after Kelsey, the pain on his face turning a knife in her chest. "Really," Kelsey said now to Knox.

He swallowed, nodded.

Glo let Tate go and followed Kelsey to the truck. Climbed into the back seat behind her.

Put her arm around her. "At least we know they care."

And she wondered just how she was going to stop herself from falling for a man like Tate Marshall.

8

So, Tate might be taking his job description a little too seriously.

Because if Kelsey was safe with anyone on the entire planet, it was Knox. The bad boy Marshall genes simply didn't run through Knox the Sainted.

Even his infamous debacle with Chelsea had been mostly about his good heart. That, and yes, pure teenage boy who'd been seduced by a girl who couldn't be trusted. But Knox blamed himself, completely.

And it clearly didn't take much to stir up the guilt of that disaster.

Tate stood at the kitchen sink, downing a glass of cold water, trying to screw up the courage to head upstairs and let Knox take a swing at him if he wanted.

Because maybe Tate deserved that. The beer *had* gone to his head, perhaps a little, because in his right mind…

Frankly, he'd been fighting to keep a hold of his right mind all night. It didn't help that Glo had picked a sexy little white V-necked top that accentuated her curves, paired it with her faded jeans, her hair in crazy, fun tousles all over her head, the kind of mess he sort of wanted to dig his fingers into.

And then there was the way she looked at him, her arms

hooked around his neck when they danced. Like if he wanted to lean down and kiss her, she wouldn't call him any names.

Or, if she did, he might actually like them.

It was all he could do to keep his brain latched around the fact that she was his boss.

Sorta. Because Carter had done the actual hiring.

Still. Off-limits.

Off. Limits.

And maybe it burned him a little—no, a lot, a full-out inferno—that Knox could kiss Kelsey, or more, or whatever happened out in the parking lot to leave Kelsey so undone, without losing his livelihood.

It went straight to his brain. Jealously, frustration, not a little unrequited desire, and it all boiled out of Tate, all over Knox.

He could hardly believe he'd nearly decked his brother because Tate had turned into a lovesick sot. Not love… but yeah, Glo had his number, and he needed to keep his distance if he hoped to not screw up the good gig he had going with the Belles.

He definitely owed Knox an apology.

Tate finished his drink. Took a breath.

Headed upstairs.

Knox's room was at the top of the stairs, right next to the one Tate had shared with Wyatt and Ford, and two doors down from the girls' room.

He knocked. Braced his hand on the frame. "Knox, open up."

Silence, then the sound of the closet closing and finally, steps to the door.

Tate straightened as Knox opened it.

His big brother considered Tate a long moment, his eyes dark and still simmering.

"Can we talk?" Tate asked quietly.

Knox stood in silence before he stepped aside.

Tate entered the room. Knox hadn't changed out of his black button-down shirt and jeans, apparently not quite ready to go to bed. Now, he folded his hands over his chest, which Tate considered a good thing because that meant he wasn't going to punch him. At least not right away.

Tate went to the window, glanced back at Knox. "There's something that you don't know."

He didn't know why he started with that. It wasn't his story to tell, but he found himself cutting his voice low, suddenly wanting to keep Knox from getting hurt and maybe from even hurting, inadvertently, Kelsey.

In truth, he'd started to care about both women as more than clients.

Kelsey, a sort of sister.

As for Glo…

Tate blew out a breath and curled a hand behind his neck. "Okay, bro, here's the deal. There's things about Kelsey that—"

"I know about the attack. She told me everything."

A gust of relief blew out of Tate, his chest uncoiling. "Oh man. I was really worried I was totally going to have to betray her here. I just…so you get that there was probably a reason she freaked out tonight when you…" He frowned. "What did you *do*?"

And Knox gave him such a look he felt like a jerk for asking. Because Knox wasn't him. Had never been.

"I kissed her. What did you think, that I grabbed her and threw her up against a wall and had my way with her?"

And the very fact that those words came out of Knox rattled Tate.

Worse, Knox blew out a breath and turned away as if,

huh?, maybe he'd been thinking that exact thing. "I surprised her, I guess. I should have asked—"

"Yeah. Maybe. I mean, she's probably pretty sensitive to any sort of physical contact, even if it's wanted—"

Knox turned back to him, frowning. "What do you mean?"

Tate lifted a shoulder. "It's not hard to figure out that a girl who's been raped needs to know she's safe. And in control, if you know what I mean."

Knox just stared at him, his face whitening.

Oh. *No…* Tate's gut bottomed out. "Knox—"

But his brother had leaned over, was grabbing his knees.

Tate walked over and picked up the trash can, set it in front of him. "I felt the same way when I found out."

Knox breathed out hard, a couple times, then stood up and ran his hands through his hair.

"Sorry. I thought… Shoot. I shouldn't have told you."

Knox glanced at him, then pressed the back of his hand to his mouth as if he might still lose it. Shook his head. "Maybe not, but…yeah, that makes sense. Please tell me she wasn't—"

"Fourteen. Mmmhmm."

Knox turned and walked to the window, bracing his hands on either side of the frame, and Tate wasn't sure his brother wasn't going to do something crazy like put his fist into a wall. Or through the pane.

"They caught the guys."

It was a statement, Tate thought, but he wasn't sure, so, "Yeah. But that's the thing. The gang leader—Vince Russell—is out on parole."

Knox rounded on him. "What?"

"Yeah. That's why we're here. Why Kelsey's so freaked out. Because we all know the bombing wasn't related but…"

"But the randomness reminds her of the attack." Knox shook his head, then met Tate's gaze. "And you're sure that this guy had nothing to do with the explosion?"

Tate frowned. "I've been trying to track him down in New York City through some contacts, but, I doubt it—"

And that's when Knox walked over to his closet and opened the doors.

Tate stilled, enthralled for a second by the masterpiece of his brother's research. A map of the San Antonio complex, pictures, news articles, lineups, schedules, itineraries, and Post-it Notes all tacked to the place where his clothes should hang.

Tate took a step closer. "What is this?"

Knox stepped up to the grid. Pointed at two sketches. "Do either of these guys look familiar?"

Tate made a face. "Uh, dude, that's like a second-grader sketch."

Knox gave him a look. "Okay, remember the guys at the bar the night Kelsey showed up?"

"In the beer tent?"

"Yeah. Maybe you didn't get a good look, but one had a tattoo of flames encircling his neck. The other has gauged ears and a port-wine stain and these two guys—" He pressed two fingers against the pictures, as if for emphasis. "They were sighted with the so-called bomber, this guy out of Lubbock."

"Arnie Gibbs, rodeo clown?"

"Yeah. Doesn't that feel weird to you? I mean, the clowns I worked with were straight-up, honest guys. Sure, they liked the adrenaline, but they were about saving lives. That's why *I* did it those few times."

Tate lifted a shoulder. "I dunno." He took a step closer to the grid. "How do you know these guys were with him?"

"An investigator from San Antonio asked me if I'd ever see Arnie before—showed me a picture, and these two guys were standing beside him."

Tate considered Knox. His brother wasn't the conspiracy theory type, but this felt a little reaching. Still, "What does this have to do with Kelsey?"

"Are either of these guys Vince Russell?"

Tate took another look. "No. I don't think so, but…I don't know. All I have are old news clippings. I need a real picture."

"Okay," Knox said. "Do you really think Russell poses a current threat to Kelsey?"

Tate lifted a shoulder.

"What can I do to help?"

Tate blinked. "Really?"

"I'm not going to have Kelsey spending her life looking over her shoulder." His face tightened. "And frankly, I'd like to have a few words with this guy."

"Knox—"

He held up a hand. "Calm down. Maybe he falls down the stairs or something."

Tate drew in a breath, tightened his jaw. "You let me do the talking, bro. This is my wheelhouse." Then he turned toward the door. "We leave for New York first thing in the morning."

"No," Knox said, reaching into the closet for his duffel. "We leave in fifteen minutes. Right after I call in a few favors."

Seriously? But Tate nodded. Stopped with his hand on the door. "I'm sorry I jumped on you tonight, bro. I just thought—"

"There's nothing going on between you and Kelsey, right?"

Tate turned, and Knox couldn't hide the question—no,

the past—haunting his expression.

Oh. Right. Chelsea. "No, bro. She's just a client."

Knox raised an eyebrow. "Like Glo?"

Tate sighed. "No. Glo is… Glo is trouble."

Knox smiled. "I know the feeling."

Tate grinned back. "Fifteen." Then he walked out the door.

She'd slept the entire night through.

In fact, she'd slept so hard, lines etched her face, the morning sun high enough to find her eyes, burn them open.

Glo was scrolling through her phone on the other bed. "You're not going to believe this, but we had fans last night at the Bulldog. At least three people posted on Instagram. And one of those pictures is you and Knox." She held the phone up to Kelsey.

They were on the dance floor, her arms up around Knox's shoulders, and the look on her face… She heated all the way through.

"Yeah, I'll bet that was right before he kissed you. Because no guy in his right mind would be able to walk away from that come-hither look."

"What— Glo!" Kelsey grabbed a pillow and shot it at Glo, who ducked. The pillow hit the wall, fell in a heap.

"I'm just saying that maybe there's a reason you're not downstairs in the recliner, all knotted up like a pretzel this morning. Sweet dreams?"

Kelsey smiled, slid down into her second pillow. "I'm a coward. I shouldn't have run upstairs last night after we got home and hid in our room. Apparently, that's what I do when I'm embarrassed."

"We had some serious debriefing to do," Glo said, closing

her app. "Girl talk."

"But poor Knox. After Tate nearly took him apart in the parking lot—"

"He did go off the rails a little."

"Talk about a look, Glo. The man is a little crazy about you."

Glo shook her head. "Nope. Nothing happening there."

Kelsey made a face but didn't circle back around for another shot. Some wounds took years to heal.

She should know.

And so should Knox. "I nearly caused a brawl between brothers. And I'm not sure why. Tate was so—protective."

Glo drew in a breath. "He *is* a bodyguard."

"He was practically convinced that Knox had done something to… I don't know. Wound me or scare me or…" *Wait—*

"Glo. Does Tate know…" Kelsey's eyes widened. "You told him I'd been raped, didn't you?"

Glo made a face. "I just wanted him to understand that… I don't know, okay? It seemed like the right thing at the time, but I know I shouldn't have—"

"Stop. Just… Do you think—" She sat up. "Oh no. Do you think he told Knox?"

Glo too had sat up, put her feet on the ground. "I don't know. I…judging by the look on Knox's face, I don't think so. He looked pretty horrified that he might have done anything to hurt you. And my guess is that Knox is pretty…careful."

Safe.

Yes. Even last night when he'd kissed her. Overwhelming, decisive, consuming, intoxicating, especially when he broke away, breathing hard, those eyes in hers.

But with such a gentleness that it turned her deliciously, wonderfully weak.

As if she didn't have to try so hard to keep herself glued together.

In fact, she'd lost herself when he kissed her, the past simply dropping away.

And for a moment, she was simply a woman in a man's arms, kissing him back.

Until...shoot, it simply wasn't fair that her past could rise up and scream at her. Taunt her. Tell her that not only was she not safe, but...not worthy. Except, in Knox's arms, she could believe she was.

Glo was right. She had nothing to be ashamed about.

Knox deserved to know why she'd freaked out on him.

And that she'd never do it again if he felt like, ever... Oh boy.

Because the memory of the warmth that had suffused her entire body as she kissed him, felt his strong arms move around her to cradle her, his big hand touching her face so gently...

Yeah, no wonder she'd slept well.

Except now she remembered how heartbroken he'd looked last night when he thought he'd hurt her, and it propelled her to her feet to grab a pair of yoga pants and a sweatshirt.

She pulled her hair into a ponytail, grabbed her toiletry bag, and headed to the bathroom to freshen up.

At least enough to face him, because the man got up early. Way early.

He was probably in the barn attending to his new baby bull.

She finished brushing her teeth and headed downstairs.

The kitchen was quiet, but a basket of freshly baked muffins sat on the counter with a note—*Help yourself to a morning glory.*

She grabbed a napkin and a muffin and headed outside, sliding on a pair of Birkenstocks by the door before she trekked through the yard toward the barn.

The door was open, as she suspected, and she stopped to pet a baby goat, its tongue wrapping around her hand, probably in search of crumbs.

Gordo had been let out into the pen, his stall open to the other side. Knox had herded the other bulls out to their own pastures a couple days earlier.

She headed toward the pen, expecting to see Knox sitting on a stool, bottle-feeding his bull—yet unnamed—and stopped, surprised to see Gerri with the bull nuzzled up to her, gulping down the bottle.

"Good morning," Gerri said. She wore a work shirt and jeans, her hair tied back in a bandanna.

"Good morning." Kelsey came up to the rail and put her foot on it. "He's getting big."

"These guys are born big," Gerri said. "Only a week and this little guy already has a temper. Knox will probably release them to pasture when he gets back."

Gets back? "Where is he?"

"I don't know. He left with Tate last night somewhere. That's Tate—he's always taking off. I'm not sure why he needs Knox. They'll probably be back later today."

Oh. She watched Gerri for a while, then headed back to the house and found Glo seated on a high-top chair. "Hey," Glo said between muffin bites.

"Did you know Tate and Knox left last night?"

Glo frowned. "Really?"

"Yeah, and they didn't even tell Gerri where they went."

Glo said nothing, but she picked up her phone.

"What are you doing?"

"Texting Tate."

Kelsey slid onto a stool. "What if I frightened the man away?"

Glo lowered the phone. "Seriously?"

"Okay, see, there's a pattern of crazy going on here, one that Knox can hardly ignore. The first night I met him, I practically plowed down innocent bystanders on my way out of the beer tent, as if some phantom was chasing me—"

"Um—"

Kelsey held up her hand. "Then, after the man saved my life, I couldn't even show up to thank him personally. Instead, I floor it to Oklahoma, where I practically have a meltdown onstage."

"That might not have been the best reaction—"

"Thanks for that."

Glo shrugged.

"And let's not forget last night, when the man kisses me with such...such...let's just say it wasn't his fault I freaked out. In fact, I'm not even sure why I freaked out."

"I know why," Glo said, putting down her phone. "It's because you're afraid that if Knox truly knows you, truly sees you and all..." She twirled her hand in front of Kelsey. "All the layers of Kelsey Jones—then he'll...run."

Kelsey just stared at her, and her voice dropped. "Is it that bad?"

"Is what—"

"My layers. My *crazy layers*."

Glo turned, took her hands. "No crazier than the rest of us. Sure, you have some darker baggage, maybe, but I'm guessing that everyone thinks their baggage is dark. So, no."

She sighed. "I'm tired of the baggage."

Glo nodded. Her phone vibrated, and she picked it up. Read the text.

"Is it from Tate?"

She nodded. "He says, 'I'm doing my job. Don't round up the posse just yet, Woody.'" She looked at Kelsey. "Why is he calling me Woody?"

"As in Buzz Lightyear and Woody," Gerri said, walking up to them. "Tate's favorite show when he was a kid. Although I think he wanted to be Buzz."

"I'll remember that," Glo said as she pocketed her phone.

Gerri set down a couple pairs of gloves on the counter. "You two girls up for taming some wicked thistles in the garden?"

Glo reached over and grabbed the gloves. "Yeah, but you'll have to show us what the thistles look like."

"They look like two grown men who sneak off into the night." Gerri winked, kidding, but the comparison stuck around as the day drew out with no sign of Knox. Or Tate.

Not even a text.

And that night, his absence turned downright prickly as Kelsey headed downstairs, turned on the television, and watched a hockey game. It brought back old memories of her father watching the Minnesota Wild.

The next day she brought her guitar out to the porch and started to work out some lyrics that had gotten tangled in her brain.

What if I let myself love you
What if I called this home.
What if my heart said forever
And never let my love roam . . .

No, that sounded silly. But she kept scrawling until she put down something that made more sense.

A ballad, really, about the unexpected turns of life. And love, perhaps, waiting at the end of the road.

"Still no word from Tate?" Kelsey asked that night as Glo was typing an email.

Glo shook her head.

Which really, was why the next morning, when Carter called, when he suggested the gig up in Mercy Falls, a mere two hours from the ranch, when he dropped the name Benjamin King and told them about the invitation to sing at King's rising star venue, the Gray Pony, and when he said that King wanted to meet with them about recording for his label, she didn't hesitate.

In fact, she didn't even ask Glo.

"We'll be there."

"You going to be okay?"

Tate stood outside the bathroom stall of the Twenty-Fourth Precinct. He was probably leaning against the sink, arms folded, but Knox had heard his brother stifling his own nausea when Detective Rayburn finally showed them the file.

Thank you, Katherine Noble, whose NYC connections had opened the doors Knox needed to track down Vince Russell, including a meet-and-greet with not only the prosecuting attorney for the case, but the detective who'd tracked down the three gang members who had jumped Clinton and Rebecca Jones and their fourteen-year-old daughter at 11:00 p.m. near 105th Street in Central Park twelve years ago.

They'd also attacked a handful of other people, but their terror spree culminated on the three tourists from Minnesota.

Knox had lost his pitiful lunch of a street hot dog when he'd opened the file. The girl in the photo had been beaten so badly Knox didn't recognize her. The first-on-the-scene officer had written that she looked tortured. Thankfully, the photo was taken after the officer had covered her naked body with his jacket.

Knox had winced, shutting his eyes to the image, unable to bear the bruises, the blood, the horror of seeing the trauma.

But oh, it ignited not only a fury at her attackers, but an admiration of the courageous girl who had climbed out of a twelve-day coma, spent seven weeks in the hospital, and had to learn how to walk, talk, and read again, thanks to her head trauma.

Oh, Kelsey, you left so much out.

But what could she say, really, to capture the horror of being fourteen and jumped by three men—two who were only a couple years older than she was. And the perpetrator, Russell, had just turned eighteen. Knox had burned the kid's image into his brain.

Dark hair, a swastika tatted between his eyebrows, a scar across his chin. Yeah, he'd recognize this guy on the street, or in a bar…or replaying over and over in his nightmares.

No wonder Kelsey dodged demons. Even if she couldn't remember the assault—which according to the court documents, she had no recollection of the entire evening, just impressions, sounds and smells—one look at this guy turned the event brutally real.

Russell, I'm going to find you.

He came out of the stall and walked over to the sink. Tate moved away, no judgment on his face. Knox ran the water, washed his face, rinsed his mouth, and grabbed and wet a couple paper towels, holding them against his tired eyes.

He could use a little divine intervention trying to find one dirtbag in a city of 8.6 million people. Two days of searching had netted them exactly nil. They'd contacted Russell's parole officer, visited his current address, a halfway house in the Bronx, talked with the resident manager, and even driven through the neighborhood on the Upper East Side of Manhattan, where his former gang hung out.

They'd finally returned to the Twenty-Fourth Precinct to talk to Detective Rayburn, a balding, thickly built man with steely, tired eyes. He'd taken them into a room with an interactive map detailing all of New York and the gang activity. Spent the last hour giving them the dark rundown of the life of a parolee.

"They can't get a job, can't find housing, and have been out of the population for so long they don't know how to integrate back into society. They're like children, in many ways, and of course the first thing that happens when the old life comes knocking is to kick back in with their gang."

Rayburn had leaned against the wall, his arms folded. "If this guy is anywhere, he's back with the Morris Park gang, an Aryan group right in the heart of a primarily Jewish neighborhood." He shook his head.

"And what about his threats against Kelsey?" Tate asked.

That's when Knox had made the mistake of opening the file again, searching for the man's statement and threats. Happened again on Kelsey's picture and had to leave the room.

Now, he threw the towels into the trash, glanced at a grim-faced Tate, and headed back into the hallway.

Detective Rayburn held a cup of coffee. "Believe me, the entire thing makes me sick too. In all my years working homicide, this was one that got to me. It made no sense— wasn't racially targeted, the Joneses had nothing of value on them. It was just a bunch of kids bent on terrorizing people. Russell may or may not have been the ringleader, but he was the only adult in the group. And, he was the rapist—we found his DNA—"

"That's all I can take," Knox said, lifting his hand. "We just need to make sure Russell wasn't in Texas three weeks ago during the San Antonio bombing. Or trying to hunt down Kelsey now."

Rayburn considered them a moment, then gestured toward a nearby interrogation room. Knox followed him in, behind Tate, and Rayburn closed the door.

Took a breath. "Okay, so if you guys can give me your word you won't take justice into your own hands..." He turned, raised an eyebrow.

Tate had folded his arms.

Knox met his eyes but affirmed nothing.

"Yeah, I get that. I just don't want to show up somewhere and find you two lying in a puddle of your own blood. These guys aren't to be messed with."

"We just want to talk," Tate said in a dark tone that Knox didn't recognize. He held up three fingers. "Scout's honor."

Yeah, the only scout in the family had been Knox, and he wasn't making any promises.

But Rayburn nodded. "He has a brother. AJ. He owns a barbershop on Cruger Avenue in the Bronx. Vince used to hang there sometimes. But I didn't tell you that."

Tate nodded, and Knox held out his hand. "If you hear anything..."

Rayburn nodded. Held on a bit longer. "Tell Kelsey... okay, maybe don't tell her anything. But I'm glad she has people. She sat in that hospital for two weeks before anyone came for her—I think it was her brother. Navy guy, if I remember correctly. But she...was alone."

"Not anymore," Knox said and released him.

They took an Uber through Manhattan, into the Bronx, onto Boston Road, and finally slowed in the residential district of Cruger Avenue. They passed two-story brick houses, some with awnings, clean and groomed, not what Knox might consider gang territory, although his understanding of gang life and criminals was limited to *Blue Bloods* and a few episodes of *Law & Order*.

Knox suspected he might be just as unassuming as the Joneses had been walking through Central Park, buoyant after a theater performance.

They crossed an intersection framed by storefront shops—a carpet place, a deli, a Chinese takeout, a nail salon. More brick houses, many with flower pots hanging from clean front porches, a green fence that cordoned off a vacant lot, Keep Out signs posted, and finally they came to the barbershop, a tiny hole-in-the-wall with a faded red awning imprinted with the words AJ's Barbershop. Next to it, a small deli featured lotto tickets and a yellow sign that read simply We Sell Beer.

Tate headed straight for the barbershop, something changed in his demeanor. But he stopped right outside the door, his grip on the handle. "I do the talking. Whatever you do, don't…just don't be you."

Huh?

But Tate didn't wait.

The place smelled of hair tonic and shampoo. An older man in a green apron sat in a chair. Another man with short blond hair, late thirties bent over him with clippers.

He looked up at Tate and Knox. Lifted his chin. "Sit down on the bench. There's a wait."

Tate didn't move. "AJ Russell?"

The man stopped the clipper motor. He held a comb in the other hand. Said nothing for a moment, then a quiet, "Why?"

Knox made to move, but Tate stepped up to AJ. "We need to talk to you about your brother." No question, just a statement, a sort of easy tone, but a seriousness in it that stilled Knox.

Especially when Tate took the clippers from AJ's hand. Set them on the counter, apologized to his customer, and pushed AJ into the back room.

AJ turned, a glance over his shoulder.

"We're just talking, pal. No worries," Tate said, his voice friendly.

But the tiny hairs raised on Knox's neck when Tate closed the office door behind them.

"Sit," Tate said and kicked out the rolling chair from a metal desk.

AJ tightened his jaw, and for the first time, Knox saw the resemblance to his brother, Vince. Square-jawed, the man bore a tattoo on the side of his neck, half covered by his smock, a German two-headed eagle.

He sat. Glared up at Tate, who didn't change his expression. Tate lowered his voice and leaned over AJ.

AJ moved so fast, Knox hadn't a clue how he'd picked it up, but in a second, he'd taken a swipe at Tate with an open shaving blade.

Little brother Tate had honed reflexes like Knox had never seen. He stepped back, the knife skimming past his gut, grabbed AJ's wrist, jerked him forward, and slammed his fist into the man's face with a cross-hand punch that had AJ's head snapping back.

Then Tate slammed his wrist against the chair, dislodged the blade, and dumped AJ on the ground with such quick force that Knox had to scramble out of the way.

Tate held the guy down in an arm submission hold, one knee in his spine, his mouth close to AJ's. "We're going to forgive that, on account of you don't know who we are."

Who we are?

Knox just stared at Tate. Apparently, his brother had learned a few tricks in Vegas.

He wasn't sure if he should help him or get out of his way.

Tate didn't look like he needed any help.

"We're friends of Kelsey Jones. That name should be familiar to you because your brother raped her and murdered her parents. Nod if you recollect this."

AJ's cheek was smashed on his grimy floor, but he nodded.

"Your brother is out of jail and gone missing, and my guess is that you know where he is."

"No, I don't! I don't know where Vince is!"

Tate considered him a moment. "He hasn't come by here once in the last three weeks? I find that hard to believe."

He must have exerted pressure on AJ because the man wheezed. Swallowed. "Fine, yes. Once. Right after he got out. Said he..." He closed his eyes.

"What? Said what?"

"He said he had unfinished business!"

Tate let out a word that seemed appropriate for the moment, then looked up at Knox.

Knox wrapped his hands around the back of his neck, squeezed. It was better than hitting something. Or someone.

"Does he have a cell phone?"

"Not that I know of."

"Anybody who he trusts, that he'd go to for help?"

AJ hesitated.

"I'm not sure who you're protecting, or why, but if your brother hurts my friend, I'm coming after *you*. And my brother won't be here to keep me from breaking your fingers." As if for emphasis, he grabbed one of AJ's fingers.

"Don't stop on my account," Knox said quietly.

Tate didn't look at him.

The man grunted, a sweat breaking across his forehead. "Listen—no. I don't know. His cellmate got out a month before he did. They were pretty tight—"

"Who was his cellmate?"

"This guy. His name was...Harris, I think. Bradley Harris."

"What was he in for?"

AJ took a breath. "I think he tried to blow up something."

Tate let him go. Got to his feet. Looked down at AJ. "If your brother comes back here, I want you to call me." He yanked AJ's phone from his pocket. No screen lock. He dialed in his number, sent himself a text. Dropped the phone on the man's back. "We'll be in touch."

Then he turned, kicked the man out of the way, and walked out.

Knox scrambled after him, not sure what had just happened.

The man in the chair had vanished, his green apron sitting in a puddle on the floor.

Tate pushed outside. Stood there and blew out a breath.

Knox came out beside him. Said nothing for a long while. Finally, "So I guess that's what you mean by just talking."

"Mmmhmm," Tate said.

"What did you do while you were in Vegas? Because I know you didn't learn that in the military."

Tate glanced at him, shook his head, his lips tight. "Nothing I want to talk about."

Fine. "So now what?"

"Now, we go back to Rayburn and see if he can help us dig up Harris."

And do more talking, Knox supposed.

He followed his brother down the street as Tate pulled

up his Uber app.

Three hours later, as the sun began to drop through the towering Manhattan buildings, they were looking at the recent morgue photo of one Bradley Harris.

"How was he killed?" Knox said as he leaned over the computer.

Rayburn sat on the table in an interrogation room. "We're still investigating. We found him beaten to death in an alley near the halfway house where he was rooming."

"The same halfway house that Russell listed as his address. Where he hasn't shown up at for three weeks."

Rayburn nodded.

Knox got up, and now he wanted to utter the word that Tate let slip earlier.

"Listen. I'll call—who was it you mentioned?"

"Torres. He's with the San Antonio FBI."

"Yeah. I'll send him Russell's picture. See if it matches anyone at the arena. In the meantime, I think this is a dead end."

Knox whirled around, just stared at Rayburn, who lifted his shoulder.

"Seriously? Kelsey is living with what this man did to her. Every. Single. Day. It's in her head, in her life. And now he's loose and we haven't a clue where he might be?" He swept up Russell's file, grabbed his mug shot, laid it on the table, and snapped a shot with his phone. "I'm not leaving New York City until this guy is found."

He left the rest of his intentions to himself. Because he wanted to do a lot more than talk.

Tate followed him out into the night, the air pungent with the day's trash, cigarette smoke, the raucous sound of traffic. Across the street, a pizza joint beckoned, his stomach nearly as angry as he was.

Tate had said nothing so far, and now he glanced at the pizza joint, shrugged, and went in.

They ordered, then sat down at a table with their slices.

Tate pulled out his cell phone. Put it on the table.

"Hoping AJ will call?"

"I'm not holding my breath." Tate folded his pizza like a sandwich. "But Glo keeps texting me. Nonstop for three days. I told her that we were fine, but she's..."

"In love with you."

Tate looked at him, frowned. "Hardly. She is...she's my boss."

"Whatever." And it was the first smile he'd gotten from Tate in three days.

As if Glo might be able to sense their conversation, a text rattled his phone. He picked it up, swiped. "What—?"

Knox leaned over. "What's going on?"

"They're setting up to play at some gig tonight."

"What—and you let them go?

"Take a breath—no! They went without my permission, but it's local."

"Where?"

"Montana—in Mercy Falls. Apparently, Benjamin King set it up. It's impromptu, and King has his own security, I'm sure. Glo says it's low-key, just a couple songs at a local bar and grill."

"Should we be worried?"

"Probably not, but I'm not thrilled. The sooner we track down Russell, the better." Tate turned his phone around and showed Knox a picture of Kelsey and Glo decked out in jeans, boots, and T-shirts that said Pony Up. The next one had Kelsey at the mic, her smile curving around her words.

All Knox wanted to do was go home. To be in the audience, for her to wink at him as she sang. To sneak backstage and maybe give her a good luck kiss. Or a hug. Or even just a high five, but yeah.

By one look at Tate's expression as he took back the phone, he wanted to suggest the same thing.

"We have to find him," Knox said.

Tate nodded. Sighed.

They finished the pizza, then took a subway to their hotel right off Times Square. Knox stood at the window, watching as theatergoers emptied into the square. Tate was channel surfing the late-late shows.

They should go home. Because what if Russell wasn't here, but somehow had found them in Montana, and was right now sitting outside, in the parking lot, waiting to, as he put it, finish what he'd started.

Knox pressed a hand to his gut. That pizza wasn't sitting right.

Especially when Tate's phone buzzed again, this time on the nightstand next to his bed. He picked it up, and his gut knotted when Tate's eyes widened, his mouth opening.

"What—?"

Tate looked up. "We're going home. Right now." His face turned grim and hard as he stood up and stalked over to his suitcase. "Their tour bus was bombed."

9

She simply had to figure out how to breathe.

"Kelsey, are you okay in there?"

The knock came through the closed bathroom door to where Kelsey sat on the edge of the bathtub, wrapped in a clean bathrobe, courtesy of Kacey King, super country star Benjamin King's wife. The tub had filled, the steam rising off it, lavender lifting from the scented oils Glo had insisted on adding.

She should be sliding in, closing her eyes. Trying to let go of the trauma.

And most of all, thanking God that they hadn't been inside the bus sleeping when the fire started.

Instead, they'd been onstage at a country-western bar and grill, Kelsey singing her heart out to a sold-out crowd, feeling like she might actually find her feet again. Not a huge crowd, but enough for her to step onstage without the panic of the big stage. No special effects, just Kelsey and Glo at the mics, their voices mingling in a set of their favorite singles.

She remembered wishing that Knox sat in the audience, grinning at her, and hoping that she hadn't scared him off.

Then, right during their last song—boom!

The propane tank that fueled their stove had shot out of the top of the bus, landing in the parking lot, setting off car alarms.

Thank God no one had been hurt.

"Kelsey!" More banging.

Kelsey sighed, looked at the water. The temptation to sink under the depths felt too powerful for her to risk it. She pulled the plug. "I'm fine."

"Hurry up. There's a cop here and he wants to get your statement."

The one she didn't give last night as she'd stood hollowly staring at her home, the flames curling around the bus, licking into the sky.

The Mercy Falls fire department showed up to douse the travesty, but Kelsey couldn't move, the realization finding her bones.

Russell had found her. This was no random event—how could it be? But how had he tracked her down in Montana?

Except, and of course—because it came to her as the crowd spilled out of the bar, snapping pictures on their phones.

Instagram. Didn't Glo say fans had found and tagged them at the Bulldog? And probably Glo, in her usual social media PR, had invited people to come out and see them at the Gray Pony.

It wasn't Glo's fault that a murderer wanted Kelsey—and by proxy, Glo—dead.

Still—why had she left the Marshall ranch? The question dogged her even as Ben and Kacey had collected her and Glo and brought them home to sleep in their beautiful log home on a ranch outside of town. She met their daughter, Audrey, who looked just like Ben, concern in her blue eyes as she showed them down the hall to a guest room.

A palatial guest room with a bed the size of Texas. And Glo got the one next door.

Clearly, they needed to sell more albums, or charge more for their gigs.

Unfortunately, she hadn't slept more than an hour in the four-poster bed, under the thick cotton quilt, in the Egyptian cotton sheets. She was standing at the window in the bathrobe when Glo came in with coffee. Took one look at her and drew her a bath.

Now, Glo banged on the door, clearly expecting her to have completed her bath.

"I need to jump in the shower. I smell, and my hair is sticky."

"For pete's—did you even get in the bath?"

She didn't say anything.

"Fine. Put your hair up. I'm leaving some yoga pants and a T-shirt on the bed. Kacey bought us packages of clean underclothes, too."

Oh, that was completely embarrassing. But incredibly thoughtful.

"I smell like smoke."

Glo paused, then quietly, through the door, "I know you. I know you're just sitting there looking out the window trying to figure out what to do next. Formulating a plan."

Kelsey said nothing. Because yes, she had been staring through the window at the grand landscape behind Ben's house for twenty minutes. To the jagged scrape of granite mountains along a pristine blue sky. To the herd of red Holsteins grazing in a nearby pasture—which only reminded her of Hot Pete and the baby bull, and then Knox, and—why *had* she left the Marshall ranch?

It was possible, however, that for the first time, she hadn't a clue what to do next.

"Or, you're contemplating running."

That thought had crossed her mind too. A crazy desire

to just get in a car and drive. Anywhere. Destination fresh start. Again.

But even that option held her hostage, because she had no car, no money, no clean clothes. She could hardly breathe through the overwhelming rush of loss.

Glo knocked again. "Please, Kels, let me in?"

Kelsey got up and opened the door.

Glo stood on the other side, no makeup, her hair back in a bandanna, wearing a pink T-shirt with PEAK SAR on the front. A pair of black leggings showed off her curves, and she ran her bare feet into the carpet. She crossed her arms over herself, gave Kelsey a sad smile. "Want to talk about it?"

Kelsey looked at her, then shook her head, her jaw tightening. "Nope."

"Kels—"

She drew in a breath, held it in check. "No. Because I'm right back there, Glo. I'm the girl waking up after twelve days in a coma, blinking and confused and bereft. I have no idea what I'm supposed to do next." She pursed her lips. "Russell has beat me."

Glo touched her arm. "No. No he hasn't. Because he doesn't know the woman I know. The one who had to learn how to walk and talk and read again. And who did it, and even went on to not just survive, but live."

"Looking over her shoulder, waiting for him to show up and make good on his threats. I feel like I've been holding my breath for a decade…and I don't know how to let it go."

"By not letting him beat you," Glo said, catching her hand. "Right?"

It sounded right, so Kelsey nodded.

"C'mon. You look fine." She gestured to the clothes on the bed. "I'll draw you another bath after you talk to Sam."

"Sam?"

"Ben's friend. He's a cop, and he's really nice."

Kelsey walked over to the clothes. Picked up the shirt. Orange, with black lettering over the pocket—PEAK—with a tiny mountain logo over the top.

"Ben has a huge collection of them. Apparently, it's part of some fundraiser they're having for a local SAR team."

"Ben? You're on a nickname basis now??"

Glo grinned, heading for the door. "I know he's famous, but he's super nice. And his daughter is pretty talented. She's been playing me a few of her songs. There's actually a slew of people here, making breakfast, hanging out. It's like a reality TV show." She stepped out of the room and closed the door behind her.

Kelsey changed clothes, pulled her hair up, and washed her face. At least she didn't have makeup stains down her cheeks.

By *not letting him beat you.*

Maybe he already had. Maybe she went down years ago.

She followed the sound of voices and padded down the hallway, past a workout room, and into a soaring great room with a giant picture window that overlooked the magnificent view of the mountains she'd seen from her room. A deck with Adirondack chairs extended from the window.

A long chandelier dangled from the ceiling, and under it, two leather sofas faced each other, flanking a tall stone fireplace.

"Hey, Kelsey," said a male voice, and she turned to see Ben walking toward her, holding coffee. "How are you feeling this morning?"

So many answers, none of them the right one, so she opted for, "Better. Thank you."

He smiled, and she could see why he'd won Entertainer of the Year. He was quite possibly even more handsome in his regular clothing, jeans, a T-shirt, with that dark brown hair all morning-tousled, those sculpted shoulders. She'd bet he worked out with the hanging bag in the workout room. A smile quirked up one side of his face, like Aw, shucks, we're all friends here.

Indeed, it looked like Glo had settled in, sitting on a high-top stool, now pouring syrup on a stack of pancakes.

A petite woman with short black hair came out of the kitchen holding a tray of blueberry muffins and set it on the dining room table in the corner of the room. Maybe Ben's cook. But she picked one up and handed it to a man dressed in a uniform, probably Sam, here to interview Kelsey. He was talking to an older gentleman with short graying hair, who sort of reminded her of Harrison Ford with his quirky facial expressions.

"Let me introduce you to Sam Brooks. He needs your statement about last night," Ben said. "I'm sorry my wife isn't here right now. She's a chopper pilot for the PEAK team—" He gestured to his shirt. "She got called out this morning to help with a hospital transport."

Kelsey followed him and got a good look at Sam when he turned and held out his hand to her. The most riveting blue eyes she'd ever seen, brown hair, a look on his face that suggested if anyone could get to the bottom of last night's attack, it would be him.

"Glad to meet you, Kelsey," Sam said.

"And this is my father, Chet King," Ben said.

Chet's hand enveloped hers, worn, warm, and solid. "Sorry about last night."

"By the way, we're doing a little clothing drive for you two, just within the PEAK team, so if you want to give me your sizes…" This from the petite cook who had added a bowl of fruit—strawberries and blueberries—to the table.

"This is Sierra. She's the PEAK team administrator. And sometimes she feeds us out of the goodness of her heart," Ben said. He reached over and grabbed a strawberry from the bowl.

Kelsey's stomach awakened, began to stir.

"We're trying to figure out how the bus blew," Sam said. "We've called in some arson specialists, but we need some help." He directed her over to the sofa and started with background information, how they'd gotten the gig—to which Ben filled in the gaps.

"I called Carter to check on the Belles. They were pretty shaken up after the bombing in Texas, and Kelsey lost her voice—"

"You were in the San Antonio bombing?" Sam asked. He'd put his phone on the table to record their conversation.

"Yeah," Kelsey said. "And uh, yeah. We were pretty shaken up. Our bodyguard suggested we hang out at his ranch—the Marshall Triple M— for a few days. But then Carter called and said Ben had invited us to sing at the Gray Pony."

"And you brought the house down, by the way," Ben said.

"Before we blew up the parking lot," Glo added, turning in her chair.

Kelsey frowned at Glo's attempt at humor.

"Too soon?" Glo said, and Kelsey nodded.

"Do you have any reason to think someone would want to harm you? A fan maybe? Or—"

"Yes," Kelsey said quietly, drawing in her breath. "I think someone is trying to kill me."

The entire room went quiet.

Then, succinctly, and without inflection or drama, Kelsey told her story. She left out the rape, the extent of her injuries, just hit the high points, the threats, the fact that Russell was free.

And apparently, keeping his promise.

When she was finished, Sam just swallowed, his expression pained. "I'm sorry, Kelsey."

"It's okay. I've lived with this a long time." But retelling it had knotted her breath in her chest. "I guess I never thought...really...that he'd come back. I'm just tired, you know? Tired of figuring out how to get back up, keep going."

"Your soul is thirsty."

Her gaze went to the voice, and it landed on Sierra, who had added scrambled eggs and sausage links to the table and now approached the sofa, wrapping her hands along the back. "You're parched and you're weary and your soul needs a drink."

Kelsey looked at her, frowned.

"There is only one source of that kind of water, Kelsey. Only one thing that will satisfy. And that's God's love." She moved her hand to Kelsey's shoulder. "He very much cares about you."

She glanced at Glo, who had raised an eyebrow, then a shoulder.

But then again, Glo had been around Dixie's family enough to hear Dixie's father preach the same thing. *Only God can satisfy.*

Except where, exactly, had God been when she lay in the weeds? Or when she was crumpled in the debris of a Texas arena? Or watching her world go up in flames?

Where was God when she was trying to find her feet, scrape out her future?

And maybe it wasn't fair to blame God. Maybe in fact, she simply wasn't important enough to protect.

At least, it sort of felt that way.

But she nodded to Sierra anyway, because really, she meant well. And Kelsey was too tired to do anything else.

"I think what Kelsey—and we both—need is to go home, back to Wisconsin, and regroup." Glo said. "We have insurance on the bus, on our equipment, and frankly, maybe this is a sign, right? Maybe God is showing us that we need to just...go home."

Which, at that moment, sounded a lot like running to Kelsey but...

"I talked to Dixie this morning, and she agrees," Glo added.

Yes. Run back to her uncle's house and hide in the attic. Perfect. But Kelsey had nothing else—

"No."

The voice rumbled through her, found her bones, and like a hot wave of fire, seared through them. She turned, and her mouth opened as—what? Knox stood in the grand entryway, flanked by Tate and Chet.

She'd never seen such a look on his face. Deeply lined with worry, a four-day haze of dark beard on his chin, his blue-green eyes so thick with emotion it stripped away every other thought but...

Knox. Was. *Here.*

She hadn't a clue how he knew she needed him, how he had figured out where they were, even, he'd found Ben King's house and made it through the front door.

But yes. In all his rumpled, large-sized, solid glory, cowboy Marshall was here.

Her mouth opened to form some sort of reply. But he simply walked into the room, his eyes in hers, not wavering, almost daring her to argue with him as he said, "She's not going anywhere but home with me. Where she's safe."

Oh.

But with his words, her chest began to slowly release, and for the first time in what seemed like years, she exhaled.

———————◆———————

It was all Tate could do not to grab Glo, drag her away from the crowd in the great room of Benjamin King's palatial home, and…and…

Shoot, he wasn't sure what he wanted to do. Strangle her, yes, for taking off from the ranch. And crush her to himself, breathing out with a hard gust of painful relief that she was okay. And then there was the other thing, the one action he kept flogging into submission…the nearly overpowering desire to pull her into his arms and kiss her. Taste and take captive those pretty lips, maybe see them curl into a smile, her eyes warming as she tucked herself into his embrace.

Tate could admit it wasn't necessarily professional behavior, and it was that truth, along with trying to keep Knox from picking Kelsey up and throwing her over his shoulder in his insistence they hightail it back to the Marshall Triple M pronto, that kept him from pulling Glo aside.

From…well, yeah. All of it.

Instead he'd listened to the account of the events, again, filing the information away, then sided with Knox when he practically dragged the ladies from King's ranch and into the rental car.

Tate didn't love the idea of Russell following them back to the ranch before he could set up a security system, but Knox had it stuck in his craw that they'd be safer on home territory.

And maybe he was right—at least about feeling better with the ladies on familiar ground—because when they stopped by the charred bus with Sam, the local cop, on the way out of town, Tate wanted to hit something.

He stood in the parking lot, his legs soft as he stared at the crumpled shell. A couple arson investigators were gloved up and inspecting burn patterns, but all Tate could think was...*What if?*

What if Glo had been asleep inside?

What if Tate had been here—would he have seen the bomber? Or caught the fire?

What if they'd never left the ranch?

And the zinger—what if he hadn't happened upon Glo that night outside the arena three weeks ago, landed this gig, and found his heart being slowly sucked out his chest?

How was it possible that he'd come back around to this helpless, frustrated ache of watching someone he cared about being threatened, without having the first clue where the danger might come from?

Please, God, he couldn't watch someone he cared about die again. Not when he was supposed to be keeping them safe.

That thought dug claws into his chest and burned the entire drive back to the ranch. And through the late dinner, as Ma fussed over the girls. They'd received some clothing from the rescue team in Mercy Falls, but his mother had purchased some toiletries, pajamas, and socks, and seeing the supplies in bags on the counter made him realize just how much the fire had consumed.

Not unlike how he'd left Vegas, with just the clothes on his back, thankful to be alive.

Ma pampered them with more homemade cookies, her answer to the perils of life, and Glo had disappeared to take a bath or something.

She'd asked him, once, where he'd gone, and he'd looked at Knox for permission to spill the truth. But a quick shake of his head suggested that Knox wanted to keep that field trip report for later.

Much later, when they found Russell. When the girls didn't have to panic about one missing criminal.

He'd offered to do the dishes, too much turmoil in his gut to do anything but prowl around the house. Darkness pressed inside, thick with night sounds—cicadas on the lawn—and a cool breeze filtered in through the open windows.

He finished the dishes, stood on the back porch for a while until the bugs began to gnaw at him. Finally came back to the kitchen, sitting in the darkness, listening to the sound of the dishwasher humming, his body still buzzing with the events of the past twenty-four hours. Their red-eye flight to Minneapolis, then Kalispell, then the drive to Mercy Falls, then back to the airport for the hop to Helena to pick up their truck. Thankfully, the ladies had had their identification with them backstage.

He buried his head on his arms. From the den, the television hummed, evidence that Knox and Kelsey might be resuming their nightly hockey game addiction.

Although, one look at Knox tonight said hockey was the last thing on his mind.

He'd been Thor, man of thunder, all day.

Probably he was doing battle with his impulses too.

Tate glanced up, to the darkness of the second story. Silent.

Put his head back in his arms. Blew out a breath. Okay, so he just needed to get a hand around his emotions, keep them from blowing up, destroying this gig he'd started to really like.

Footsteps on the stairs, and the third step groaned. He lifted his head.

He sat in the darkness, behind the table, nothing of moonlight on him, but made out pretty clearly Glo's outline as she tiptoed into the kitchen. Fumbled at the cupboard for a glass. Filled it with water.

Then she set the glass on the counter and headed for the pantry. Stood in the darkness for a while, rummaging around, making funny sounds of frustration.

He got up, moved over to the door, and flicked on the light.

"Oh!" She jumped, turned, her eyes wide. Mouth open.

He raised an eyebrow and reached up to the second shelf, right above her arm's length, and pulled down the cookie jar. "Looking for these?"

His mouth tightened, and she lifted a shoulder.

He clutched the jar to his chest.

She made a move for the cookies, and he turned a shoulder into her reach, deflecting it.

"What are you, the cookie police?" she whispered.

She wore a long T-shirt and leggings, her feet bare. And her freshly washed hair hung in free tousles around her makeup-free face. It only made her eyes that much bigger, sparkling with that hazel-green glow, threaded with hints of gold, and for a second, he simply couldn't breathe.

Glo, you are so pretty.

The words nearly tipped his lips, but like the professional he was, he bit them back.

Instead, "Maybe. But for the right password, I might give you one."

She set her hands on her hips, considered him.

"What? Are you trying to decide if you can take me?"

"Maybe, Rambo."

He smirked. "Oh please. Please make a move." *Please.*

She gave him a look. "Fine. What's the password?"

"Why did you hire me if you weren't going to listen to what I said?"

"What—"

"I told you to stay put."

"You told me not to get my knickers in a knot. That is hardly *stay put*, Shakespeare."

He raised his eyebrow.

"Mean what you say. Be clear. 'Glo, don't leave the ranch. I'll be back from my secret mission in three days.'"

"Fine, Glo. I'm the boss of you. Don't go anywhere without me."

Her mouth opened. "You're hardly the boss of me."

He took a breath, aware that his voice was shaking. "You could have died out there, Glo. Don't you get that? And it's my job to keep you alive. So, from now on, I'm *absolutely* the boss of you."

Her mouth closed, and if she could shoot fire from her eyes, she probably would have.

Suddenly, "Fine."

He stared at her. "Really?"

He had nothing when she closed the gap between them.

When she touched him. She put her hand softly on his chest, right in the center where she could probably feel his heart thundering.

She took another step closer, looked up at him, something soft in her eyes. "Yeah. I know you are bigger and stronger than me, Tator, so, please, please, rescue me."

He knew there was something wrong with her words, but when she licked her lips, he simply…he couldn't move.

Then she reached up and touched his face, her fingers whisper light, as if drawing him down to her.

He simply stopped breathing, lost the feeling in his body, just his heart hammering in his chest, the forbidden stirrings inside loosening—

She curled her hand around the cookie jar and grabbed

it from his arm.

Danced back from him.

It took him too long to react, to realize she'd played him, to shout an indignant, *Hey!* because even in her play she was grinning at him, her eyes sparkling, practically an invitation to follow her deeper into the pantry.

"You gotta be faster than that, McDraw." She opened the cookie jar and pulled out a fresh sugar cookie. Tilted the jar toward him. "Want one?"

Yes. Very much.

He shook his head.

"Really?"

He nodded.

"Your loss." She put the cap on the jar. Set it on a nearby shelf.

Turned back, smiling, and took a bite. "See, not the boss of me."

He stilled. And the game was gone. She was about to take another bite of the cookie when he caught her arm. She looked at his grip, then met his eyes.

Swallowed. "Sorry."

He stepped closer to her, cut his voice low. "Don't you get it, Glo? You are my responsibility. You and Kelsey and Dixie, and you nearly burned to death. And I *wasn't there.*"

Her smile vanished, and she set the cookie aside. Caught her lip between her teeth. Met his eyes, and they glistened. "You're right. And I am sorry. I...I'm sorry I scared you."

He loomed over her, aware of how small she was when he got up close, and a painful surge of protectiveness swept through him. He cut his voice low. "Please, please don't do that again. Don't leave without...without telling me."

She looked up at him, nodded.

"And while we're at it, enough with the name-calling. My

194

name is Tate. Not Tator, not Shakespeare, not McDraw—"

"Not Magnum? Because I like that one." Her lips curled into a smile.

Oh. Shoot. Because now all he was thinking about was how he really, oh so very much, wanted to taste those pretty lips.

And as she looked up at him, her smile vanished, leaving just the rise and fall of her chest.

She reached out and splayed her hand over his chest.

"Tate," she whispered.

He lowered his head.

His back pocket buzzed.

He jerked away, realized he'd been holding his breath, and blew it out as he turned, yanking the phone from his pocket.

A text from AJ Russell, four providential words.

My brother is dead.

He stared at the screen, blinking. Walked out of the pantry as he texted back. *How?*

The return text came almost immediately. *Murdered. Found this morning in Bronx River. Dead three days.*

Which meant he couldn't have possibly been in Montana, firebombing the Yankee Belles' trailer.

He pocketed the phone. Turned.

Glo—and the cookie jar—had vanished.

But she'd left him a sugar cookie on the counter.

———————◆———————

We need to talk. Four easy words, but Knox couldn't seem to get them to emerge from his mouth as he sat on the sofa, the remote control in his hand, eyes glued to the Blue Ox hockey game.

At least they were winning. And, on their last game of

the regular season, which meant a few days off for Wyatt.

He just might make it home for the big day next week.

Knox glanced at Kelsey, curled up in the recliner, just as avidly staring at the game. He wanted her to meet his siblings, for them to see how talented and brave and amazing she was.

But of course, no one would know that, really, because she wore nothing of the past on her face. He couldn't fathom how the battered face and body in the pictures had turned out to be the beautiful Kelsey Jones.

It was all he'd been able to think about for the past eight hours. No, more. How had she put herself back together again?

Except, maybe she hadn't. Not to the naked eye, but if he were honest, he'd seen the cracks. A few quiet moments of sheer panic in between her stage presence.

But give the girl some grace—she'd nearly been crushed in an explosion. And it made perfect sense why she hadn't wanted to face him after that.

But why had she left the ranch? Had she been planning on returning?

What about their kiss?

What if she didn't want to remember that? Frankly, all the questions simply had his brain in a knot—

"Thank you for showing up at Ben's place."

Her voice was so quiet he nearly didn't hear it over the game announcer, but he looked at her, and she met his eyes, a soft smile tugging at her mouth. "I didn't expect you, and there you were, showing up."

He nodded, his chest thick.

"Where did you go for the last four days?"

Oh. Shoot.

But she deserved to know that he'd been hunting for

Russell. And frankly, deserved to know that he knew about…
well, more than even what Tate had told her.

He'd entered her pain, seen it up close, and admired the
heck out of her that she'd overcome it. So he held on to that
and turned to her.

"I was in New York City."

Her smile fell, and she simply blinked at him, absorbing
his words slowly.

He nodded. "I know about Russell and the fact he's out
of prison. And that you think he might be the one who
bombed you, twice."

She drew in a breath, and he could nearly see her closing
up, so he delivered the rest quickly.

"Tate and I went to find him and shut him down. To tell
him to leave you alone, forever."

She stared at him so intently, with so much undisguised
hope, that he hated the answer to her next question.

"Did you find him?"

He shook his head. "He's missing."

She swallowed hard and looked away, back at the game.

"But we'll find him, Kelsey. And until we do…please…"
And he didn't care that it sounded like begging. "Stay here,
with me. I know I'm not a bodyguard, but I promise I'll do
whatever I have to in order to keep you safe."

She drew her hands into the long sleeves of her shirt,
her knees up to her chest. "But that's the thing, Knox. You
can't." She wiped her face with her sleeves, shook her head.
"Oh! I promised myself I wouldn't do this."

"Do what?" he asked softly.

"Fall apart. Be weak. I hate it!" She drew in a breath, and
when she looked at him, her jaw was stiff. "Listen. I know
you mean well, but…please, don't make me a promise you
can't keep."

Like, *I'm going to get you out of this?* And maybe she didn't mean that at all, but it sat at the top of his mind like a dagger.

"I won't—"

"But you'll try, and that's the problem." She closed her eyes. "I suppose you...you probably talked to Detective Rayburn."

He said nothing, so she looked at him.

He nodded.

Her mouth tightened. "Read the police report? Saw the pictures?"

He nodded again.

Her breath shook, and she looked out the window. "You know the worst part about the entire thing?"

He had some guesses—like waking up naked in a tangle of weeds, nearly bled out, hypothermic? Or having to learn how to walk, talk, and dress yourself again? Or maybe the moment when, at fourteen, she realized she'd had her innocence stolen.

"When my brother Ham came to see me."

He didn't see that one coming.

"He was deployed at the time, and since he was my closest relative, they brought him home. He was sitting by my bedside one morning, a couple days after I woke up. Alone, mind you. Disoriented, in the ICU, beeping and hissing all around me. But then one day, he just appeared."

She leaned her head back against the recliner. "He was my father's son, from his first marriage, and Hamilton was... larger than life. Tall, like my father, and muscled—he played football in college before he dropped out to join the Navy. The SEALs, actually."

Huh.

"He'd come to visit on the farm in the summers and was the only one who knew how to put the saddle on the dumb horse without it falling off. Then we'd ride her all over the farm, pretending we were settlers of the Old West. He's ten years older than me—can you imagine, a sixteen-year-old playing *Little House on the Prairie* with a six-year-old?"

Maybe.

If she was as cute as Kelsey.

"I wept for weeks when he went off to boot camp. I was eleven. And when I opened my eyes that day and saw him, I just knew…I knew everything would be okay."

She turned to Knox. "He stayed with me every day I was in the hospital, through rehab and even flew out with me to Wisconsin to settle me with Dixie's family. Her dad was a cousin on Mom's side that I'd never even met before." She drew in a breath. "Silly me, I thought Ham was staying, too."

Oh no. He wanted to reach out, touch her hand.

"The worst part about the entire attack was the day he packed his duffel bag and walked out of my life."

"Walked out?"

"Yeah, I know that sounds harsh, but that's what it felt like. He emailed, sometimes, and came to my high school graduation, but really, he simply faded away, busy with his deployments and saving the world or whatever he did. And I realized…you can only count on what you make. What you do. Because people will leave you."

"Not me."

He didn't know why the words came out, but he'd never meant anything more in his entire life. A tenor of heat consumed him, and he sat up. "Not me, Kelsey. Have you not met me? I'm the guy who sticks around. Who keeps his promises—or tries with everything inside him to. I show up. And I stick around. You can count on me."

She was consuming his words, her eyes in his, and he couldn't help it—he reached out to her and pulled her over to himself on the sofa.

He couldn't believe it when she surrendered, sitting on his lap and sliding into his arms.

"Kelsey. I made you a promise back in Texas, and I intend to keep it."

"You did? What—"

"I won't let you fall. That I'm going to get you out of this."

She drew in a breath, the hope back in her eyes. Then she leaned down and kissed him.

And as much as he'd dreamed about it, the fact she'd made the first move told him that this time, please, there wouldn't be panic, running, or God help him, tears.

He hoped.

So he let her be in control, let her caress his face with her thumb, let her explore, taste him, let her be the one to wrap her arms around him, sink into his embrace.

The warmth of her touch enveloped him, and he purposely kept his hands on her back, not moving her down onto the sofa, not deepening their kiss.

But it cost him, his breath coming hard when she leaned back.

Met his eyes.

"Safe is a good thing, you know."

He frowned.

"And so is Nice."

He nodded. Maybe.

Especially since she was bending to kiss him again. He was leaning in to meet her when—

"Hey, Knox—oh, whoops! Sorry!"

He leaned back and caught Tate turning in the threshold, his back to them, hand over his eyes.

"What?" Knox growled.

Kelsey made to scramble from his lap, but he touched her hand.

"Stay?"

She smiled at him, and Tate had better have a very good reason—

"I have some news." Tate turned and cast a look at Kelsey, who had settled back into Knox's embrace.

A beat. Huh. "And?"

He considered Knox a moment, then held up his phone. "AJ texted."

Oh, uh...

"AJ *Russell?* Kelsey said softly.

"You know him?" Knox said.

She nodded. "He sent me flowers. Even showed up once at the rehab center, but Ham made him leave. He was pretty upset about what his brother had done to me."

Knox glanced at Tate, but the man showed nothing of remorse for nearly breaking the man's fingers. His mouth tightened.

"Just say it, Tate."

"Vince Russell is dead. His body was found this morning in the Bronx River."

Kelsey stilled. "Really?"

"Really, Kels. It's over."

She looked at Knox, her eyes shiny, her breath starting to shudder.

"C'mere," he said softly and reached for her, pulling her close, her body shaking against him. "You're all right. You're going to be all right." Then he looked up at Tate. "It's time for you to leave, bro."

Tate closed the door behind him.

And Knox held Kelsey to himself as she dissolved into wracking, relieved sobs against his chest.

10

The morning dawned bold and bright, the sky striated with lavender and gold, the clouds over the snow-capped blue mountains tufted pink, just like every other day in Montana.

But today wasn't every other day. And neither had been yesterday, or the day before.

Today, Kelsey woke with her nightmares declared dead, the strings that held her to fear snipped.

She lay in the bed and stared at the ceiling. Four days after the news of Russell's death, Kelsey should be happy.

And not just with the news of Russell's death, but she could still feel Knox's arms wrapped around her last night, taste him on her lips, smell the cottony, cowboy redolence of him on her skin.

They had a routine, of sorts. She and Glo spent the days helping his mother as she prepared for her birthday weekend. Yesterday, they'd made pies. The day before, enough cookies to feed a couple hockey teams. They spent two afternoons prepping the garden, replanting the pots and window boxes, and even feeding the baby goats, which Glo had developed a particular craziness for.

In the evenings, while Glo and Tate squared off with a

board game, she snuck into the den with Knox. He would turn on an old episode of *Bonanza* or *Gunsmoke*, neither of them interested in watching.

They would talk about the day, her life on a farm in Minnesota before the tragedy, and his growing-up years on the ranch. And somewhere in there she'd end up on the sofa in his arms, tucked tight against the curve of his body, her head on his bicep.

He took his time kissing her, his fingers wrapped between hers. Warm, lingering, deep kisses, the kind that confirmed that she was, indeed, safe.

No running necessary.

And then, when she thought she might lose her mind, he'd tuck her back against him, drape one muscled arm over her, his breathing in sync with hers until she fell off to sleep, his whiskers against her skin stirring up a desire in her that she hadn't ever thought possible.

In fact, with Knox, she began to tiptoe into the realm of too much glorious, unexpected possibility.

She could blame him for this crazy thinking. He'd started it last night when he'd helped her onto the back of his horse, where she could put her arms around his trim waist, cuddling up close to that wide back, and trotted her out to the perch overlooking the waterfall.

The sunset had glinted copper off the distant rush of water, the sky mottled with amber and gold. They'd dismounted and walked out to the benches. There, they'd sat, her back against his chest. He'd tucked her into his embrace and just let her listen.

Listen to the rush of the wind, the rise of cicadas into the evening, listen to her heartbeat slowing, her own thoughts unwinding.

"There's a little cave behind the falls," Knox said in her

ear, his late-afternoon whiskers brushing her neck. "It always reminds me of that scene in *The Last of the Mohicans* when the hero, Hawkeye, is being chased by the Huron warriors. He and Cora, the heroine, are trapped on this ledge behind the falls. He tells her he'll rescue her and dives over the edge."

"'You stay alive, no matter what occurs! I will find you! No matter how long it takes, no matter how far. I will find you!'" She had lifted her head, turned to meet his eyes. "One of my favorite movie lines."

He made a sound, searched her eyes. "I would, you know."

"What?"

"Find you."

"And then what?" Her own gaze had landed on his lips.

He said nothing, but a small smile tweaked his face. "I guess I would bring you home."

Home.

The world filtered through her, and she gave a sad smile. "I don't have—"

"Yeah, you do. If you want it."

She turned in his arms and looked up at him. She must have worn surprise in her eyes because he nodded. "I know it's soon, and fast, but…" He looked away from her, back to the waterfall. "My mother told you that I dreamed of being a professional bull rider. She left out the fact that I was good at it. I'd won a junior national championship and had big dreams of winning the PBR. I saw myself being a champion, a star…someone who could outshine my bigger-than-life big brother." He'd given a small, humorless chuckle. "Then Dad died, and it all crashed down. I'd made a promise to my dad to take care of the place after Reuben left—and when Dad died, I had to step up to that promise."

She'd touched a hand to his chest, under his flannel shirt,

felt the heartbeat there. Steady. Dependable.

"I turned the ranch finances around, started our bucking bull line, and yes, we are very successful, but...I felt suffocated." He turned his gaze on her. "Until you showed up. Until I started to see the ranch through your eyes. This is a safe place. A place to dig in roots and stop running. A place to grow a future."

"Have a happily ever after," she said quietly, almost trying the words out, and they tugged a smile from his mouth.

"Sort of like a country song." Then he'd touched her chin and kissed her, such an achingly sweet touch she couldn't help but wonder...*What if?*

She could stay. Be happy.

If she were honest, she was tired. And not just from the gigs and endless travel, but...from waking every day afraid. Fear did that—made a person exhausted. And edgy and demanding and even controlling. Fear kept her from freedom. From life.

She wanted to be free. Truly free, even from the ghosts. And maybe she could do that here.

With Knox.

Now, she turned over in her bed, staring out the window. *What if I stayed?*

After all, she had no bus, no more gigs, her band was scattered.

And she'd begun to truly sleep, the nightmares receding.

So then, what was her problem that a knot still coiled, deep inside?

She would have attributed it to the unknown bomber of their bus—except for the call from Deputy Sam Brooks, who told her that the arson investigators ruled the fire an accident. The old propane tank had been jarred loose from under the stove, probably for some time, and a smoldering cigarette thrown nearby had ignited it.

An accident.

So, really. Breathe, Kelsey.

She threw off the covers, grabbed her clothes, took a shower, and came down for breakfast.

Knox was gone, as usual, up early for chores. Tate, too, who'd taken to helping him ride fence or haul feed out to the far pastures, just until the grass turned green and rich for foraging.

Gerri stood at the counter in the kitchen, wearing a checkered blue apron, her hair back in a headband, rolling out bread dough. And beside her, tossing flour onto the dough, stood a woman with dark hair tied back into a messy bun. She wore a gold-and-maroon UM Griz shirt and a pair of yoga pants and possessed blue eyes and the same intense, probing gaze of a Marshall.

"Hey," she said, looking up and wiping flour from her hands. "You must be one of the famous singers Ma keeps bragging about."

Kelsey gave a laugh. "I don't think so. We're more like the homeless waifs she's taken in. But we can sing for our supper."

"I'll look forward to that." She came around the counter. "I'm Ruby Jane." Went to hold out her hand, then pulled it back. "Sorry. I arrived just in time to make cinnamon rolls."

"And I arrived in time to eat them."

A deep voice, even deeper laughter, the kind that rumbled through a woman's body. She turned, half expecting Knox, and startled at— "Wyatt Marshall, goaltender for the Blue Ox—?"

He had shoulder-length dark hair still wet from a morning shower and tucked behind his ears to fall in unruly tangles. A smattering of dark whiskers, and whiskey-brown eyes that looked her over, a tug at his mouth. "Yeah. Actually. How did you—?"

"I've been watching your games for the better part of two weeks," she said as he walked toward her. Bare feet, low-hanging faded jeans, an open denim shirt to a sculpted chest. The saunter of an athlete, or maybe the cockiness was simply embedded in the genes of the Marshall men. He was taller than Knox, but his muscles had nothing on Knox, whose weren't honed by the gym but by the hard work of everyday life.

"A fan," Wyatt said, coming up to her and sliding onto a stool. "I like it."

"Maybe you could explain how the Oilers' right wing slapped in two goals last week. Taking a little nap there between the posts?" She winked, but Wyatt's grin faded.

"Listen—"

"Calm down, Wyatt, and button your shirt," Gerri said. "This isn't a locker room. Kelsey, honey, do you want some coffee?"

Kelsey slid onto the stool next to him. "I can't believe I slept so long. I didn't even hear you guys come in."

"We got here late last night. Wyatt picked me up at the airport in Helena, and we drove over. I saw my room was occupied, so I slept in the den," Ruby Jane said. "Although I had to kick out Knox."

Yeah, he'd been asleep when Kelsey had sneaked away last night, although the sight of his eyelashes soft against his cheeks, his strong face in repose made her want to stay.

Oh, she'd wanted to stay.

The thought swept her up as Gerri handed her a cup of coffee and nudged a bowl of popovers her direction. She handed Wyatt a cup of coffee too.

Wyatt helped himself to a popover, grabbed some honey,

and filled the pastry. "Ma, no one cooks like you."

Gerri grinned. "I know they're your favorite, Wy."

What would it be like to have a family like this? People who felt as comfortable with each other as they did in their own skin?

"Is Ford going to make it?" Ruby Jane asked. "I haven't heard from him in a few weeks."

"I don't know," Gerri said. "You never know when Ford will turn up. I can't keep track of him."

"What about Reuben?" Ruby Jane asked.

"Tate and Knox are down at the airstrip right now. Gilly is flying them in for the weekend."

"Oh, fancy, his own private pilot," Wyatt said, waving his hands.

"Who happens to be his fiancée and his jump plane pilot," Ruby Jane said. She was taking the cinnamon roll dough from her mother as she cut them and put them into a round pan. "We really need to pin them down on a wedding date. Three years is simply too long to date." She looked at Kelsey and winked, as if she knew what she might be referring to.

She'd never had a boyfriend...ever. She didn't know what to call Knox.

In her mind, four days felt like a lifetime.

And crazy fast for her to feel so connected, so...

She sighed.

"Do you think Coco..." Wyatt shook his head. "Never mind."

And just like that, all the air sucked out of the room, Gerri focusing on her rolled dough, Ruby Jane looking up, something of sadness in her face. "Wyatt—"

"It's no big deal. She's got a different life now. It's good." He smiled—something so forced it pained even Kelsey— slid off the stool and walked over to the coffee pot.

Ruby Jane leaned over, and said, sotto voce, "Coco's name is really Katya—her mother was a family friend who passed away a few years ago. Coco lived with us for four years, and Wyatt sorta—"

"I'm standing right here," Wyatt said, turning to lean a hip on the counter, bringing the coffee cup to his lips. "Coco and I were good friends, nothing more."

Ruby Jane rolled her eyes.

"I just worry about her."

"She left shortly after Orrin died, although she came back about a year later for a week or so to see us. Wyatt came home for that weekend. You remember that, right Wyatt?"

He nodded, a strange emotion flashing in his eyes. It vanished as Gerri continued.

"We haven't heard from her except for once—a post card from Russia a year ago."

"It's like she got sucked back into the Cold War," Wyatt said. "My coach is trying to get a game with one of the Russian teams, sort of an exhibition, and it's like we're asking them to defect." He lifted a shoulder. "A couple more degrees and we'll be back in the Cold War and she'll disappear into the Siberian tundra. We need to find her and bring her home."

Something about the earnestness of his words tugged at Kelsey's heart. She'd bet they'd been more than 'good friends'. The poor man carried a flame for this woman, even now.

"Thank you, Wyatt, for that political downer," Ruby Jane said. She finished packing the tin with dough balls. "The fact is, Katya is an American, too." She picked up the tin and carried it to the oven. "Her mom married a Russian while she was a foreign exchange student in college and she stayed in Russia. They separated, and her mother moved back to

Geraldine, bringing Katya with her."

She set the timer on the oven. "And don't believe for a second that Wyatt considered them just friends. There's a reason we don't let him out in the barn alone with a girl."

"Hey! Everyone is overreacting."

Ruby Jane returned to the counter and pulled out another round tin. "Ford found Wyatt and Coco in a clench in the barn right before Wyatt went to play for the Minnesota Blue Ox junior team."

"She wasn't my sister or anything. Sheesh. Everybody overreacts." Wyatt stalked away toward the den.

Gerri turned to Ruby Jane, bending over laughing, her eyes shining, her floury hand on her daughter's shoulder.

The gesture stirred up a bittersweet memory, one camped out in Kelsey's subconscious so long she hardly remembered it.

Christmas baking, age thirteen. She and Mom in the kitchen cutting out cookies. The movie *White Christmas* playing in the background, the snow piling against the windows.

Her throat tightened, and she forced a smile. "Wyatt sounds like he's not quite over her."

"No, sadly, he's holding pretty tight to that old flame," Ruby Jane said. "Poor guy. I don't think Coco liked him as much as he liked her. But Wyatt is…a charmer. And Coco had a lot of wounds back then that she was covering up. Wyatt was just a Band-Aid."

"We all have our Band-Aids, don't we?" Gerri said, lifting her apron to wipe her eyes. "Coco was an eighteen-year-old girl who'd lost her mother at fourteen. That's a rough time to lose a parent. You're going through puberty and you have this terrible mix of emotions, and then suddenly, you lose everything? She just couldn't grapple with it all. I don't blame her for trying to stop the bleeding any way she could. But that's the problem, isn't it? You put on a Band-Aid, but you don't really deal with the infection inside. You don't really dig down, clean it out, deal with the pain, and heal. And after a while, the Band-Aid just feels normal."

She looked up at Ruby Jane. "I actually think she loved Wyatt. Or wanted to. But she was too scared to feel it. To let him into her life. She'd been so busy numbing herself to her grief, she also numbed herself to the real feelings she had for Wyatt. So she let him Band-Aid her wounds."

"That's an awfully generous description of what was happening in the barn, Ma," Ruby Jane said, grinning.

"I would call it grace, honey. Something that we need to give as well as receive, every day."

Kelsey stared at Gerri and heard her words from nearly a week ago. *He gave me just enough grace for that day to keep going on with my life.*

Ruby Jane finished filling the second tin. "She was so embarrassed, she returned to Russia."

"Your brother probably blames himself, so go easy on him, RJ."

Ruby Jane went silent as the buzzer went off on the oven. She walked over to switch the pan to a lower shelf and add the second tin. The tangy aroma of cinnamon and brown sugar filled the air, and Kelsey nearly wept with the smell.

"She was my best friend as well as my sister, and I miss her." It was the first hint of hurt in Ruby Jane's voice.

"I know, honey. We all love her. And I'm hoping she'll come back and realize that her wounds aren't handicaps but are what make her beautiful."

And Kelsey couldn't stop herself. "What do you mean, *beautiful?*"

Gerri pulled another roll of dough from the pan and set it on the board. "We're all wounded, Kelsey. But it's our wounds that allow us to have compassion for each other. It's how God shows us He loves us too—through the way we reach out and hold on to each other."

Maybe. Like Ham reached out to care for her after the attack. And Dixie and Glo, when she moved to Wisconsin, and…and Knox.

How Knox had wrapped his arms around her, kept her from falling.

"But of course, we have to be vulnerable. Share our lives with others if we want to connect. And then maybe people will share theirs with us." She looked up and winked at Kelsey. "Sort of like you do in your songs. What's that one—'One True Heart'?"

"That's Glo's song. I just sing it."

Gerri dusted cinnamon onto the dough. "You do it beautifully. It's so…"

Fake. Kelsey kept her smile, but…yeah, Glo had written a song from her soul and Kelsey turned it into a performance. Something she could cocoon around her, make her seem authentic and honest and…

Frankly, it had probably been only a matter of time before the stage exploded around her. Before her performance cracked and people saw through her.

Dix, Glo, Carter, and Tate had saved her from that moment.

"It sounds like Glo wrestled through a dark night of the soul with that song. So honest and raw and…it makes me cry every time."

"I've never heard it," Ruby Jane said.

"It's about lost love and the fear of starting over," Gerri said.

"Glo lost the love of her life in Afghanistan," Kelsey said quietly. It wasn't really her secret to tell, but it just spilled out.

"She said she gave David her whole heart and has decided she'll never fall in love again."

"I felt that way, too, until..." Gerri didn't finish that sentence, but instead she pushed the rolls toward Ruby Jane. "That's the last pan."

The second buzzer went off and Gerri went after it. Retrieved the pan and set it on a cutting board to cool. "Maybe that's why I love that song so much... I understand how it feels to lose everything and be afraid to love again, having had so much of it the first time."

Ruby Jane looked up, gave her mother a sad smile.

Gerri squeezed her daughter's hand. "Ho-*kay*, do you think we have enough here to feed the brute squad?"

"Who are you calling brute?"

The voice came from behind them, deep and gruff, as if it had been whisked from the wilds of some northern Montana wilderness.

"Reuben!"

Ruby Jane grabbed a towel for her hands as she rounded the counter and headed for the big man at the door.

They just grew them bigger and bigger up here on Marshall land. Reuben seemed the size of a small buffalo, with hulking shoulders, a trim waist, and arms that could tear a tree from its roots. He caught Ruby Jane up and twirled her around. Kelsey slid off the stool, taking in the petite redhead who came in behind Reuben. Her aviator glasses were perched on her head, and she carried a backpack over her shoulder.

"Gilly!" This from Gerri who had also crossed the room. She pulled the woman, dressed in army-green cotton pants, a T-shirt, and a jean jacket, into a hug.

Knox pushed past them both, and Kelsey's insides released a little. Apparently, she'd been holding her breath again.

He came over to her as Wyatt emerged from the den and caught Reuben in a hug.

"That's my brother Reuben and his fiancée, Gilly. He's a smokejumper on a base northwest of here," Knox said.

Reuben looked like Paul Bunyan, as if he could put out a fire with one breath of his mighty lungs.

"C'mon, I'll introduce you."

But she didn't move under his nudge.

"What?" he said softly.

"It's just...there's...so many people." And it was just an excuse, she knew it, but...

"This isn't a crowd, Kelsey. This is a family."

She took a deep breath. Yeah. That's what she was suddenly, oddly, afraid of. So many people to *know* her.

But wasn't that part of freedom too? Being known...and still being loved?

She glanced up at Knox and found his gaze on her. Warm, the kind of smile simmering at his lips that made her insides turn to flame.

This is a family.

She wove her hand into his and nodded, the words bubbling up. *I want to stay.*

Maybe he saw her intent, because his mouth edged up in a smile. For a second, his gaze dropped to her lips, and she had the sense that if his family weren't here, he'd be wrapping his big hand around her neck and pulling her close for one of his smoldering kisses.

Later. Maybe tonight under the beautiful cascade of Montana stars.

After she told him that she'd stay.

She turned to meet the rest of his family when Glo came through the back door, off the porch. She caught Kelsey's arm, glancing up at the crowd. "I need to talk to you for a second."

Tate had come inside, and Kelsey saw his gaze falling on Glo, then off, as if it stung him.

She turned to Glo. "What?"

Glo sighed, glancing up over her shoulder at Knox, then back to Kelsey. "I got a text from Carter. We…we did it, Kelsey!"

Kelsey frowned, shook her head—*Did what?*

"We landed the NBR-X tour. Our first gig is next weekend."

Oh. Kelsey drew in a breath, turned and looked at the crowd—no, family—gathering at the front door. At Knox. Then back to Glo.

"So, what do I tell him?"

———————◆———————

It should be a magical night. With the stars strewn across the sky like fairy dust, the mountains cordoning off their pocket of paradise. The entire family, save Ford and of course Coco, had made it home for the weekend bash, and Knox was still holding out hope that his brother might show up. At least on Skype.

He'd done it—brought them all home.

And all he could think about were Glo's words to Kelsey about NBR-X…and Kelsey's response to Glo's question—*So, what do I tell him?*

So, he'd eavesdropped a little. A lot. The entire thing, really, his gut in a knot as he pretended to listen to his family's chatter.

Kelsey was going to break his heart. Knox knew it in his soul as the night deepened. Every time she looked over at him, offered a tiny smile, so much pain in her eyes, his chest tightened, claws digging in, tearing him apart.

He bit back the crazy, dark edge of tears as he stared at the flickering flames of the campfire.

He didn't blame her. This was her big break.

And what was he going to do? Run after her? Be a groupie? He couldn't leave the ranch.

But the old stirring had only deepened with the thought of watching her sing every night, being in the wings to catch her up when she ran offstage, triumph in her eyes.

She was the adventure he'd longed for. And he might be boring, and nice, but she made him feel like the safe, dependable guy was the hero after all.

It was all Knox could do to smile and not let the howl inside escape.

Reuben sat on the ground, leaning back on his hands, Gilly pocketed between his legs as she extended two marshmallow sticks into the coals around the edge. The fire turned his face hard-edged and gritty, but he wore a sappy grin as he watched his fiancée.

Happy. The guy looked downright happy.

And then there was Tate, who had gotten up to hand Glo a beautiful brown-crusted marshmallow, now sitting down on the peeled, smooth log next to her. Oh, the guy was so perfectly whipped for the tiny blonde, he practically wore his tough-guy heart on the outside of his body.

In truth, Tate's actions in New York City had rattled Knox. But he didn't want to dig too deep around Tate's past. Especially since it seemed he wanted to leave it behind, start new.

Apparently, that was the theme of the night, with the appearance of their neighbor, Hardwin Colt. He'd simply come around back to the campfire pit about an hour ago, his hands shoved into his pockets, freshly shaved, and wearing a clean button-snap shirt. He wore a brown cowboy hat over his gray hair and a warm smile, especially when it landed on Knox's mother.

Huh.

She introduced him around, and when Hardwin reached him, Knox met Hardwin's eyes, studying him.

Hardwin didn't flinch, just stood there.

Knox finally nodded. He said nothing when Hardwin went to sit by his mother. Nudged her, got her to laugh.

Wyatt and Ruby Jane sat together, and now Knox picked up snippets of their conversation.

"You were lousy in the game against the Bruins," RJ said.

"Hey, that's not all my fault. Rusk was trying to play goalie—he opened up holes and screened the shooters. They just need to stay in their lane, let me do my job. If I see the puck, I'll stop it."

Wyatt stuck a marshmallow on his stick, set it deep into the coals.

Knox's gaze lifted to Kelsey, across the fire. She was gazing into the flames, the fire flickering in her beautiful eyes.

Please don't leave me, Kels.

"Yeah, but that shootout! That was crazy."

"People forget that I had thirty saves in that game."

"And one that slipped through."

"Oh, you're brutal, RJ."

Knox wanted to smile at their laughter, at the fact that in one moment, it all felt exactly how he wanted it to be. With a few gaps, of course.

Their dad would have been talking about setting fire to one of the fields, or repairs he needed to make to the house. Maybe telling the epic story about the time he rode rodeo, competing in roping and bull-riding events. Or worked as a smokejumper in Glacier.

He'd even played hockey. So much of their dad spread out amongst his sons.

Dad, I hope you're proud of us.

Me. I hope you're proud of me.

His mother made a sound of delight as she pulled out her cell phone. "It's Ford! He's video calling."

Ford, you champ, you.

She answered, and Ford's face filled the screen, just a gray wall behind him. "Hey, Ma, happy birthday."

She held up the phone and ran her hand across her cheekbone. "Where are you calling from?"

"Aw, Ma, he can't answer you," Ruby Jane said. "Just tell us, are you hot or cold?"

He laughed, his pale green eyes shiny. He wore his hair shaved short under a blue cap. "Neither. I'm hungry!"

They laughed at the old joke. His mother caught him up on the festivities in the making—tonight's campfire, tomorrow's barbeque—Knox had spent the day hauling in charcoal to the barn and cleaning out the massive chuck-wagon grill. Last time they'd used it might have been for a wedding they'd hosted a couple years ago.

"When are you coming home next?"

"I dunno. We have another four weeks in country, and then...I'll try." He glanced away, then back to the phone. "I gotta go, Ma. Love you guys."

He hung up, and they sat in silence for a moment.

Then Ruby Jane turned to Wyatt. "Remember that shootout between you and Ford? He totally smoked you!"

Wyatt made a face.

"I think we have it on tape," Tate said. "In Dad's VCR collection." He stood up.

Kelsey was still staring into the flames. Knox longed to go over, pry open her thoughts. *What are you going to tell him?*

But really, what did he expect from her? That she'd settle down here, on the ranch, and live happily ever after with him?

Maybe, yes. After all, he had.

And it hit him. He was happy here. Loved the smell of the land, the hard work, the bone-weariness at the end of the day. The sense that this family depended on him. *You can count on me.*

His words to Kelsey from a few nights ago, but now they burrowed deep.

Please, Kelsey, count on me.

Around him the hockey argument had stirred to flame, and suddenly Wyatt, Tate, Reuben, Gilly, and Ruby Jane were headed into the house.

Tate grabbed his shirt. "C'mon. We know you took over the den—we need to find Dad's tape."

Knox met Kelsey's eyes a moment, and she gave him another enigmatic smile that only tightened his gut.

Fine. He would get the tape, then he was going to get her away and tell her…what? That he loved her? Maybe. Beg her to stay?

He drew in his breath, screwing up his courage to do exactly that as he followed Tate through the house.

His siblings were rooting through the built-in book-shelves and cupboard at the far end of the room. He moved RJ aside, bent, and found the old shoebox of Dad's videos, tucked behind his saved newspapers from pivotal events in history and a couple old *National Geographic* magazines.

"Where is the old VCR?" Tate asked, and of course, Knox pulled that out next. He handed it to Tate, who set it beside the television, unwinding the cords. Reuben pulled the television from the wall, and in moments they had the thing hooked up, the screen fuzzy as they changed inputs.

Reuben shoved in the tape, pressed Play, and in a moment the grainy image came up.

Not the Ford versus Wyatt after-game shootout, but the game itself—the Garnet County Wildcats against a Kalispell team. Wyatt, a senior, at goal, Ford, a sophomore playing defenseman. He'd wanted a glory position, but back then, he was bigger and tougher than the other guys his age, and the coach slotted him where they needed him.

The camera panned to Wyatt and Ford, bracing for a fast break, and when the puck pinged off Wyatt's glove, bounced out, and Ford shot it back down the ice, a fist crossed the screen, a *hooyah* rising above the cheers.

Dad.

The camera flicked to him—probably their mother at the controls—and then the room went quiet as Dad glanced into the camera. "Way to go, boys!"

Dark hair, brown eyes, a smug smile. He wore such pride in his eyes, Knox's throat simply tightened.

The air in the room seemed to empty, and in his periphery, he saw Ruby Jane wipe her eyes.

Tate took a deep breath.

Gilly put her arm around Reuben.

The camera turned back to the game, but no one spoke.

Shoot. *Dad.*

A knock came at the door, and Reuben reached over to pause the tape.

Hardwin stood in the threshold. He glanced at the television. "Sorry to interrupt. Looking at an old game tape?"

Tate nodded, like they hadn't all just been sideswiped by the past.

"Um, I wanted to talk to you all, and I thought this might be the only time—without your mom around."

Knox stiffened. Reuben got up off the floor, folded his

arms.

Hardwin came into the room, closed the door. Took off his hat.

What in the world—

"So, I'd like your permission to court your mother."

Knox stared at him.

Reuben's gaze didn't move, either.

Tate looked at the ground.

"Really?" Ruby Jane said. "I thought you were…I mean…you and Ma?"

"I moved out here five years ago, and then lost my wife suddenly two years later. I never thought I'd meet anyone who…well, your mother is amazing, and we like spending time together, and I'd like to see if…I mean…with your permission, I'd like to see if we have a future together."

"I don't want to see Ma hurt," Reuben said quietly, darkly.

"I won't hurt her," Hardwin said. "I promise."

Knox's mouth tightened.

And then, Reuben took him out at his knees when he held out his hand. "Okay, then."

What—? Since when was he the family spokesperson?

Hardwin shook his hand, nodding. "Thank you, Reuben."

But—

Knox waited until Hardwin left, then he closed the door behind him and rounded on his brother. "Seriously? Who appointed you family boss? Listen, you left here, kicked the dust off your boots, and left me in charge. If anyone should be giving permission, it's me—"

"No one needs to give Ma permission to date. She can run her own life—" Ruby Jane interjected.

"Yeah, well, I'm here, I'm the one who has kept the ranch running, who is paying the bills and keeping us in the black. Of course Ma doesn't need permission, but if Hardwin is asking, then I'm the one handing it out."

"I don't think so, Knox. I'm the oldest. I'm the one who the responsibility falls on—"

"You're not even here!"

"Actually, I want to talk about that. I'm glad everyone is here." Reuben turned, sliding his arm around Gilly. "We want to get married soon. And then…" He met Knox's eyes. "I want to move back and help run the ranch."

Knox just blinked at him.

"Gilly and I are ready to settle down, start a family, and I want my kids to know the childhood I had. Working the ranch side by side with my dad—"

"You played *football!* I worked the ranch!" Knox fought to cut his voice low. Took a breath. "Reuben, you left because you hated working the ranch—"

"I left because you drove me away," Reuben said quietly, something of a lethal tone to his voice.

Knox felt it like a gut punch.

"I wanted this ranch too. I loved working with Dad, and if I hadn't broken both my legs while I was *working the ranch,* then he would have never turned to you."

"Rube—you wanted to go away, play college ball. The ranch was never on your radar."

"It is now."

Knox opened his mouth, not sure how to form the words that boiled inside. Finally. "Fine, yes. Come back as our foreman."

Reuben shook his head.

And Knox never wanted to hit his brother more than he did at this moment.

"Hey, guys, so long as we're sharing secrets, I've got one." Ruby Jane to the rescue, but Knox just couldn't tear his gaze away from Reuben.

Of all the arrogant—

"So, you know how I said I'm a travel agent...that's not quite accurate..."

Knox looked at her. Frowned. "What are you talking about?"

"That's just...a cover story. Sorta."

Now she had Reuben's attention too.

"What—are you a spy or something?" Wyatt said.

She made a face, lifted a shoulder.

"I knew it!" Tate said, then cut his voice lower. "I knew it. I thought I saw you in Vegas once—"

She glanced at him, raised an eyebrow, and he went silent.

"You're a spy? With the CIA? The FBI?" Reuben said darkly.

"CIA. And not a spy. An analyst."

"More travel agency speak?"

She gave Knox a half smile. "That's all I can tell you, but I thought you should know."

"Why, so if you disappear we know who to blame?"

"Or maybe where to start looking for me?" She laughed. No one else did.

"That's great, RJ. It's not enough that Ford is out there risking his life and that Tate disappeared for three years and shows up with the skills of a mafia thug, but now you've decided to make us live in secrecy."

"Tate was a mafia thug?" Wyatt said.

Knox shook his head, turned back to Reuben. "No. You can't come back. Not as the boss. Dad wanted me to run it."

"Dad defaulted to you when I got laid up. You took this ranch, just like you took Chelsea!"

Knox jerked back, shook his head, his eyes meeting Reuben's, hot in his.

Gilly put her hand on Reuben's arm. "C'mon, Rube.

That's not fair."

Her soft words put a dent in his anger. He pursed his lips. "Fine. Yes, I know." He blew out a breath. "Shoot. Bro, I didn't mean that—"

"I think you did. I think you've been spoiling for this fight for over ten years. You want to finish it, we can."

Reuben recoiled. Drew in a breath.

"Geez, you just can't say you're sorry, can you?" Reuben snapped.

"And you just can't let it go, the fact that finally, I was as good—no, better than you! Finally."

Knox didn't know where those words came from, and they hung there, ugly and sharp-edged, with everyone staring at him.

The air had gone out of Rueben's argument, his face pained.

Knox shook his head. "Do whatever you want, Rube." Then he turned and headed out of the den.

He couldn't face Kelsey right now and what she might say to him, so he turned and headed out the front door. Crossed the grass to the parking lot and hopped in his truck. The keys lay on the seat, and he scooped them up, turned the ignition, and threw some gravel as he backed out the drive.

"Knox!"

His name lifted into the night as he drove down the road, not sure where he was headed. Just…away.

Except their land extended for a couple miles and by the time he got to the end of the gate, he felt a little silly, like he might be a fourth grader having a tantrum, so he turned the truck around and headed toward the airfield.

Toward the best memories he had.

Gilly's plane sat on the runway, a red-and-white striped Otter that she used to herald smokejumpers to the sky and drop them over a blazing fire to save the planet.

He pulled his truck up next to the plane and got out, now breathing less like he'd been punched.

He ran his hand over the wing. *You have the yoke, Knox.*

He'd been twelve the first time his dad let him fly. Soloed when he was sixteen.

Just hold it steady.

I'm trying, Dad.

A truck pulled up next to his, and he didn't turn as he heard the door open, the grass crunching under booted feet. Knox walked away from the plane, staring at their house tucked inside the hill, up to the Milky Way, and beyond.

"I'm sorry, Knox."

He drew in a breath at Reuben's voice.

"You're right. I left, and you stayed, and you have done something amazing with this place. You've built it beyond what Dad could have asked or imagined. The truth is, all my life I've wanted to be like you."

Knox glanced at him. Reuben had come up to stand beside him. "C'mon."

"Okay, not your bull riding or football skills, but…you're smart, Knox. Smart and solid and dependable and so much like Dad. I was so jealous when Dad took you under his wing after I got hurt. It was like you belonged beside him and I was the outsider."

Knox looked down, shook his head. "Remember the rodeo down in Cardiff? I was…ten, I think."

Reuben looked at him. "Um…"

"My first try at bull riding. Only then it was steer riding, but…"

"Oh yeah," Reuben said. "I think it was my idea."

"Yeah, but Dad was all over it. I remember you guys leaning into the chute, helping me adjust my bull rope, the bell jangling everywhere. You were shoving my hand up under the rope, Dad was telling me to scoot up, and I was sweating inside that crazy helmet thinking…I'm going to get killed."

Reuben laughed. "If I remember right, you rode that thing for…almost eight seconds."

"Six point four."

"You had the makings, bro…" Reuben shook his head.

"You rode it all eight that day," Knox said quietly, glancing at him. "And Dad's comment as I got off the ground—he'd come running down the dirt to get me—was, 'Keep it up, and someday you'll be just like Reuben.'"

Reuben went quiet beside him.

"He let you drive the truck home that night," Knox said.

Reuben nodded. "I had just turned twelve."

"I wanted it." Knox looked at him. "To be like you. To be you. You were larger than life, bro. And then…then suddenly I was *you*. I was taking Chelsea to the prom and driving the truck and Dad was teaching me to fly and…" He shook his head. "Maybe it did all belong to you."

Reuben drew a breath. "No. It belongs to all of us. But Dad chose rightly when he asked you to take over."

"Actually, he didn't. I was just the only one who showed up. I made him a promise to take care of the place."

"I'm back, with my own promises, Knox. Because you don't have to do it alone. Not anymore. Let me help. Teach me what I don't know, and maybe someday this will be the Marshall Triple M again."

Knox looked at him. "Oh no, I'm not letting Tate run the place."

"Hey!"

The voice shot out of the darkness behind him. "What are you talking about? I'm a great rancher."

227

Knox turned and wasn't really surprised to see Tate and the entire posse behind him. Gilly walked over to Reuben, a grin on her face. Wyatt looped his arm around Ruby Jane's neck.

"You can barely stay on a horse, Tate, let alone rope a steer."

"That's not true. I just…okay, so I won't be the third M. Maybe Wyatt—"

"Not me." Wyatt held up his hands. "I'm buying a condo in Big Sky."

Tate came up to Knox. Grabbed him by the shirt. "But, if you need us, we're here. You don't have to carry it all on your shoulders, right?"

Knox nodded, the fist in his chest releasing a little.

Tate's smile faded, and he looked over Knox's shoulder, released his shirt. "What the—"

Knox turned, and his gut hollowed out.

"Is that—" Wyatt started, but Knox had already turned, started for his truck.

"Get in the truck!" Reuben shouted. "The barn is on fire!"

11

ot Gordo, please not Gordo.

N The fire had reached the top of the southeastern corner of the barn by the time Knox pulled up the drive. Sparks bit into the night sky, the smell of cinder and ash and burning hay and wood saturating the air.

The rest of the Marshalls piled out of the bed of his truck—more out of Reuben's as he too pulled up.

Knox had already grabbed the hose that ran into the giant water trough for Gordo's pen. He shoved it into Tate's hands just as Wyatt ran to turn it on.

Reuben and Gilly were shouting directions even as Reuben headed inside.

The wind that gusted into the barn from the open doors fueled the flames, and they licked into the sky.

Reuben grabbed a pitchfork and headed up to the loft.

"What are you doing?"

"Throwing the burning hay out—we need water up here!" he yelled to no one in particular, but probably Knox.

But Knox had opened Gordo's pen, walking through it to the other side. The animal shoved at him, panicked, but he pushed him away, opening the doors. "Get out!"

"Knox!"

The animal bolted into the yard, and Knox closed the pen and ran down to the end.

"I have to get Daisy and her bull!" Oh, why hadn't he put them out to pasture already? He'd meant to, but he liked having the bull in the barn where he could keep an eye on his growth.

Now, smoke turned his eyes gritty, and he grabbed a railing, doubling over, coughing.

"Put something over your face!" Reuben yelled, also coughing. He was pitching hay out the window, even as water dripped down the side of the barn from Tate's—and now probably Wyatt's—hoses.

Knox covered his mouth with his arm and groped his way to Daisy. She was in a panic, slamming against the gate, and he opened it, flung it back.

She lunged out, and he went after the bull. It lay on the hay, its eyes wide. Knox jerked it up. "C'mon, little guy." And in a second, the bull found its legs.

Tufts of hay dropped from the mow overhead and flamed in the middle of the barn, crackling, sizzling. Knox barely dodged it, pushing the bull out of the way as they escaped the building.

He grabbed the hose curled by the door, turned the water on full, and doused the mound of hay.

"Up here! We need some water. The fire's getting into the rafters and if it reaches the ridge pole, it's all over!"

Knox coiled the hose and tossed it up to Reuben, who caught the unraveling snake with one hand. He got a good view of his brother in that moment, backdropped against the smoke and flames, wide-shouldered, fearless, almost more alive in the middle of the flames than Knox had ever seen him.

Was he sure he wanted to give up his life on the edge of

wildfire for…well, they might not have anything left after tonight.

He climbed up the ladder, took the hose from Reuben, and kept spraying the rafters as Reuben grabbed up the pitchfork again and tumbled the rest of the smoldering hay out the window, separating it from the unburned green mounds. The smoke clogged the mow, and with the steam, Knox could barely see Reuben, who kept shouting at him, pointing at glowing cinders and new burns.

The sound of bleating rose, churned panic through him, but he could do nothing for the family of baby goats.

His mother's shouts rose, mixed with a male voice he didn't recognize.

Oh, Hardwin, helping to rescue his mother's pets.

The flames finally sizzled out, steam pouring through the barn, through the windows, water dripping from the hay mow, a summer's work ruined. Sweat ran down Reuben's face, but he grabbed the hose and ran water into the rafters, a final sousing.

They stood, breathing hard, meeting each other's eyes, the water dripping out of the hose.

"How did this happen?" Reuben said.

"I don't know." Knox climbed down the ladder, stood in the shadows of the barn. He bent over, gripping his knees.

Reuben followed him down and laid a hand on his back. "You okay?"

"We could have lost Gordo. And the baby bull out of Hot Pete…" He blew out. "If you're going to take over the ranch, you should probably know that we're just on the line here. When Dad died, he left a double mortgage on the house. We had a number of cows who were bred out, and our only bull couldn't keep up. Dad's insurance went into the herd, and I took the rest and bought Gordo. And we've slowly climbed out of the red. But…" He stood up. Water saturated his arms, his shirt. "I had a lot riding on Hot Pete. His purses, his future straws. He paid off our first mortgage over the past two years. But we need the insurance on him to keep the ranch afloat, acquire another breed cow." He sighed. "Not rebuild a barn."

"The barn is insured, I hope."

Knox nodded. But he let out another long breath.

"You're overwhelmed."

Knox nodded.

"That's what we're here for, bro." The words sunk in, found his bones. "You don't have to do this alone."

He again had the crazy urge to weep.

Reuben squeezed his shoulder.

Outside, Tate and Wyatt were winding up the hoses. Ruby Jane and Gilly had rounded up the goats, Gilly petting one as if she might be in love.

Daisy and her bull stood in the drive, not far away. Knox walked over to her, opened his arms, shook his hand to direct her. "Hup, hup." She started to move toward the pen, and he clapped his hands, walking behind her. Reuben opened a pen, and she ambled in, her bull behind her.

Then he stopped to oversee the damage. In the darkness, it was hard to make out the extent of the fire. The headlights from the trucks poured over the pens, across the blackened walls of the barn. Could be mostly surface damage, but he'd have to wait until tomorrow to investigate.

"How do you think it started?" Tate asked, which was clearly the question of the hour.

Hardwin came over. "Did you bale your hay wet?

"I don't know. I was on the road last fall. I left it to Lemuel."

"How about electrical wiring? This barn is pretty old,"

Ruby Jane said, coming over with a barn cat.

"I replaced all the wiring, I think." He ran a hand behind his neck. "I don't know."

Tate stood on the outskirts of the group. "This is awfully coincidental, given that Glo and Kelsey's bus also burned a week ago."

"That was a propane leak," Knox said, but…wait— "Where are they?"

Tate stepped back, looked around. "Glo?"

"Last time I saw them, they were sitting by the campfire," his mother said.

Knox took off toward the house, but he cast a glance at the barn.

Kelsey liked the barn…

No, he would have seen her— "Kelsey?"

He rounded the house and headed for the campfire pit.

Just the embers smoldered in the rock pit.

Tate burst out of the house. "They're not inside." He looked at Knox. "Why do I have a terrible gnaw in my gut about this?"

"Maybe they just went for a walk."

"In the dark? With the barn on fire?"

"I'll get the others. Spread out—they couldn't have gone far."

"Shh, Glo, stay quiet."

Although, granted, it had to be hard for Glo to clamp her mouth shut with her arm bleeding, whatever had hit her causing her to pull her arm into her shoulder. And, Glo was bleeding—Kelsey could feel the ground beneath them getting damper.

"Do you see him?"

They were crouched under a bench at Gerri's overlook, Kelsey practically lying on top of Glo to hide them both. And out in the darkness somewhere prowled someone who'd grabbed Glo as they'd sat at the campfire alone.

Someone with a gun.

Kelsey had seen him in the barest of light—gauged ears, an eyebrow bar, and a look on his face that suggested he meant business.

Kelsey wasn't sure what business that might be.

She just knew he wasn't going to drag someone she cared about away to do who knew what, so she did the only thing she could think of.

She stabbed him with her hot marshmallow skewer. Pitiful, she knew, but when he shouted and dodged away from her, Glo kicked him in the instep.

Which caused him to swear, cuff her, and turn on Kelsey.

She had picked up a nearby log and clubbed him with everything inside of her.

Grabbed Glo's hand and ran.

They scrambled up the path etched out in the rock, nearly impossible to see in the darkness, and somewhere in there, she'd heard shouting.

Then a scream from Glo as she stumbled beside her.

Kelsey grabbed up her friend, clamped her hand over her mouth, and kept running.

Not until they reached the overlook did she pull Glo down and in the wan moonlight see what she'd grunted about.

Her flesh was torn, right through her shoulder, maybe even to the bone.

"Glo, I think you're shot," she'd said, and pressed her hand over the wound.

Glo had groaned again, just a whisper of what she

probably wanted to do. Kelsey had to give her props for her guts.

And to think her biggest problem seconds before was trying to decide how to tell Glo that she wanted to turn down the NBR-X gig.

That she liked—no loved—living on the ranch. It brought back her life on the farm, the memories she harbored deep inside, and being with Knox...

Knox. He felt like home. He was the exhale, the soft place to land.

In fact, since Gerri's words this morning, lyrics had begun to form in her head.

Something dug out of the griefs and sorrows of her heart.

She wanted to feel the love Knox offered, and if that meant digging down into the darkness...

She'd never expected the darkness to climb out and go after her.

But maybe Glo was right—they'd worked so hard for this moment. This opportunity.

She couldn't run from her past. And maybe hiding wasn't the right answer, either.

"Who is he?" Glo whispered, pain tremoring her voice.

"I don't know." *Knox, please find us.* But she hadn't seen him since he'd gone into the house with the rest of his family.

His amazing, overwhelming, embracive family that she very much wanted to belong to with each passing moment.

Then they'd simply lain there, trying not to breathe. Kelsey practically willed her heartbeat to slow, to become silent.

In the distance a glow lit the sky, and she watched as it flickered against the night. The smell of smoke burned the air.

Oh God, I'm not sure what's happening, but…

She stopped, aware of the crazy, desperate prayer.

She hadn't actually prayed in years, although Dixie's family were friends of Jesus. *Jesus loves me! This I know, for the Bible tells me so.* She'd learned the song, along with a dozen other hymns Dixie's family members were always singing around the house.

It simply hadn't been enough to heal the wounds inside.

Now, Sierra's words rushed at her. *He very much cares about you.*

A crack against the dry grass sounded nearby, and she stayed perfectly still next to Glo.

It moved away, but she lay like the dead.

Okay. *Right now, God. If You're there, if You care, please show up.*

She tried to sort out where she'd seen the man in the yard before. A deep, buried memory she couldn't nudge forth.

But he moved away, so she finally peered up, watching the light dimming in the distance.

It looked like the bull barn on fire.

I'm sorry, Knox. Because she couldn't get past the idea that maybe this had to do with her. That maybe Vince Russell wasn't dead after all, or maybe he'd simply come back from the grave to haunt her. Keep her running, bleeding, pretending that she was okay.

Because if she were honest, she would always be a little broken from her past. Maybe that's why sometimes, when she tried to take a full breath, the shards crashed against each other, like broken ribs, stirring up the ache.

Although maybe that was okay, too, because like Gerri said, if it made her more compassionate, more willing to give grace…

More steps and she ducked her head again.

Glo was shivering beneath her.

"Kelsey!"

That voice. Like a flame, burning through her, finding her bones, igniting them.

Knox!

She lifted her head just as he knelt beside her.

"Are you okay?"

His face was black, sooty from the fire, and sweaty, his eyes so full of worry it whisked the breath from her. She could only nod—

And then Knox simply lifted her up into his arms, pulling her off Glo, a strange sound in his chest. His entire body shook, and oh, he was wet, maybe from sweat, but under his cool shirt his body heat swept through her.

She hung on.

"*Glo's been shot!*" Tate's horrified voice erupted as he crouched beside Glo.

"Are you kidding me?" Knox roared. He put Kelsey down and bracketed her face with his hands, searching her body for injury. "What happened?" Sweat ran from his hair in grimy streaks. "Tell me you're okay."

Kelsey looked over just in time to see Tate pulling off his shirt. He wrapped it around Glo's arm, securing it to her body. "It's going to be okay, honey."

Honey?

Then Tate scooped Glo up into his arms. The man looked shattered.

Oh, *honey.*

Kelsey turned back to Knox. "I'm okay—"

And then he kissed her. Not a tender, you're-in-control-because-you've-been-damaged kiss, but a desperate, heart-outside-his-body clench that she could only surrender to, like a tsunami.

Yes, this was what it would be like with Knox. Him, showing up in full force.

Into her disasters.

His eyes were glossy when he let her go. "What happened?"

"I don't know. We were sitting by the fire, and suddenly this man came up and just grabbed Glo. Tried to drag her away."

Knox stared at her, clearly trying to take all this in. "A *man* grabbed *Glo*?"

"Yeah. Maybe she was the closest, I don't know, but—I poked him."

"You...poked him."

"Then I hit him with a log."

His hands cupped her face and he leaned his forehead against hers, just breathing.

"Is he still out here?" A woman's voice, and Knox released her. She turned to Ruby Jane.

"I think so. I don't know."

"Let's get in the house." Knox took her hand and practically ran with her after Ruby Jane. Tate was long ahead.

"What did he look like?" Knox said as they followed Ruby Jane's light across the hill.

"He had gauged ears. An eyebrow bar. Maybe a dark tattoo?"

Knox's hand tightened in hers. "Could it have been a port-wine stain instead of a tattoo?"

"I don't know. Maybe."

Wyatt and Reuben stood by the fire. Reuben held a gun in his hand.

"Get inside, guys," Knox said. "But yeah, keep that out, Reuben. There's someone on our property, and he's armed too."

He pulled Kelsey into the back, waited for the others, then shut the door.

"Stay away from the windows," Tate said from the kitchen. He'd set Glo on a chair and was kneeling in front of her. Kelsey went over to her. Glo looked a little light-headed.

"The bullet seems to have nicked her shoulder. I'm not sure if it's broken or not, but she needs to get to a hospital."

"It's a two-hour drive to Helena," Wyatt said.

"And a twenty-minute flight," Gilly said. She looked at Reuben. "Let's go."

Gerri came over with a box of gauze bandages. "Let me tape her up. Tate will bring her down to the airstrip in a minute."

Reuben and Gilly headed for the door.

"I'll get our stuff," Kelsey said and went upstairs. She didn't even realize Knox was behind her until she entered her bedroom.

He closed the door behind her. "You're not going with them."

She rounded on him, and for a second, had nothing. "What—of course I am. Glo is my best friend—"

"And someone is out there, trying to hurt—maybe kill—you! You need to stay here, where I can take care of you."

So much emotion in his eyes, and in that moment, crazily, she heard...shoot...her father.

Run, Kelsey!

The memory swept through her, buckled her knees, and she pressed her hand to her chest.

Looked up at Knox. He wore such a fierceness in his countenance, as if he'd walk through fire for her—and without a doubt, she knew he would.

But trouble, disaster and danger seemed to simply follow her, and...

It wouldn't be long before he got hurt too. That he went down fighting.

That she lost someone else who had become her entire world.

"Knox—"

"No, Kelsey." He stepped closer, touched her shoulders. "Please, don't leave. We can drive to Helena, but...let me protect you."

"You can't, Knox. You can't—"

"Yes I can!"

Oh, she wanted to cry with the desire to just collapse into his arms. Somehow, she shook her head.

"Listen." He took a breath, as if schooling his voice. "It's what I do, Kelsey. You pegged it. I'm safe. I'm nice. I'm boring. I might even be an old soul. But that's also what makes me the guy who shows up to do the hard stuff, the dirty work, the manual labor. I'm the guy who makes dinner for his wife and does the laundry and stays home with the kids while she hangs out with her girlfriends. I'm the guy who builds a house on the rock and doesn't move when the storm hits. God *made* me to take care of you, to protect you."

Oh, sweet Knox. Kelsey ran the palms of her hands under her eyes. "I know."

He drew in a breath.

"I know you are," Kelsey said again, this time quietly. "And I know you'd like to promise me that nothing will ever happen to me again, but it's impossible. Don't you see—crazy things happen, and...I don't know why. Even if Russell is dead—"

"He is."

She held up her hand. "Even if—I need to be honest." Her eyes filled. "Meeting you, being here has been the most wonderful two weeks of my life. But clearly I've dragged you into something…"

He was shaking his head, something of horror on his face. "Maybe I've dragged *you* into something."

What? And her question must have emerged through her frown.

"Come with me." And in case she said no, he took her hand. Pulled her down the hall to his room. A cowboy's room, simple, with a dresser, a king bed, a rocking chair, and—

"Oh my. Knox, what—?"

He'd opened the closet and stepped back.

She stared at the collage taped to the back wall. "What is this?"

"I…I think there is more to the San Antonio bombing than they're telling us. And I've been doing some digging. I hired a private eye in San Antonio to track down these two guys." He had a photograph and now showed it to her. "I got this from a camera in the arena. Paid the security there to pull it for me, but do you recognize this guy?"

He pointed to a man, tall, dark, gauged ears, a port-wine stain that crept up his neck.

"This isn't a good view."

"No, but…" He took the picture from her. "Could it be?"

"I don't know—what is going on, Knox?"

"I think these guys were behind the bombing. And now one of them is here." He shook his head, ran a hand behind his neck. "Maybe they're after *me*."

He was simply being desperate, now. She kept her voice soft, hoping not to bruise him. "I don't know, but I have to go with Glo."

His mouth pinched tight.

"I'm sorry, Knox. I…"

"Fine. I'm right behind you."

"No, you're not." She reached up to touch his chest but made a fist and drew her hand back. "I've made up my mind…I'm taking the NBR-X gig, if Glo still wants it. I can't…I can't hide here with you. Clearly, I'm not safe anywhere. I need to keep moving. On the road, I'm in control. I know what I'm doing. Here—"

"You've gotten so used to living on the edge, it scares you to stop, to feel, to trust."

She stilled, his words stinging.

No. She'd…she'd just been fooling herself. She'd never outrun Vince Russell, never outrun the random tragedies of life, and the longer she hung around Knox Marshall, the sooner he'd get hurt. Or killed.

Protecting her.

But he wouldn't ever get that.

He stood there, his gaze fierce, shaking his head. "It's easier to pretend, isn't it?

"I don't—"

"You can't fake what we have between us, and that scares you more than whatever is out there, doesn't it? It's easier to be the performer onstage than the person who is scared and vulnerable and…who just wants to be loved."

She drew in a breath, so many words—

He took a step forward. "You don't need the bright lights and the cheering audience—"

Her voice pitched low and tight. "Are you seriously asking me to give up my career?"

That closed his mouth. Silence pulsed between them.

His voice softened. "I'm asking you to stop pretending that is enough."

She looked away. "It's what I've worked for, what I've always wanted."

He touched her arm. "Please, Kelsey. Don't let your fear keep you from us. From this."

She stepped away, crossed her arms, steeled herself before she met his eyes. "I'm just trying to be honest, Knox. I love your ranch, your life. But...I have a different life. It can't work. I'm sorry, I gotta go."

He turned, his jaw hard, but didn't follow her as she walked back to her room, collected her and Glo's belongings into a couple donated backpacks, and headed down the stairs.

She did see him, however, standing at the balcony as she followed Tate, carrying Glo, out the door.

I'm sorry, Knox.

Glo needed to fire Tate Marshall.

Because she simply could not fall in love with her bodyguard. It was too painfully cliché, too romance-novel-ish, too pitiful.

He'd practically carried her all the way to the hospital in Helena, clutching her to his chest.

His body had started to shake when he picked her up on the mountainside. Never mind that he'd taken off his shirt to bandage her, held her to that wet, hair-roughened chest—yeah, the pain nearly went away just breathing in the smell of him—smoky, sweaty, and desperate.

Oh, she was a goner because really, he smelled like a boys' locker room after a football game. And she would gladly bottle the smell and pay millions for it.

Her mother would be horrified.

Which was a point in his favor, actually.

When Tate had brought her into the house, she'd also gotten a good look in the light at the words of the tattoo that ran across his chest. *Surrender Is Not a Ranger Word.*

Huh.

His brother Wyatt had tossed him a shirt then, and her world calmed down a little. Enough that she didn't completely swoon when he picked her up again and brought her to a truck outside. He slid with her into the back seat and held her against the bumps as they drove down to the Marshall airfield.

The plane's seats were against the wall. He sat with her cradled on his lap, Kelsey beside her, looking stripped and heartbroken, trying to hide it behind her worry over Glo.

Really, Glo wasn't that hurt. Or perhaps it was the adrenaline, because it didn't feel like a gunshot wound should.

At first. The pain curdled in as they drew closer to the hospital. Reuben must have called ahead. An ambulance waited for them on the tarmac.

They had her under blessed pain killers, then in surgery, in an hour.

Which didn't bode well for her imagination. Every time she woke up, Tate sat by her bedside, his dark brown hair rumpled and cast up as if he'd been running his hands through it. And looking at her with those blue eyes that hung on to her as she sank back into the aftereffects of general anesthesia, as if begging her not to leave.

And then she dreamed. Saw him standing in the wings, his hands folded, his biceps thick as he listened to her sing. Felt his big hands on her when they'd danced, pulling her against him, twirling her out. Smelled his cottony shirt, the cologne he'd started wearing, something woodsy and rich. Tasted his breath, inches from her own, reeling her in, those lips millimeters from hers.

It left her breathless and hoping he'd be waiting when she came to again.

And he was, every time, all the way until morning when

the sun cascaded in through the large square picture window of her hospital room. Except now, his head lay on the bed, cradled in his folded arms, his eyes sweetly closed, exhaustion winning. The whiskers had returned after yesterday's shave, a light dusting of brown.

Oh, the man was handsome. And strong. And dependable. And her *bodyguard.*

Yeah, she needed to fire him, and pronto because…

Because she wanted more. Wanted to respond to that desire she saw in his eyes every time he looked at her. Wanted to fold his fingers between hers, sway to the music without warning sirens screaming and worse, tabloid headlines ticking across her brain.

Oh, Glo, what have you done now? Don't you know how this will look?

Thankfully, her mother was two thousand miles from here.

Probably Senator Reba Jackson hadn't the wildest clue what her only daughter had experienced the last few weeks.

But Tate did.

And clearly, so did Kelsey, because she lay on the sofa under the window, curled up on her backpack, her only belongings. Glo noticed her pack on the floor.

So, they were on the move again. She'd wondered how long the fairy tale with Knox would last. Although, she'd hoped for a happy ending. She'd half expected Kelsey to tell her last night that she wanted to stay.

Glo wasn't completely sure she'd argue.

Tate moved, and she touched her hand to his arm.

He lifted his head.

If she'd wondered at his feelings for her, they emerged right there in his eyes as he caught his breath, stared at her, his voice roughened. "Tell me you're okay."

"I don't know," she whispered. "You tell me."

He leaned up then and got her a drink of water, held the straw to her lips. "You didn't break any bones, and they just stitched you up. You're going to be fine."

She took a drink, the water freeing her parched mouth to clear her throat. Her hand closed on his arm. "How are you doing?"

He swallowed then, something raw and torn in his gaze. "I've never been so scared in my life, Glo."

Oh. Uh…

"And, yeah, okay, that's saying something considering the things I've seen and been through. But when I saw you lying there—you had so much blood on you I wasn't sure how badly you'd been hurt and I…" He drew in his breath, swallowed hard like he might be revisiting that moment.

His voice emerged shaky. "You were so…frail. And…" He closed his eyes, looked away as if trying to gather himself.

Oh, Tate. And with everything inside her she wanted to reach up and pull him to herself, to kiss him and tell him that the best day of her life was the day he'd invaded her life.

That she was terrified of reliving her worst fears, but maybe…maybe she could start calling him by his real name, could start letting him into her life.

Could believe that she could love again.

One true heart.

"Tate—" she whispered.

He looked over at her, his heart in his eyes.

And then he must have read her because he leaned over her, his gaze roaming hers, his fingers caressing her face. His mouth opened just slightly, and she grabbed his shirt with one finger to tug him closer. The smell of the night—smoke and fear and raw desperation—hung on his skin, and his beautiful eyes held hers.

"Glo," he said softly, "I—"

The door opened behind him.

"And then I want to have a press conference— Gloria. Sweetheart—there you are."

Tate jerked away from her.

She froze. "*Mother?*"

Senator Reba Jackson strode into the room like the presidential contender she was and stood at the end of her bed. She was sporting a fresh wash of amber-red in her shoulder-length hair and wore a pair of black dress pants, a white blouse, and gray blazer, and she looked like she'd already hit the gym, had her first cup of coffee, and was snapping her fingers at her assistant to deliver her a kale-orange-banana smoothie along with the freshest foreign affairs briefing. Only the slightest smudge in her mascara hinted that she'd probably taken a red-eye from DC to land in Glo's hospital room in the first blush of morning.

She hadn't changed a bit in the eighteen months since Glo had last seen her, at least in person. Her mother had made a point of FaceTime-ing her regularly in case Glo forgot she wasn't really a country music sensation. Heaven help her if her hobby overtook her true calling as spokeswoman for the Elect Reba campaign.

"Mother, what are doing here?"

Tate stepped back from the bed, and a glance in her periphery said he didn't know what to do, his arms folded across his chest.

Kelsey, however had risen, and who knew if she'd been witness to the almost kiss between Glo and Tate.

Glo's entire body still tingled.

"Senator Jackson," Kelsey said and walked over to her.

"Kelsey, honey. How are you?" She gave Kelsey a hug, something with a shade of warmth. Oh, look who was trying. She'd never been a fan of the Yankee Belles, although admittedly, she did like Kelsey.

The warmth stopped when she turned to Tate, however, and she gave her best shot of sending him to his knees with a look.

Oh. So they hadn't been quite quick enough...

Clearly, Tate would pay for that.

"And, who is this?" Glo's mother said, no smile.

And right then, Glo had a choice. She could end the game between them and yank Tate into her world with a simple *He's a friend.* Or she could keep him at a stiff-armed distance—

"He's our bodyguard," Kelsey said, answering for her.

Her mother raised an eyebrow, glanced at Glo, then back to Tate. "Keeping my little girl safe, are you?"

Tate's mouth thinned. "Yes, ma'am."

"I think you might need to work a little harder at it."

"I agree." He glanced at Glo, a fierce resignation in his eyes.

Her mother slid up to her bed and sat in the chair Tate had just vacated. Sighed. "This is all my fault."

Glo stared at her. "What—?"

Reba took her hand. "I'm so sorry to get you mixed up in this mess, honey, but when I heard about the bombing, I had my people look into it, and then last night's shooting—"

"How on earth did you find out?"

Reba frowned. "Honey. I'm your mother. I know things."

Maybe Glo didn't want to know.

"But the fact is...and probably I should have told you...I have recently received some death threats."

"Oh, Mother, you are always receiving death threats. You're on the Senate Armed Services Committee."

"Yes, but these relate to the campaign. The fact that I'm

rising in the polls."

"Excuse me, ma'am, but what death threats?"

Tate, behind her, sidled up. He wore an expression that scared Glo a little. "How serious are they?"

Reba leaned back and looked over. "I'm sorry, Mr.—"

"Marshall. Tate Marshall."

"You haven't been cleared by my security yet to know—"

"I'm *her* security. Your daughter's and the rest of the Yankee Belles, and if their lives have been in danger because of something you did, or know or—"

"That's enough." Reba got up. "I think your services are no longer needed here, Mr. Marshall."

His mouth opened, closed, and he shook his head. Then very quietly, "I'm sorry, ma'am, but you're not in charge here. Glo is."

Tate looked at her, something of possession in his eyes. As if he wanted to belong to her.

Yes. But not like this.

However, if she let him go, then...

Then her mother would have her under lock and key so fast Glo's world would close off at the top, strangle her. At least with Tate by her side, she could pretend she had some control over her life.

And if she had to spend twenty-four seven with personal protection...hello, Tate.

"Gloria," her mother corrected.

He took a breath, seem poised to argue—

"He works for me, Mother. And he's good at his job."

"You were shot."

"But he got me to the hospital and hasn't left my side, and if we had known we were in real danger—"

"This won't happen again, Senator. I give you my word. And my life, for Glo—Gloria's."

It was so sweet, resolute, she wanted to weep. Instead she met her mother's eyes and swallowed. Nodded. "Vet him, Mother. We did. You'll find that he knows what he's doing."

A flicker of a muscle moved in Tate's jaw.

Carter had vetted him, right?

Then Tate was nodding. "I'll keep her safe. All the Belles safe—"

"Oh no, she's done touring. Enough of this—"

"Mother. I have commitments, and my own life."

"And you may resume them as soon as we neutralize this current threat."

Glo glanced at Kelsey, who met Glo's eyes.

"No, Mother. We just accepted a six-month gig with the NBR-X. I can't let Kelsey and Dix down."

Kelsey sighed, nodded.

"I'll keep her safe, ma'am. It's my job," Tate said. No flinch, no glance in her direction. His job.

Yes.

"If you'll have your security people brief me on this threat, I can start working with my team to prepare for our next event."

His team? But good save, Tate.

Her mother's mouth tightened. But she took a breath and nodded.

She turned back to Glo. "You just rest, sweetheart. We'll get this sorted out. Everything is going to be okay."

Then she turned and motioned for Tate to follow her outside.

Kelsey took Glo's hand, met her eyes, and gave her a small, pained smile. "So, the adventure continues."

Apparently, no one was getting a happy ending.

12

Tate wasn't going to let it happen again.

Nearly kissing her. No, nearly losing her twice.

And it wasn't just losing her by some terrorist shooter, but by Glo's very large and in-charge mother who came with a security team to rival a Gambino mob boss.

He was used to mob boss security personnel types—dark, beefy, and focused. Had been one, once upon a time.

What had him on edge was the very serious, very lethal threats on Reba's—and Glo's—lives. The fist in his gut had only tightened reading the emails from the Bryant League, a group of social revolutionists.

Tate prowled the hallway outside Glo's room, his Bluetooth to his ear, on the phone to Knox.

Inside, Glo was getting ready to check out of the hospital after her twelve-hour stay. She'd move to a nearby hotel, then tomorrow they'd fly to…and his chest tightened.

Vegas.

He blew out a breath. He'd just have to keep his head down, hope that Malovich's men had dispersed, forgotten him.

Not hardly, but he couldn't think about that now.

Now, he had to figure out how to keep the Belles safe.

Which meant his own team, buddies he'd put a callout to under the radar, but the kind who would have his back.

And then there was his family.

"So, you're telling me none of this had to do with Vince Russell?" Knox said through the line. He had the phone on speakerphone, and from Tate's understanding, the entire remaining Marshall clan, with the exclusion of their mother, crowded into Knox's office to get the update on Glo and Kelsey.

Today, the town of Geraldine would congregate in the Marshall yard. Apparently, when Knox and the rest of the family had sat her down to cancel the party, she responded with, "We're not going to let evil win. As long as Glo and Kelsey are okay, I'm going to celebrate my family and my friends—and the fact that no one died, again."

A small part of him still died every time he closed his eyes and saw Glo lying in a pool of her own blood. He blew out a breath and continued the debriefing with his family.

"According to Senator Jackson, the threats started coming in weeks before the bombing in Texas, very specific about her stepping back from her run for office, or her—and her family members—getting hurt. Specifically, Glo."

"Who is this group?" Reuben's voice came over the line, and Tate imagined his big brother leaning over the desk, one strong hand bracing him.

"They're called the Bryant League, an offshoot of a group called the World Can't Wait, or WCW."

"Aren't they an affiliate of the Revolutionary Communist Party?" Ruby Jane asked. And of course, she would have heard of the radical left-wing group. "The RCP is an isolationist group—anti-war—but they're also for isolation and socialist reform, calling for individual groups to fight back against government crimes, everything from the torture of military detainees to wiretapping. Which has led to a number of wildcat terrorist strikes that have been attributed to them."

"Wildcat?" Wyatt asked.

"Unsanctioned attacks meant to put pressure on governments—or even the organization—to act," Ruby Jane said. Her voice got closer. "Want me to do some checking into recent activity, Tate?"

"Yeah. And especially Arnie Gibbs, the so-called bomber from Texas. See if he has any affiliations. So far, Jackson's people haven't dug up much, but I think they're just trying to get in front of it. She has a number of events coming up, including a huge fundraiser in Nashville in a few weeks that is drawing a lot of media attention."

Silence, and he looked around to see if his voice bounced down the hallway. But he'd stalked down to a far corner of the waiting room and stood next to a wall and window, his voice low.

He didn't need Jackson's people hunting him down and accusing him of leaking something to the press.

Still, they all needed to prepare for the worst, so, "Knox, now is the time to show Ruby Jane your closet."

"He already did," RJ said. "Scary, but...now we have something to start connecting the dots."

"And what about you...and, um, the Belles?" Knox asked, and Tate knew he was fighting the urge to ask about Kelsey.

Tate wasn't sure what went down between them last night, but from the dark, pained looked on Knox's face as Kelsey had followed him and Glo from the house, it didn't look good. Add that to the fact that Knox wasn't here, prowling the hallways with him, told him that Kelsey had put the kibosh on the romance between them.

Sorry, Knox. Because frankly, given the hollowed-out, whitened look Kelsey wore today after Senator Jackson's news, she could probably use Knox's solid presence.

In truth, *Tate* would appreciate Knox's solid presence. He wasn't thrilled about stepping his foot back on the soil of Sin City. But he wasn't going to leave Glo—or the rest of the Belles—unprotected, or worse, protected by grunts who didn't know them.

Didn't know the demons that chased Kelsey, that she needed extra time in her dressing room to get out of her head and onto the stage. Or how Dixie's neck got so tight that she needed an ice pack after her set. Or that Glo had to figure out how to slough off her stress. She'd spent the few minutes before she went onstage during their last gig waging a thumb war with him. Of course, he'd let her win.

C'mon, McClane, don't let me take you down.

No, he wasn't going to let anyone else be the recipient of Glo's nicknames.

Which meant he'd have to tame the flame she'd stirred up inside him, the one that nearly flashed over when she'd tucked her finger into the neck of his shirt, tugging him toward her lips.

His mouth had gone a little dry, the look in her eyes rising to thump him in the chest.

Finally.

Except, no. Not now.

Maybe not ever.

And maybe he'd been reading her wrong anyway, because she sure went quiet when Kelsey assured her mother that he was just her employee.

That was enough. It had to be.

"I'm heading to Vegas. The NBR-X has an event at the end of the week, and the band is flying in, meeting there for rehearsal, then the gig."

Silence, and yes, they'd heard him right.

"They're going to perform? After...how's Glo?"

"She says she'll be fine." Tate leaned against the wall, glancing down the hall. "She's tough. No broken bones, but she's pretty bruised and hurting. Honestly,"—he ran a hand through his hair—"I think she's just trying to stay out of her mother's clutches. Senator Jackson is...she's a real piece of work."

"Why would this group be after the senator?" Reuben asked.

"She's progressive. She wants peace and global connections and alliances...all which the Bryant League translates into America's illicit activity in foreign countries. Add to that she's a member of the Armed Services Committee and is probably solely responsible for deaths in Iraq and Afghanistan, if you ask them."

"And Glo and Kelsey are involved, how?"

"Proxy. Pressure. In other words, collateral damage."

"I'll do my homework," Ruby Jane said. "And ask around."

"I should be there," Knox said darkly. His sigh of frustration blew through the phone line. "I knew there was more to the bombing than just Arnie Gibbs."

"Any trace of the shooter?" Tate asked.

"Nothing," Reuben said. "We searched the yard, found some tracks that led to the lower pasture. We figure he parked there and approached from the southeast. Fired the barn to get our attention, then went after the girls—no, Glo."

"How's Kelsey?" Gilly asked.

Tate hadn't known she was in the room. "Seems okay. Quiet."

He heard the muffled sounds of the phone going off

speaker, then Knox's voice, closer. "Are you sure about this, Tate? It's Vegas and...should we be worried for you?"

Huh. Tate hadn't figured that Knox knew anything about his past, of what went down in Vegas, of the Malovich takedown.

Of Tate's own collection of death threats.

"No. I'll keep my head down. Besides, what was it that you said—I have the skills of a mafia thug?"

He got a slight chuckle.

"Listen. We'll be okay. Nothing is going to happen to Glo, Dixie, or Kelsey on my watch. I promise, bro. How are things going with Ma's party?"

"You're missing some serious barbecue. And the barn isn't as bad as we thought—mostly surface damage."

"Tell Ma I'm sorry."

"She gets it, Tate. And..."

He trailed off, and Tate wasn't sure if he wanted to give Kelsey a message or maybe offer to help or...

"Stay safe, Tate."

Oh. He shrugged away the tightness in his throat. "Of course. It's me. I make trouble, not the other way around."

Knox harrumphed but hung up.

Tate slipped the phone into his pocket and was just turning when he spotted Glo and Kelsey emerging from the room. A nurse pushed Glo in a wheelchair.

He headed down the hallway. "I got this," he said to the nurse and took the handles as the nurse walked with them to the elevator.

"No wheelies, Andretti," Glo said, glancing up at him, offering a tentative smile.

Not Tate. That was probably for the best.

"I got this, boss," he said and winked at her.

"Is that the insurance adjuster prowling around outside?"

Knox looked up from where he stood at his window, watching the portly, bald man from Helena traipsing around his barn, taking pictures.

He turned to Reuben's voice, spotted him standing in the doorway to his office.

"I'm staying out of his way."

"Or feeling like you want to hit somebody, so you've decided to brood in your office." Reuben came in and shut the door behind him.

"I'm not brooding." Knox turned away from the window. But even from his countenance, flashing so quickly in the reflection in the window, he had *miserable* written in his furrowed brow and gritty, bloodshot eyes.

Five days had passed since a terrorist showed up at the ranch, but Knox kept reliving seeing Kelsey crouched over Glo, kept feeling his heart jerk out of his body. Most of the time he woke in a cold sweat, biting back a shout.

It can't work. Translation. He wasn't enough to keep her here. To build a life with.

Then, unable to sleep, he'd sit in the darkness, the moon waxing through his room, listening to her words, fighting them.

Except, maybe she was right. What was he going to do, give up his ranch, his life to be her—what—groupie?

And no, he couldn't ask her to give up her career, her dreams, everything she'd worked for.

Which meant he spent another hour staring at the ceiling, thinking about her sweet voice, the woman he'd seen onstage, and the cruel words he'd thrown at her. *It's easier to be the performer onstage than the person who is scared and vulnerable and...who just wants to be loved.*

Yeah, what a jerk. Because didn't they all feel that way?

It was easier for him to bury himself in work, in the to-do list on the ranch than to let himself acknowledge for a moment that he'd met someone who made him feel like he was exactly who he should be. Nice. Safe. And the guy who believed in the old-fashioned, happy ending.

Which then made him throw back his covers and spend the rest of the night unsnarling the finances of the ranch. At least it made him feel as if he might be accomplishing something. Instead of sitting around letting the woman he loved become—what had Tate called it? Collateral damage.

Brooding might be exactly the right term.

"Dude," Reuben said now, "you're the definition of darkness. I've never seen a guy so determined to pretend he's happy. I thought your face would crack on Saturday from the forced smiling."

"What? I was happy. It was Ma's birthday."

"Like a man tied to a stake in the sun is happy he's getting a tan. C'mon—you just lost the woman you love."

"I don't..."

Reuben raised an eyebrow, held up his hand. "Listen, I get it. Believe me, I didn't want to face the fact that I was in love with Gilly until...until I thought she'd *died*. And it was the worst few hours of my life."

Knox stared at him, still a little bruised from the excruciating hour it'd taken to find Kelsey and Glo. "Fine. Yes. Okay. I'm in love with her. Around her, I feel like I can be me. And maybe I am boring and safe and nice, but...she makes that okay."

"I've never, not once thought of you as nice, just so we're clear." Reuben was smiling.

"Funny." Knox shook his head. "Truth is, with everything

inside me, I want to go to Vegas. And every second that Tate doesn't call me, I'm losing my mind."

"Then go."

"I can't—I need to get the repairs on the barn going and finalize the purchase of Calamity Jane with the bank and start the training on the younger bulls and—"

"Oh, for Pete's sake—*stop!*"

Knox raised an eyebrow.

"This is what you do, bro. You pile up your life with stuff, then brood about how stuck you are. Has it occurred to you that God has given you a chance to have something more, if you have the guts to take it?"

Knox just blinked at him. "What are you—"

"For the smart one, you are so bad at the math. First, Kelsey is in love with you."

He shook his head against the words, the swift rush of desire. What if? But, "No, she said she doesn't want me."

"C'mon. Yeah, she does. She's just scared." Reuben sat down in one of the leather chairs.

"When did you become an expert on women?"

"I'm not—this is Gilly's insight, but she's probably right. A woman who has been through what Kelsey has is going to run from the first sign of getting hurt. Physically and emotionally."

"I would never hurt her."

"Yeah, actually, you will, even if you try not to, but that's beside the point." Reuben leaned back and crossed his leg across his knee. "She needs you to be bigger than her fears. Stronger than her rejection. And yes, if you truly believe that she doesn't want you in her life, then you have to let her go. But a woman who opens her heart up wants to know she will be protected."

"How can I protect someone who says they don't want

to be protected?"

"You show up. You wait. You give. You sacrifice. You love anyway."

Knox nodded, looked out the window. The sky arched blue, the clouds wispy over the dark-edged line of mountains. "People need me here."

"Oh, bro. You and Kelsey are so much alike, and you don't even see it. She thinks she needs to keep moving to stay safe. You're afraid to leave."

Knox frowned at him. "I'm not afraid—"

"You're terrified, bro. You think it's all going to fall apart without you."

"The ranch is my responsibility! Dad counted on me to be here, and...and I wasn't. *I wasn't here.* I was off chasing some silly dream of being a bull rider, and...it got him killed."

A muscle pulled in Reuben's jaw. "Yeah. You're not the only one who thinks that."

Knox frowned at him.

"Dad wanted me to be a firefighter—after he told me to leave, he sent a letter to my old jump boss, Jock, and asked him to teach me. But I never got over the sense that I should have come back, should have been here. If I had then maybe Dad wouldn't have been alone."

Knox drew in a breath, this throat tight.

"And you wouldn't have had to give up your so-called silly dreams of being a bull rider. You were good at it. Much better than I ever was, and you deserved your shot."

Knox looked at him.

"I'm sorry, bro. I should have been a better big brother to you. I was so angry about my life, and stupid Chelsea, I abandoned you. And you had to stick around and pick up the pieces. But...I'm here now. And I want to help." He leaned forward. "And for the record, I forgive you for Chelsea." He shook his head. "She was wild and I knew it, and frankly, you probably saved me from getting into big trouble there."

Knox pursed his lips. "You finding us probably saved me...well, you know..."

Reuben gave a soft nod.

"I've tried very hard to be the man Dad wanted me to be," Knox said quietly.

"Me too," Reuben said. "Still trying."

Knox let the silence pass between them, his fingers absently running over the taped song lyrics on the desk. His gaze went to it, then back to Reuben.

"Who do you see when you look at Jesus?"

Reuben frowned, then, "Oh, you're being Dad. He used to ask us that. I never knew what to answer—"

"Me either. But ever since Dad died, and maybe even since you left, whenever I dared look at Jesus, I saw anger. But what if...what if I was looking at Jesus through the lens of my own shame. My own self-judgment. I saw what I thought I deserved."

"Okay, I take it back, you are smarter than you look."

Knox offered a small harrumph. "And then, I just stopped looking, put my head down, and kept working."

Reuben nodded. "Yeah, I get that. Sometimes it's just easier to do the things we know will make us feel better than simply stopping to...I don't know, receive. It's like what happens when we get a water dump—we take cover and let the bombers take out the fire around us. They do all the work."

"Stand back and see what I will do," Knox mumbled. "Remember that verse Dad used to quote, from Exodus? After Moses tried everything with Pharaoh?"

"Exodus 14:13. 'Do not be afraid. Stand firm and you will see the deliverance the Lord will bring you today,'"

Rueben said softly.

Knox nodded, his eyes turning gritty. "What if that's the key to the entire thing? To stop and look up and...truly see Jesus. Believe Him at His word, that He loves us. That we shouldn't assign how we feel about ourselves to Jesus. Maybe He loves us. Nothing else."

"I think I figured it out. You're sitting in the big leather chair. Dad is rubbing off on you, because now you're starting to sound like him," Reuben said.

Heat rushed over Knox, through him, touched his bones, and he looked away, his eyes burning.

"You know, bro, maybe if we saw love more in each other, it might be easier to look up and accept it from God."

Knox looked at him. "Clearly it's not the chair."

Reuben lifted a shoulder. "Gilly's dad is a preacher. Something might have stuck."

Knox sighed. "I'm sorry, Reuben. For everything. I was...I was so jealous of you. And Wyatt and Tate and even Ford. Jealous that you got to run off and live your lives, and I pined for my stupid bull-riding dream. And who knows if I would have made it into the PBR, but—but that's not the point. I kept looking at your lives, and I hated mine. I thought it was...boring, I guess."

"And then Kelsey walked in," Reuben said, smiling. "And your boring became her sexy."

Safe is a good thing, you know. Kelsey walked into his head, took a seat on his lap, leaned her lips close to his, and his mouth dried. Especially when he heard his own words to her.

Have you not met me? I'm the guy who sticks around. Who keeps his promises—or tries with everything inside him to. I show up. And I stick around. You can count on me. I made you a promise back in Texas, and I intend to keep it.

He shook his head. Some promise keeper he was. "Maybe it's time I was reckless."

Reuben gave him a slow grin. "Maybe." He got up. "The insurance guy is headed this way. I'm going to go talk to him—I'd like to get started on the barn, and I need to see how much we might get for it." He got up, but then stopped at the door. "Let me be the brother you need me to be. You—go do something crazy."

Knox nodded. He ran his fingers over the lyrics on the desk.

Be Thou my Vision, O Lord of my heart
Naught be all else to me, save that Thou art

Oh, Dad. How Knox missed him.

Who is Jesus to you, son?

He closed his eyes, heard the question.

He'd have to look up to find out, perhaps.

You'll never find your path by looking at yourself, Knox.

He drew in a breath, hearing his father's voice, that last time they'd ridden fence together. *You want to find your way, keep looking up.*

Except, he hadn't even been moving, too safe.

Not anymore.

Lord, help me to see You. To put my focus not on myself, and not on my brothers, but on You. On Your love. Be my vision, Lord.

The phone buzzed, and he opened his eyes. Read the caller ID.

"Rafe. What's up?" He glanced outside, saw Reuben talking with the insurance man.

"Hey, Knox." Rafe's easy tone was clipped. "NBR-X is in trouble. I need you to come to Vegas. And I need you to bring Gordo."

"I'll get the pizzas."

Tate glanced around the room, his gaze landing on Kelsey, then Glo before he added, "Don't let anyone in but me, but I have my key, so, just don't let anyone in."

"Aye-aye, Master Chief."

Tate gave Glo a small glare but didn't hide the tiny grin as he left.

"What's with you two?" Kelsey asked. They'd been acting weirdly since they left the hospital in Helena.

Glo looked at her. "Nothing." She adjusted her sling, something she put on after today's rehearsal. She sat on the sofa of the suite, her head against a mound of pillows Tate had built for her. She wore a pair of yoga pants and an over-sized T-shirt down to her knees, probably in defiance of her mother's attempts to clean her up in case the press tracked them down between rehearsals.

Senator Jackson had already made a statement about her daughter's "accident," leaving out the death threats. She'd added a couple security personnel to Glo's detail, under Tate's direction.

Tate had spent the last five days working with the security team at the Las Vegas Western Complex, a venue used for everything from sporting events to motorcycle shows. And of course, rodeo and country music. He had also briefed the security team about the bombing in San Antonio, and they created another layer of security around the stock areas.

Dixie came in from the kitchenette area of the suite holding a couple ice teas and handed one to Glo before she slid onto the sofa and put Glo's feet on her lap. "I think we have the finale nailed."

"Just like you planned it, Kels. Way to go." Glo lifted her

bottle.

"As long as I don't freak out." She hadn't, not once, in practice, but the threat sat in her gut, tugging.

Vince Russell was not out there in the darkness waiting to kill her. She hadn't even been the target.

She'd just been an innocent bystander, a tourist in the park.

A random victim.

Her words to Knox kept pinging back to her every time she walked onstage and took the mic, looked out over the auditorium. *I need to keep moving. On the road, I'm in control. I know what I'm doing.*

Or not. Because yes, she knew all the harmonies, had the show embedded inside her, but frankly...Knox was right. It was easier to be a performer onstage than to...

Than to rely on someone to show up just when you needed them. To reach out and hope that person—even God, maybe—would catch you.

I won't let you fall. I'm going to get you out of this.

She had to stop thinking about Knox. The way he folded his fingers between hers, the way she lost her name when he looked in her eyes.

She hadn't slept well for a week, not until she turned on the television and found a hockey game. Wyatt's team had lost last night. Probably she should stop watching the Blue Ox.

"You're not going to freak out," Dixie said. "But I do have an idea..." She picked at the label of her bottle, glanced at Glo. "What if Glo sang 'One True Heart'?"

Kelsey looked at her, then Glo, who stared at Dixie as if she'd asked her to streak across stage.

"No—"

"Yes," Kelsey said. "It's a great idea. You're not playing

tomorrow night, and you need your own spotlight. This is a great idea!"

"No!" Glo said. Took her feet away from Dixie. "I…I'm not ready."

"Yes, you are. I hear you singing it all the time, in the shower, in the bus—"

Glo was shaking her head.

"Glo," Dixie said, touching her foot. "I see the way you look at Tate, and I know…he's just your bodyguard." She finger-quoted the words.

"Our bodyguard," Glo said, a little fire in her words.

"Hardly. Sure, he'd take a bullet for me, but he'd do it walking across fire for you, honey," Dixie said.

"It doesn't matter. He can't…we're not—"

"Fine. But it doesn't mean your heart isn't ready to love again. And…it's time you sang your song," Kelsey said.

Glo's chest rose and fell. She looked at Kelsey, then Dixie. Then, "If I have to bare my soul onstage, then Kelsey does too."

Huh?

Glo turned to her. "I heard the song you were working on at the Marshalls'. And in your room. I wanna hear it."

Kelsey froze. Shook her head. "No, it's not finished. It's…it's…"

"About Knox, isn't it?" Glo said.

Kelsey looked away, at the darkness pressing into the windows, the lights of the Vegas skyline glittering, a kaleidoscope of colors. "It's about fear and…love. And what-ifs—"

"So, that's a yes," Dixie said. "Let's hear it." She slid off the sofa and headed over to her violin case, opening it. She grabbed her violin, then Glo's Dobro and walked over to the sofa.

Glo sat with the instrument pocketed into her lap. Dixie

sat down, raised an eyebrow.

"Fine, but…it's not done. It's…a mess. I told you that I can't write a song."

She reached for her guitar. Took a breath. "It's a little sappy."

"Please. It's a country song," Dixie said. "It had better be about lost love, or I'm turning in my bow."

"Fine." Kelsey had worked out a few chords but let her voice lead the way.

He said hold on to me, and don't let go
Don't be afraid, don't say no.
Hold on, lean in
What if I said yes, what if I believed
What if I reached back until I could see
That my tomorrow was with you.

He said don't cry, honey, you're safe with me
My love, babe, can set you free
Hold on, lean in
What if I said yes, when he asked to dance
What if I reached out, grabbed hold of his hand
Said my tomorrow was with you.

She let the song die out. "So, I need a chorus and a final verse…"

But Glo had picked up the melody and looked at Kelsey. "My mind said no. My heart said yes…"

Dixie was nodding. "My mind said whoa… My heart felt his caress."

Yes. She had felt Knox's caress on her heart. Something pure and right and beautiful.

Hold on, lean in.

She was humming, let the words spill out. "Hold on, lean in. I'd do it right this time, if I could do it all again…"

Her breath caught, and she looked up as Glo nodded, continued playing.

He took my hand, said babe, let's fly away
To our tomorrows, we'll start them today
Hold on, lean in
So I will trust you, I'll give us a try.
Take my love, baby, please don't let it die
There is no tomorrow, not without you.

Glo finished the song with a lick, and then looked up, grinning. "It's a start."

"It's more than a start," said Tate. He closed the door with his foot. "It's good." He brought the pizza over to the counter. "A new Yankee Belle hit."

"It's Kelsey's song," said Glo.

"No, it's—"

"It's about Knox," Dixie said, and Kelsey closed her eyes.

"Really," Tate said quietly.

She couldn't look at him. Instead she set the guitar down. "It's not. It's about…what-ifs, and…I don't know…"

Tate grabbed a stack of plates. Turned. He wore a dress shirt and a pair of jeans, and the resemblance to Knox that night at the Bulldog could almost knock her over.

What if.

She blew out a breath. "I need some air." She was heading for the hallway when Tate came over and put his hand on the door. "Not so fast."

"Tate."

"Fine. But I'm going with you." He turned, glanced at the girls. "Don't—"

"Let anyone in but you. We got it, Captain America," Glo said as she got up.

"I was going to say don't eat all the pizza, but that too." He released the door, and Kelsey opened it.

"Really, I am safe—"

"Yeah, I agree, but humor me," Tate said. "Besides, I think I know what you need. Follow me."

He led her toward the stairwell at the end of the hall, then walked them up more flights to the top. But didn't stop there. He pulled down the stairs hooked to the top level and affixed them to the floor. "The skyline is amazing from up here."

Oh, she liked Tate, especially when he wore the same look Knox had the day he'd suggested the Ferris wheel.

He opened the door to the roof, climbed out, and held out his hand. She hesitated only a moment, then took it and let him pull her up.

A gravel surface, filled with electrical and HVAC boxes, but beyond the edge of the roof, Vegas sprawled glittering under the black sky. Tate walked her over to the edge and then let go of her hand.

Silence edged between them. Then, "You okay, Kels?"

She took a breath, then, "Oh Tate, I...I don't know." She curled her hands around her waist. "I know what I did was the right thing—I can't take your brother away from his life. But...I..."

"What if?"

She looked at him and slowly nodded.

"Yeah, I know," he said quietly.

She sighed. "He accused me of hiding inside the person I am onstage...and maybe he was right. I know this world."

"But you wanted the other one."

"I don't know. I...I think I just wanted..." She sighed.

"It doesn't matter."

Tate stood beside her, saying nothing, and just his presence made her ache for Knox.

"Knox used to drive me crazy. We'd be out riding fence, hours and hours of mundane work in the spring, looking for breaks in the barbed wire, and I'd just...I'd want to go home. I hated every minute of it, but Knox—no, when you rode fence with Knox, you rode to the bitter end. You checked every cotton-pickin' inch of that fencing because he refused to be the guy who let one of our cows get hurt or wander off our land." He shook his head. "Knox is the guy who gets it right."

"Safe. Nice. He even called himself boring."

"Oh, Knox is not boring. He wanted to be a bull rider, but my dad said he had to learn how bulls think, too, so he made him be a clown for a while."

"A clown?"

"Yeah. They distract the bull after the rider is bucked off. It's dangerous, but Knox...he was crazy good at it. He could read a bull, tell which way it would go, taunt it, then run the other direction. He'd pull the bull rope and play with the animal, herding the animal right into the pen like it was coming home for dinner. And then he'd work the audience for the next cowboy. Everybody loved Knox the rodeo clown."

"I can't even imagine him doing that."

Tate lifted a shoulder. "He gave it up when he started seriously riding bulls—mostly did the clowning for local rodeos. But it's still in him—the desire to protect. Only now he channels it into the ranch."

And, toward her.

She looked away, nodded. "I've never felt so...safe as when I was with Knox."

"I'll try not to take that as a criticism."

She laughed. "No, I mean…he just…he has a way of looking at me. And yeah, he has those eyes…that…well, they're a little dangerous…"

He glanced at her, but she didn't meet his eyes.

"But he also calms the churning inside," she said softly. "Something came back to life inside me when I was with him. He made me believe that maybe…maybe I didn't have to be afraid all the time."

"'Lead me to the towering rock of safety, for you are my safe refuge.'"

She glanced at him. "Your mom said that."

"It's one of her favorite psalms. She said that you always have to look for the high places to get a different view and for a firm place to stand." He glanced down at her. "Of course, Ma always means Jesus, but I suppose it could work for Knox too. He's a pretty big guy."

Tate's words wove through her, settled, and in their wake, she heard Gerri.

It's how God shows us He loves us too—through the way we reach out and hold on to each other.

Like Knox had held on to her.

God made me to take care of you, to protect you.

She ran her hands up her bare arms, her gaze on Vegas.

What if…what if God had shown up in her life through Knox? She drew in a breath. *Your soul is thirsty.*

It was. So very thirsty.

Lord, if You're out there, please… She didn't even know what to ask for.

Or rather, she did.

But she'd already said no to her tomorrows.

13

Kelsey, you're wound so tight I think I'm going to lose the hotdog I had for supper just looking at you. Please, take a freakin' breath. Everything is going to be okay."
Tate stood in the doorway of the Yankee Belles' dressing room, one hand on the jamb, the other looking out toward the concourse of the Las Vegas Western Complex.

The smell of animal flesh, dirt, beer, and a hint of manure filtered down the hall, mixed with the concession area offerings of popcorn, pizza, and ball park dogs, and didn't help the mess in Kelsey's gut.

And not because she was afraid. Tate had distributed the two pictures of the men suspected in the bombing in San Antonio. Plus, he'd cordoned off the Belles' dressing area with double security. He wore an earpiece and had spent not a little time briefing the crew of the arena of possible threats.

No, they were probably safe from whoever wanted to hurt Glo.

And she'd run through her set without a glitch in rehearsal. Not a moment of hesitation as the lights fell, nothing to take her by the throat and send her to her knees.

Tate was right—everything was going to be okay.

Except she'd probably put too much hope in the idea that Knox might show up. Had shot a bullet prayer into the heavens with too much expectancy.

Silly.

He wasn't coming, and of course not because she'd walked away. Told him not to follow.

The man probably came to his senses. Who wanted this life anyway—playing in dirty stadiums, staying up until all hours, pasting on a smile…

Down the hall, the crowd cheered as another poor cowboy got thrown from a bull. She glanced at the clock. Thirty minutes to showtime—the rodeo was nearly over. And NBR-X had sold out tonight, thanks in part to a killer bull they'd brought in to impress the crowd. Were pitting some old PBR rider against him.

Apparently, rodeogoers had been spooked by the events in San Antonio, but maybe after tonight—and her concert— they might get back on track.

Dixie's violins were lined up against the wall, and now she sat in a chair, checking her phone. She looked amazing tonight in a pair of black leather pants and a white, sequined shirt, her long blonde hair down and twined with flowers.

Glo sat with one leg over the arm of a lounge chair, picking at her Dobro. Her arm had healed fast, but not enough for her to play tonight. Carter had hired a guy from Vegas who'd rehearsed with them for the week.

Elijah Blue was out in the wings, hanging with him somewhere.

Glo had opted for a short, black tiered dress with flouncy long sleeves, and red cowboy boots that showed off her legs. One look at Tate's face when he'd knocked on the door to check on them, his gaze lingering on Glo, said that despite her efforts, he still saw her injury. What he'd nearly lost. Poor man, he recovered quickly, hiding it, but she sort of hoped that she'd see that look of desire on Knox's face again, someday.

Apparently not.

Kelsey wore a pair of cutoff jean shorts, a white over-sized blouse with cutout shoulders, and fringed boots. No feathers tonight, but she did braid one thick section of hair and let it fall into the tousles of the rest.

"C'mon," she said, pushing herself out of the chair. "Let's go watch the rodeo."

Dixie looked up at her, raised an eyebrow. "Really?"

"I have to get out of my head. So, I'll go watch strong, brave men try to cheat death."

"I'm in," Dixie said and got up.

Glo put down her Dobro. "I'm always in the mood for eye candy."

Tate's mouth tightened as he stepped back to let them through. "Just stay in the hallway. I don't want anyone to see you."

Tonight's stage would be pushed out onto the arena floor after the rodeo. Kelsey walked down the tiny hallway, standing at the opening that led out to the auditorium. A walkway ringed the arena floor, a shelf that separated the dirt from the stands.

NBR-X had thrown everything into this night. American flags hung from the ceiling in between banners printed with the pictures of rodeo and stock champions. Her gaze fell on the one of a white bull and a handsome cowboy with a half smile, a dangerous twinkle in his eyes. He looked familiar, but she dismissed him as one of the regular bull riders who competed in the NBR-X events.

She hoped the man lived through this night.

She heard a shout, then the crowd roared as in the arena a black-hided bull burst from the pen, twisting its body as a cowboy gripped the bull rope, his red chaps flying.

"It looks so painful," Glo said, coming up to stand beside her. Dixie was leaning against the wall across from her.

"It is. You can sprain your wrist, tear ligaments in your arm, break fingers, strain your back, not to mention break your neck and get gored," Tate said. "It's for the crazy, or maybe the not real bright. These guys have landed on their heads one too many times."

"Knox was a bull rider." She glanced over her shoulder to Tate.

He was grinning. "I know."

Oh. She grinned back, and it eased the deep ache for a moment.

As if he might be suggesting that Knox was an idiot for not running after her.

She turned back to the rider, now scrabbling through the dirt toward the rail. The rodeo clown distracted the bull, then ran to the rail to dodge the animal as it charged.

Tate's words about Knox the rodeo clown thrummed in her head. *He could read a bull, tell which way it would go, taunt it, then run the other direction.*

She refused to apply that comparison to her. Maybe she'd done the taunting, then ran the other direction.

This clearly wasn't working to get him out of her head.

The lights suddenly went down in the arena, and a spotlight hit the center floor as a cowboy walked to the middle. He looked familiar.

Right. Tori's dad, from San Antonio.

He raised his mic and waved to the crowd. Good-looking with brown hair, a lazy smile that tweaked up one side, and a lean, sculpted body outlined in a teal blue snap-button shirt, and a pair of black chaps and a black Stetson. "Hey, y'all. My name is Rafe Noble, and I'm one of the NBR-X organizers. Thanks for comin' out tonight! I hope y'all are having fun!"

The crowd rose to his greeting with a roar of applause.

"Rafe is a three-time champion bull rider with the PBR," Tate said as the applause died.

"We have a special treat for you tonight. A couple of old cronies coming out of retirement for one spectacular ride tonight, just for you."

The crowd began to murmur.

He turned, and someone was running out into the area holding a protective vest and a helmet. Rafe handed the man the mic and donned the vest as the murmurs grew. He grabbed the mic again.

"It's a great night to get back on a bull."

"Oh my…" Tate said, almost in a whisper. "He's going to get killed."

The crowd was roaring, and Rafe held up his hand. "And the bull I'm going to ride is a champion himself, a three-time PBR Bull of the Year, with a power ranking of 90.14 and an average buck off rank of 86.7 percent. Out of fifty-one attempts, only seven cowboys have stayed on this powerhouse. He's a nineteen-hundred-pound monster, nine years old, and was the sire of PRB champion bull Hot Pete, who passed away recently. And tonight he's back, for one show only, to see if he can get another old dog off his back!"

The spotlight shifted away from Rafe and over to the bucking pen.

Kelsey drew in a breath as the light lit up the animal. But her gaze didn't land on the massive, leathery white Brahma bull who bucked in his chute, giving life to Rafe's words, but—

But on the man who stood on the gate, settling the bull down. He wore a red shirt with the NBR-X logo on the front, a white hat, and as the spotlight settled on him, he looked up and waved.

"Let's give a warm welcome to Gordo the Bonebreaker!"

Knox Marshall smiled, reached down and patted his animal as if he might be the family dog.

And if she'd forgotten the stun power of this man, it swept back through Kelsey, his smile, the dangerous stubble across his chin that made her clench her hands. Wide shoulders, lean hips, and he looked a little like a bull-riding champion himself.

The crowd roared—for Gordo, probably also for Knox—and then the lights went back to Rafe. "You ready to get 'er done?"

Kelsey turned her back against the cement wall as the crowd cheered whatever was happening down in the arena. She pressed her hand to her chest.

"Are you okay?" Tate said, turning to her, his eyes clouding.

She closed her eyes. "He's here. Knox is here."

Tate went silent.

She opened her eyes. He was pinching his mouth tight.

"Wait—did you know?"

He shook his head. "He called and left a voice message, but I've been too busy to check it. I didn't know. I'm so sorry..." He glanced back at the arena. "Rafe's getting on Gordo."

Knox was here.

And...he hadn't called her. Hadn't tracked her down.

Her eyes burned, but she refused the emotions that filled her throat. *Don't let your fear keep you from us.*

She turned, her hands around her body, holding on, watching the jumbotron as Rafe stood over the old bull. Gordo was moving around in the chute, but Rafe pounded his hand down onto the bull rope, then settled on the bull.

Tate sucked in his breath as the entire arena went quiet.

Knox bent over Rafe, holding his arm. Rafe wrapped his free hand around the gate. Hit his chest once, then nodded and lifted his hand.

Kelsey clamped a hand over her mouth as the bull released. Gordo came out twisting, his back hooves kicking high, but Rafe bore down, his legs viced around the monster's body.

Gordo landed on a run, then writhed again, both sets of legs leaving the earth.

Rafe's body jerked hard to the right, but he clung to Gordo's back. Gordo didn't just kick, he curved his body midair, so when he landed, the cowboy was already off balance.

Rafe was thrown forward and narrowly missed Gordo's cropped horns.

The crowd had gone wild, on their feet, pumping their fists.

Terrifying, wild, reckless—Kelsey couldn't look away from the spectacle, suddenly rooting for Rafe to hang on. To ride Gordo's violence out for the win.

Gordo dipped back, his hindquarters hunching down as his chest arched.

Rafe flew off the back, doing a near flip before he landed in the dirt.

The buzzer sounded as Gordo, still bucking, ran down the length of the field.

Rafe got up, ran to the railing, and Kelsey's breath caught as Knox hit the dirt, waving for Gordo. The bull turned to follow him, and the crowd gasped as Knox ran toward the pen, dodged Gordo's advance, and led the bull right into the gate.

Then he walked over to Rafe, and they high-fived, Rafe grinning.

"Six point nine seconds," Tate said. "Almost."

But she couldn't take her eyes off the triumph on Rafe's face.

Maybe that was it—what she was missing. The triumph. She simply hadn't held on long enough through the fear and recklessness and wild ride of letting Knox into her heart.

Safe, nice, protective Knox who'd just run down a bull to protect his friend.

Who had shown up tonight. Because...because God had answered her prayer.

And maybe it was time to stop letting fear rule her life.

"C'mon, girls, we have a change in the program." She grabbed Glo's hand and pulled her close as they walked to the dressing room.

"What?"

"You're singing your song tonight."

"No, I—"

"Stop being so afraid!" She glanced at Tate, a few steps ahead of them. "Poor man deserves a little hope."

A smile tugged on Glo's face. "Maybe I do too," she said softly.

Maybe, in fact, they all did.

Kelsey called in the band, grabbed her guitar, and laid out the new program. "Just one big change—aside from Glo singing her song. I'm debuting mine."

Dixie grinned, folded her arms over her chest, nodded.

"Really?" Glo said. "We haven't worked out any arrangements, there's no...are you sure?"

"Yes. Just a simple acoustic performance." No polish, just heart.

Please, God, make Knox be in the audience.

She ran the song a couple times with the band, and Glo offered a few ideas. But yeah, it was enough. *Please let it be enough.*

Even if it killed him, slowly, from the inside out, Knox planned on watching Kelsey sing. He'd stand in the shadows so he didn't distract her, but when Kelsey walked out onstage, he'd lose himself for the space of her show in the what-ifs.

Clearly, however, she wasn't interested in having him back in her life, because Tate would have texted him. When he'd left the voice mail—something he regretted almost instantly, thanks to the pleading in his voice—he'd left the decision with her.

Hey, Tate, it's me. I'm here with Gordo—the show needed a boost, so they've brought us out for a one-night event. But...I was hoping...so, um...how's Kelsey? I'd like to see her, but...she might not want to see me. I'm going to hang around for a while tonight, maybe catch the show, so if she's...oh brother. Just text me if she wants to see me.

Yeah, desperate, weak, and pitiful.

He'd just have to figure out how to live with the ache in his chest.

And the lingering hum of fear of *collateral damage*. Ruby Jane had called Knox with an update on the Bryant League. According to her, the two men in the photo had vanished, which meant they could be anywhere.

Not necessarily Vegas, but...

"There he is!"

Knox turned to the voice and spied Rafe, limping just a little as he walked down the corridor. Katherine, his wife, and little Tori were with him, and when Tori saw Knox, she broke into a smile and a run.

He scooped her up, amazed at how easy it was to sink into the idea of having his own beautiful, dark-curly-haired daughter. "How are you?"

"I'm good. Are you here to see the Yankee Belles?"

He put her down. "I guess so." He tried to keep a smile, but oh, yes, this night would hurt.

"Still walking?" he said to Rafe.

"I'm going to be on ice for a month, but thanks. I'm just glad to have lived through it."

Katherine gave him a hug, kissed his cheek, leaned back, her eyes warm. "How did things go in New York City? Did you find what you needed?"

"Yeah, thanks for the introductions. Detective Rayburn was a big help."

"He helped me track down Rafe years ago when he tried to hightail it out of town after crashing into my hotel."

Knox looked at Rafe. Who lifted a shoulder. "It really wasn't my fault. But I did get the girl, so…"

And Knox knew Rafe didn't mean for his words to pinch, but…shoot, why couldn't *he* get the girl?

Rafe stepped up beside him and looked at the assembling crowd. The pre-music was still playing, a giant disco ball lowered from the ceiling, the floor of the arena crowded as the audience was let in. A giant black stage now jutted from the side of the arena, massive speakers and spotlights angled around to hit the metal rafters.

Only the lights from the hallways would be lit once the concert started, which meant he could hide in the back.

Wow, he was pitiful. Maybe he should just leave, pull the Band-Aid off fast, live with the fact that Kelsey really meant her words.

I'm just trying to be honest, Knox. It can't work.

"I can't believe our little plan paid off. I thought for sure it was a long shot—bringing Gordo back and me riding him. And it looks like the Yankee Belles will be a hit." Rafe turned to him. "So all we need now is for you to say yes as our Director of Livestock."

Knox nodded, looked away. Not if he had to endure this every night. "I'll let you know," he said, glancing up at Rafe.

Rafe considered him a moment, then, "You know, I can study a bull, watch his moves, even feel his breathing and how he stands in the gate to get a sense of how he'll buck. But then, I just have to let go and let the instincts take off. Let the bull take me where he wants—and just hold on."

Knox stared at him. "Is that some sort of metaphor for, Take the job, Knox?"

Rafe grinned. "Or maybe, follow your instincts, hold on, and don't let her go?" He patted Knox on the arm and held out his hands for Tori and Katherine. They headed into the arena.

Knox stayed in the periphery, wishing he knew what instincts to hold on to. Because half of him wanted to run.

The other half couldn't move, especially as the lights dropped. As the familiar a cappella voices lifted, as the Belles walked onto the stage in the dark, their song haunting and beautiful, the blend of female voices finding his soul.

The drum rolled, the lights came up, and there she was. Her beautiful hair was down, curled in soft waves around her face. She wore a white shirt, and her legs looked about a mile long in her cutoff shorts and fringed boots.

No, he couldn't trust his instincts at all, because the strongest one told him to rush the stage and take her in his arms.

So sweet bull-doggin' man, take me home tonight
Sing me a song, pull the stars from the sky
Make me believe your words, that everything will be all right.
Cowboy don't lie—Take me away and make me fly.

He should leave. Right now. But just watching her up

there in her element, wooing the audience, had lifted his heart right from his body. He'd even stepped out of the hallway, into the darkened crowd, as if pulled by her voice.

They finished their first song to the screams of the audience, then Kelsey took the mic, waving, introducing the band, then diving into the next song.

He knew them all. The one about the high school crush, the high energy songs everyone liked to sing along to. His gaze began to roam the crowd, landing on the security guards posted in the tunnels. Four tunnels plus the one behind him. Tate was probably backstage.

He barely noticed when the song ended and Kelsey took the mic. "We're changing things up tonight. I usually sing the song written by Glo Jackson, but tonight, she's going to take the mic for that one, and I have something new for you."

One of the stagehands brought a stool out onstage. Kelsey sat on it and picked up the guitar from its stand, slipped it over her shoulder. Took a breath.

"This is actually the first song I've ever written. See, up until recently, I couldn't write songs…too much stuff on the inside holding me back, I guess. But I realized that I was tired of my past cluttering my future, so…anyway, once I figured that out, this song sort of came out."

She let her pick strum along a few chords.

His gaze landed on a security guard in the lighted tunnel closest to him. He wore the dark pants and white shirt of arena security, but something about him…

"This song is for all those who want a second chance at their first love. Who wish they'd said something differently, maybe turned around and tried again. Who realize that they made a mistake…"

He tore his gaze off the man and back to Kelsey, so sweetly sitting on the stool, her knees drawn up. He could picture her sitting across from him at the family campfire.

She looked up then, as if searching the audience, and his breath caught.

What if—

No. She was just performing, acting like—

"I can't see beyond the front row, but…Knox Marshall, if you're out there… This is for you."

He couldn't move.

She began to strum, adding a beat with a thump on her guitar body and moving slightly to the rhythm. Looked up at the audience, her eyes clear and full. Then leaned into the mic and released her beautiful voice.

> *He said hold on to me, and don't let go*
> *Don't be afraid, don't say no.*
> *Hold on, lean in*
> *What if I said yes, what if I believed*
> *What if I reached back until I could see*
> *That my tomorrow was with you.*

He couldn't breathe, his chest so tight he thought it might simply close in on him.

Kelsey.

She hit the chorus, and his eyes freakin' welled up.

> *My mind said no.*
> *My heart said yes…*
> *My mind said whoa…*
> *My heart felt his caress.*
> *Hold on, lean in*

He couldn't tear his eyes off her, but something in his periphery buzzed his attention away, just for a second.

The security guard. He held—

The man had a rifle. And maybe that wouldn't have stunned Knox if he hadn't seen the tattoo—a swastika between his eyebrows—hadn't recognized the scar across his chin.

No. *What—?*

He swiped up his phone and pushed through the crowd toward the platform that ringed the arena, his eyes on Vince Russell.

He speed-dialed Tate, who of course didn't pick up. "Tate, I'm here, and so is Vince Russell. The jerk isn't dead—"

Someone jostled him, and he dropped the phone.

But he left it, refusing to take his eyes off Russell who had stepped into the shadows, climbing up the steps.

Probably to send a well-aimed shot into Kelsey's head.

He started to run.

He said don't cry, honey, you're safe with me
My love, babe, can set you free
Hold on, lean in

He broke through the crowd. "Russell!" He hoped his voice rose above the song, hoped that Russell heard him enough to stop, to know he'd been spotted.

What if I said yes, when he asked to dance
What if I reached out, grabbed hold of his hand
Said my tomorrow was with you.

It worked. Russell popped up on the far side of the wall, and for a second, Knox's body shook with the image of Russell aiming into the crowd.

But the man jumped the wall and took off down the

corridor.

Yeah, run, buddy, because I'm comin'.

Knox broke through the crowd and took off.

Russell's footsteps pounded down the hall, and Knox glimpsed him headed toward the exhibit area.

Which led into the cordoned-off backstage.

Nope.

Knox sprinted down the hallway, past the concession stands, the T-shirt and souvenir booths. No one seemed to care about his pursuit until he realized that Russell was wearing a security uniform. Probably people were simply staying out of his way.

"Call security!" he shouted to a hot dog vendor.

He rounded the curve of the building. Russell had vanished.

The exhibit area was lined with rows and rows of stock—calves, steers, quarter horses, and bulls. But Gordo's pen sat in the middle, set apart from the rest beside a sign with a listing of his legendary accomplishments.

A row of sheep pens bumped up to the temporary wall that led to the backstage area. Knox slowed, giving a cursory search for Russell.

Certainly Tate had posted guards at the backstage entrances.

He stopped at Gordo's pen. The animal stood in the middle, staring at him through the bars, dark, glassy eyes in his. Knox was breathing hard, searching for security. *Please.*

"I know you."

The voice emerged from behind Gordo's sign.

Knox stepped back, on the other edge of the ten-by-ten pen. The shooter held his rifle on Knox, and he wasn't a weapons expert, but the thing had a scope, a handgrip, and looked like a semiautomatic.

Thank You, God, that Russell hadn't pointed at the crowd.

"And I know you, Vince Russell," Knox said. He lifted his hands, more instinct than surrender, something he'd do to calm Gordo.

The animal grunted, shifting to stand between them.

"You came to see AJ. Tried to scare him," Russell said, a slight accent to his voice. His dark hair hung uncut and greasy, tucked behind his ears. Graying, colorless tats squirreled up his forearms.

The thought of this man beating…raping…

Knox fought to keep his breathing even, to think. "Clearly not enough. I heard you were dead."

"Yeah, well, you can't believe everything you hear."

Apparently.

And from the nearby backstage wing he heard the last of Kelsey's song.

So I will trust you, I'll give us a try.
Take my love baby, please don't let it die
There is no tomorrow, not without you.

"I'm not going to let you hurt her again."

"This thing will shoot right through your champion bull here, no problem, and come out the other side." He pointed the rifle at Knox, through Gordo.

Knox drew in a quick breath, but kept his voice cool, even. "Go ahead and try, buddy. But I can promise that both Gordo and I are tougher than you think—" With a shout, he exploded. He hit the cage to scare Gordo and dove for the floor.

A shot flared off.

He rolled, came up hot a few feet away from Russell.

Knox couldn't look toward the pen—just launched

himself at Russell.

Russell was already crumpling. Knox landed on top of him even as Russell slammed the butt of his gun into his shoulder.

The hit barely registered, not with all the rage behind Knox's punch. He slammed his fist into Russell's face, saw the man's head snap back. Reared back for another.

Someone caught his wrist. "Knox! He's down!"

"Not down enough!" But hands came around his shoulders, jerked him back, and he landed on the floor. Watched as a security guard retrieved the rifle, as Tate grabbed Russell and jerked him over, onto his stomach.

The man had been shot in the leg. Not a life-threatening wound, but enough to slow him down.

Tate had a knee in his back, and the first guard handed him a zip tie.

Knox was breathing hard. "You got my message?"

"No. I saw you from backstage, all lit up and dangerous as you took off."

Knox scrambled to his feet, but his head rushed with the adrenaline of the moment, and he had to lean over, grab Gordo's pen.

The bull looked over at him, nudging his hand with his snout, unhurt.

Knox could have wept with relief except— "Did Kelsey see?"

"I don't know."

Tate handed off Russell to his other security guard as two more arrived.

"He needs medical help. And call 9-1-1. He's a fugitive."

Tate looked at Knox. A slow smile spread across his face. "Would you like a backstage pass?"

Knox took a breath. Then followed his instincts and

nodded.

———————◆———————

Kelsey opened her eyes and raised her gaze to the audience. The applause thundered around her, but for a moment, she'd forgotten them all. Just listened to her song, rising lonely into the rafters.

Hold on, lean in.

Only it wasn't her voice in the final notes, ringing through her.

Something deeper, in her bones, in her soul.

Hold on. Lean in.

Yes.

She breathed it in one last moment, then let out a smile, raising her hand. "Thank you!"

She put the guitar away and called Dixie and Glo forward. "We're so glad to be here tonight. It's my first appearance after the bombing in San Antonio. We're thanking God that no one was seriously injured. And we thank you for your support tonight."

More cheers and she launched into their sing-along song, something fun and upbeat. But even as she pasted on a smile and led the crowd in "Let him go, go go, bye, bye," she stared out into the darkness and…

Knox was right. It wasn't enough. Sure, she was grateful for the fans, the following, but…the music, the applause was just a taste of what she truly longed for.

Hold on. Lean in.

She pumped the air, grabbing the mic, but inside heard the words of the woman back at Benjamin King's house.

There's… only one thing that will satisfy. And that's God's love.

Oh, she could not—would not—start weeping onstage. But she wanted it. All of it—yes, Knox and the life she'd tasted, but even more, the love she'd seen from him, from his family, from…maybe even from Hamilton when he'd shown up all those years ago to stand by her. And Dixie and her family, and Glo and…

Yeah. God had shown up, over and over again, through the people who loved her.

She finished her song, the truth welling through her, nourishing her.

The crowd applauded, and she stepped back, introducing Glo and her amazing song.

Then nodded at Glo to take the mic. Picked up her guitar.

Glo blew out a breath, smiled, and lifted her voice.

She met him on a night like any other
Dressed in white, the cape of a soldier
He said you're pretty, but I can't stay
She said I know, but I could love you anyway

Kelsey's eyes filled, the song finding her cracks, so much want, so much hope.

Glo unsheathed the mic from the stand and walked to the middle of the stage.

So they started their own love song
Found the rhythm and tone
He said he'd never found anyone
Who made him want to come home

Kelsey looked away from the audience, away from Glo. Closed her eyes into the song. Glo's voice rose, sweet, vulnerable, touching down into her soul.

She…don't wanna cry,

But she ain't gonna fall for another guy.
It's too hard to be apart
Not after she's waited for…one true heart…one true heart…

She glanced at Dixie, into the bridge, and then her gaze landed on Tate who stood just offstage in the shadows, his arms folded, his face tight, gaze pinned to Glo.

Clearly listening.

Glo stood in the middle of the stage, her face lifted, her eyes closed.

He said I'm leaving, baby don't cry.
No, Stay with me, please don't die.
Always, forever, together, with me
She lay in his grass, clutching eternity.

When she opened her eyes, tears edged them.

She…don't wanna try,
It's too hard to fall for another guy.
But you don't know if you don't start
So wait…for one true heart…one true heart…

The music faded out and she bent her head.

The crowd erupted, but Glo looked over at Kelsey, something sad and broken in her expression.

Maybe they were all showing up with their best performance, trying to hide the broken places inside.

Oh, she wished Knox had been in the audience. But maybe…maybe it was enough for her to simply sing something from her heart.

And to realize that she wasn't alone onstage. Ever.

She stepped up to the mic and gave Glo another round,

then set up the finale song, the beat fast, the entire band showing up to bring the house down.

She noticed that even Glo had grabbed her banjo. Oh Glo—she just couldn't stay out of the fun.

The crowd was dancing, and she reached inside, heard the words as she belted them out.

So, when life doesn't make sense
when you want to run away
When the songs seem over
and you ain't got nothing to say,
Stick around, boy, and give us a chance.
Take my hands…and let's just dance!

Just dance. Whatever life had for her. Maybe, like Knox said, she didn't always need to keep moving. Didn't always need a destination in the front windshield.

Maybe she could let God take the wheel—as Carrie would say—and simply enjoy the view.

The finale went off just like she'd planned. The chorus sung twice through, then the lights went down, just the starlight cast from the giant disco ball twirling overhead.

And a second later, the explosion of silvery confetti.

The crowd kept singing, and the Belles sneaked offstage, followed by the band.

Kelsey felt Dixie's hand in hers and Glo taking the other as they exited toward Tate.

The crowd, behind them, was still singing.

Take my hands…and let's just dance!

Maybe the Yankee Belles had reached in and healed a few wounds tonight.

Or maybe God had simply done the healing, in her. Through her, sharing her wounded places, letting God's love pour out and back in to heal. To give hope. *You are enough, God.*

Tate was there, his flashlight flicked on as he lit a path away from the stage, toward their dressing room, but Kelsey grabbed her Yankee Belles in a hug.

"You were magnificent!"

The song had ended, and the applause turned thunderous.

But she didn't hear it. Because Tate flashed his light on someone emerging from the shadows of the backstage wing. Tall, he wore a red shirt, the arms rolled up past his forearms, as if he'd been working, his hair tousled, those dangerous forest-blue eyes on her.

How had she ever thought him safe?

"Hey there," Knox said. He had his hands in his pockets like, aw, shucks, but she didn't wait for him to catch her before she simply walked forward and threw her arms around his neck.

He caught her anyway, of course, and he was so solid and real and...here. Of course he was here. He smelled of the rodeo—roughed-edged, hard work, pure cowboy, but under his exterior, she felt the thunder of his heartbeat, the slightest tremble in his body.

"What is it?" She pushed away from him, met his eyes.

But he caught her face in his big hands, running his thumbs down her cheeks. "You. Just you. I...I love you, Kelsey. I have since the day you kissed me on the cheek and told me I was old and safe."

"You're neither old, nor safe, Knox Marshall. And I love you too."

A slow, hot, dangerous smile slid up his face. "Good. Because you're not getting rid of me. I'm going on the road with you."

It took her a second, then, "As a groupie?"

His eyes turned warm. "Something a little more up close and personal, I hope. And far from boring." And then, just to prove his words, he kissed her, right there, in front of her band, with the stands still cheering, so much strength and sweet possession in his kiss that she knew...

No more running. Nor more fear.

This was enough.

And it was time to go home.

What happens next...

All this sappiness didn't solve the biggest problem. Sure, Tate could cheer on his brother, the fact that he'd ended up with Kelsey in his arms.

But someone had to raise their hand and point out the obvious—someone had tried to kill Glo—and that someone was still on the loose.

Although, yes, it seemed Kelsey's nightmare had ended. Russell would be heading back to prison without another shot at parole—and a stack of other sentences to serve, no doubt.

Knox and Kelsey sat on the white leather sofa overlooking the massive fountain of the Bellagio hotel, a two-bedroom penthouse suite that apparently Rafe Noble had pulled connections to secure. And gifted it to Knox to give to the Yankee Belles.

Tate and Knox had nabbed a similar suite, so Tate wasn't exactly complaining, but just being in the Bellagio, or even in Vegas proper, raised the little hairs on the back of his neck.

The sooner they hit the road, the more likely he'd live through his under-the-radar return.

"Room service show up yet?" Glo came out of a bedroom wearing a fluffy white bathrobe, her hair wet and tousled as she dried it with a towel. She hadn't cinched the robe and he spied a T-shirt and a pair of yoga pants underneath, so maybe she was simply basking in the luxury. She slid onto a green leather high-top stool pushed under the granite countertop of the long, mirrored bar.

"Not yet," Tate said, the scent of her catching him, and he had to look away.

The adrenaline of running down Russell still spiked his system, and he'd barely stopped himself from grabbing Glo and holding on when she walked offstage.

Just because.

Knox got up, his hand woven into Kelsey's. "We're going for a walk."

A walk. Right. Euphemisms. But he could play along. "The fountains go off every fifteen minutes."

Knox grinned at him.

Lucky dog.

Dixie had gone with Elijah Blue and Carter to check out the famed chocolate fountain.

Which left—aw, shoot. He hadn't done the math in time. The door clicked behind Knox and Kelsey.

Glo was still drying her hair with the towel.

Now, she looked over at him, her hair in short, nearly white-gold curls around her head. "How do you know so much about the fountains?"

Oh. He walked to the window, stared down at the night, the strip alive and always moving. The 460-foot Eiffel Tower replica sparkled gold against the pane of night in front of the Paris Las Vegas. At its feet, the Chateau Nightclub was rocking, spotlights alerting the world to some headliner, and to the left a little farther, blue light cast upon Bally's casino. The real action was happening just northwest of Bally's at Drai's nightclub in the front yard of the Flamingo.

He knew every cranny and dark alley on the Vegas strip,

not to mention what happened under the bright lights.

"Tate?"

He hadn't noticed Glo join him. She had stuck her hands into the robe, and without her boots on, she seemed like a tiny, delicious package of curves and smarts and talent.

For a second, he was standing offstage, watching her sing her solo. So much of her heart on the outside of her body, her voice sweet and honest and…

And the words felt like they might be for him.

But you don't know if you don't start
So wait…for one true heart…one true heart…

He knew, right to his bones, that Glo was the one he'd waited for. Wanted to start over with. And he would. As soon as they got clear of the specter and the death threats stalking them, he would quit this job.

Create his own sappy happy ending, hopefully.

But until then, he had to keep his hands fisted in his pockets.

"I used to work here," Tate said, finally answering her question.

"Doing what?"

He simplified his answer. "Protecting people." And other things.

"Of course you were." She glanced up at him then. Such beautiful hazel-green eyes, with tiny specks of gold. He could forget the past, the knot in his gut, even his sins when she looked at him like that. A trust.

As if he might actually be a hero.

He couldn't move, his heart nearly frozen in his chest.

Especially when she moved toward him. Touched his arm. "Thanks for taking down Russell tonight. You set

Kelsey free."

"I didn't—"

Her hand touched his chest. "Yeah, you did." She stepped in front of him, her back to the window panes. She put her other hand on his chest. "Thank you."

The heat of her hands turned his entire body to fire. He swallowed, stared down at her. "Glo—I—"

"Kiss me, already, hero."

Oh, uh—

But she wasn't hesitating. She leaned up, running her hands around his neck and pulling his head down, and then her lips were on his.

Sweet, tasting of toothpaste, and soft against his.

And it just took a second for him to catch up, because he had to get past the warning bells bonging in the back of his head.

The past, rising to convict him.

But he ignored it and swept his arm around her back, pulled her against him, and returned her kiss. Let all the emotions of the past month sweep through him, flood over him, and pour out in his ardor.

She made a sound, something of desire deep in her bones, and it only sparked heat in his own, only made him press her against the glass, move his other arm around her.

Glo—

The knock at the door was a hand between them, and he came up breathing hard, his heart pounding. Glo, too, and she bit her lip as if struggling with her own emotions.

Yay for pizza, because yes, he needed a deep breath, something to help him tuck his emotions back inside and escape the hot temptation that he knew could only cause trouble.

Maybe he and Glo needed a walk, too, and pronto. "Get

dressed," he said over his shoulder as he headed into the foyer. "I'll show you the strip after we have pizza."

"It's about time." She headed for her bedroom.

Lock the door behind you, honey. Because he was about three seconds from following her and frankly she made him want to stay *out* of trouble, possibly for the first time in his life.

She turned the lock, as if reading his mind. He heard the click just as he opened the door to their suite. "Room service. Finally."

Except, it wasn't a waiter with a white-clothed serving cart containing pizza and drinks.

Unless the Bellagio had upgraded their room service staff to a six-foot-five Russian dressed in a black turtleneck and a suitcoat and missing a right incisor.

Tate's reflexes let out a word. "Slava—"

"Look who's back in town." He shoved a foot in the door before Tate could slam it.

Then the Russian's big hand hit the door, banged it open, and Tate had just a second to brace himself as Slava sent a fist into his gut.

It knocked Tate, doubled over, back into the suite. He fell to the floor as Slava stepped over him. Knelt and slammed his cement mitt on his chest, pinning Tate as he tightened his fist.

"I warned you what would happen if you ever came back to Vegas," Slava growled.

He had. Oh, he had.

Please, Glo, stay in your room...

Author's Note

Be Thou my Vision, O Lord of my heart
Naught be all else to me, save that Thou art
Thou my best Thought, by day or by night
Waking or sleeping, Thy presence my light

There is no peace, no healing without the secure knowledge of God's love. But when our lives are shaken, it can be nearly impossible to reach out and hold onto the truth that we are loved. Even when life and people betray us. Even when the unthinkable happens. Period. Full stop. And God's love is not dependent on our actions.

He loves us because He Is Love.

And because of that, we can trust him with our hearts. Our hurts. Our need for justice, healing and hope. He is our provider, or healer, our protector. He. Is. Enough.

But getting that through our heads to our hearts is a life-long process. And it was this journey that I wanted to convey when I set about penning the Montana Marshalls series. A journey of faith through struggle, through joys and through an unknown future. Knox had to see that God had a great plan for him if he would be willing to let go of the one he'd planned for himself. The logical one. The one he'd promised to his family. And Kelsey had to step forward into healing. Into peace, into the home God had for her, if she would simply surrender.

These are life lessons I'm still learning. But I'm excited about the journey the Montana Marshalls will take us on!

My deepest gratitude for their help in creating this series goes to my amazing SDG publishing team: Rachel Hauck, for her amazing encouragement and help on the journey. Alyssa Geertsen, my key beta reader, Barbara Curtis, for her almost magical editing, Rel Mollet, for her awesomeness in countless ways. I'm deeply grateful for my cover designer, Jenny @ Seedlings Design Studio, and my talented layout artist, Tari Faris. Thank you also to my fabulous beta readers (any mistakes are all mine!) Lisa Jordan, Lisa Gupton and Bobbi Whitlock. You all are fabulous! Appreciation also goes to my amazing Masterminds. You know who you are. Thank you for pushing me and believing in me.

Finally, to the Lord, who is always and forever enough. Thank you for proving this to me every day.

Thank you, dear readers, for reading book 1: Knox. I invite you to continue the journey with book 2: Tate!

Susie May

Susan May Warren is the USA Today bestselling, Christy and RITA award–winning author of more than sixty novels whose compelling plots and unforgettable characters have won acclaim with readers and reviewers alike. The mother of four grown children, and married to her real-life hero for nearly 30 years, she loves travelling and telling stories about life, adventure and faith.

In addition to her writing, Susan is a nationally acclaimed writing teacher and runs an academy for writers, Novel. Academy. For exciting updates on her new releases, previous books, and more, visit her website at www.susanmaywarren. com.

Continue the Montana Marshall family adventures with TATE.

THE MONTANA MARSHALLS

TATE

RITA AWARD-WINNING AND USA TODAY BESTSELLING AUTHOR

SUSAN MAY WARREN

What will it cost this bodyguard to save the woman he loves?

Personal security guard, Tate Marshall, has always been the family troublemaker. Maybe it's his propensity to get entangled in problems that don't belong to him. Now, he's in over his head because he's desperately in love with the woman he's tasked to protect, the beautiful Gloria, "Glo" Jackson, daughter of US Senator and presidential hopeful Reba Jackson. A member of the country band, the Yankee Belles, Glo was targeted in a recent terrorist attack designed to deter her mother from running, and Tate will do anything to keep her safe.

As stubborn as her mother, Glo isn't about to hide from threats, at least the kind that won't cost her heart. She's already paid a terrible price for the war on terror, and she refuses to let herself love a man who might die, especially because of her. Better to keep him away from her, even if it means losing the man she loves.

As the presidential campaign heats up and the threats deepen, so does the attraction between Tate and Glo. But what will it cost Tate to keep her alive?

And what will Glo do to keep from losing another man to the cost of war?

The gripping second installment of the Montana Marshalls series.

Available where books are sold
JULY 2019
Also available in ebook format